I0654084

Praise for the Dakota Sunrise series

"The second book in Leavell's Dakota Sunrise series has action, adventure, secrets, romance and gunfights. The characters are witty, cunning and out for revenge. The storyline is fast-paced, with some twists and heart-pounding turns that enhance the overall plot. Leavell is an amazingly talented author, who brought his A game to this series. They will be longtime keepers."
—**RT BOOK REVIEWS** on *Shadow of Devil's Tower*

"Leavell has spun a nicely textured narrative with complex main characters . . . There's enough here to keep western fans awaiting the next installment, with faith elements nicely woven in. This absorbing read is a good counterweight to the West as it is often envisioned by inspirational romance writers."
—**PUBLISHERS WEEKLY** on *West for the Black Hills*

"Peter Leavell writes a compelling story of coming to terms with the past in western style. Research for the time and setting is blended in nicely to deliver a story of one man's search for justice."
—**TRACIE PETERSON**, award winning, best-selling author of over 100 books, including The Lonestar Bride series on *West for the Black Hills*

"A wonderful historical Western with amazing characters who are bent on revenge, trying to right a wrong from their pasts. The storyline is plausible and runs smoothly throughout. Leavell is a talented writer and brings to life a good old-fashioned Western with a twist."
—**RT BOOK REVIEWS** on *West for the Black Hills*

Shadow of Devil's Tower

SHADOW OF
DEVIL'S
TOWER

Peter Leavell

Mountainview Books, LLC

Shadow of Devil's Tower
Copyright © 2017 by Peter Leavell. All rights reserved.

Edited by Carol Kurtz Darlington

Cover photograph of horse copyright © istockphoto/cgbaldauf
Cover photograph of Devil's Tower copyright © istockphoto/dlerick
Cover photograph of landscape copyright © istockphoto/kentarcajuan

This novel is a work of fiction. Names, characters, places, and incidents either are the product of the author's imagination or are used fictitiously. Any resemblance to actual events, locales, organizations, or persons living or dead is entirely coincidental and beyond the intent of the author or the publisher.

ISBN: 978-1-941291-33-7 (paperback)
ISBN: 978-1-941291-34-4 (ebook)

Brothers three, ride trail.
One is carried away.
The other two keep to the trail.

For my brothers.
Joe, who still sits across the campfire from me. And Chris, who took his
guitar to heaven. This world can still hear his music.

Acknowledgments

This novel is the first I've written since my brother died of cancer. At times, I found living in the scenes therapeutic. At other times, as I read through edits, I don't remember writing them at all. That's the nature of grief. Memory loss. There are so many people to thank, but I'm afraid I'll miss the most vital due to the moments I've forgotten.

Usually a writer pleads for minutes, stolen from family here and there. I'm thankful my wife Tonya, and kids Jost and Kade, carve time for me to write. If not for them, this novel wouldn't have been possible. If they ever asked me to stop writing, I'd gladly comply. They ask the opposite.

My parents, Monte and Jeneen, are more than simply genetic links. My mother is an artist, painting pictures that spark my imagination. My father grew up in a saddle in Cody Wyoming, and has helped with horse lore. Thank you, you two. Stay forever young!

Mountainview Books has been an inspiration—C. J. for her encouragement and kind words, and Carol for her edits. If there are any errors in this book, it's because I put them in later. It's an honor to write for them.

A few obsessive friends made the series popular—especially Mike Ehret, Clarice James, Terrie Todd, Jim Hamlett, and Kimberley Graham. Also Susie Finkbeiner and Rachel McMillan and Karen Barnett and Nancy Kimball and C. J. Darlington. They all have excellent books.

Thanks to everyone in Fowler, Colorado. I hope you noted the part near the Apishapa. The scene is located there because I think you're all awesome.

Cathryn Swalia helped with Arabian characteristics. Cathryn, did you notice Raven doesn't always listen to you?

Thanks to you, reader! Without you, the series wouldn't have won awards and found success. And thanks for buying your dad, mom, grandfather, and grandmother a copy. They sent me a note of encouragement! I've received hundreds of notes! Thanks again!

1

Love is the feeling that eats your insides when you're not with the girl. And mine were as cold as the driving wind around me.

The world crippled my sight with brilliant white. I wanted to turn back to the warmth of the barn, the horses, my dog Trevor—but the thought of the missing boys drove me deeper into the storm. If it were any colder, I would need to move to Antarctica to warm up.

Bitter winds pelted snow against my cheeks. Every breath shot ice shards into my lungs, freezing my core from the inside out. A feeling like missing Anna.

Yeah, an expedition across Antarctica instead of the Dakota Territory sounded more pleasant.

A fence ran along each side of my lane, and I found the top few inches of wooden rail, the rest buried in swirling snow. I couldn't see far enough to spot the other side of the road.

The men who'd just left my barn said this morning had been forty degrees. Jackets! The boys from the Hutterite camp had worn jackets to school. No one would have guessed the temperature now as they made their way home would be forty below zero.

I wore long underwear, knitted socks, thick pants, a heavy felt shirt, a jacket, coveralls, my duster, a fur-lined cap, a hand-kerchief over my face, and gloves. Yet the roaring wind still froze my skin. The boys wore jackets.

The thought drove me deeper into the late afternoon.

I would do anything to save their lives.

The men from the camp told me their names, but I only remembered one—Jake—whom they said was a smart boy. He would find a fence and follow it, knowing the poles led to a shelter or house.

White drifts nearly covered my fence.

I cupped my hand around my mouth. "Jake!" The name was instantly lost in the thundering wind. I wouldn't stop, though. "Jake!" Every intake of breath shot cold air into my core.

Black tugged at the edges of my mind.

My legs sunk into the snow, my knees buried. My feet felt heavy, as if I wore enormous horseshoes instead of boots.

The thought of telling the men I found dead bodies in the spring thaw sent a new shiver that had nothing to do with the cold down my spine. "Jake!"

God, please!

A mantel flashed into my thoughts.

No, not now. Not a vision. I will die out here.

"Jake!" My voice drifted with the snow.

The mantel again.

My childhood home.

No, I can't get lost in my visions.

Atop the mantel, large black-and-white photos of family. My father's fine face, firm jaw, a touch of Spanish Moors heritage in his dark skin, and black hair that I'd inherited. There was no sign of his cruel manner in the dark eyes.

Please no, not the memories. Not now.

My mother's picture stood next to his. A beautiful, compassionate smile, high forehead, dark hair, all like mine. Her long, athletic frame was her gift to me as well. Despite the black-and-white image, her eyes shone, eyes that passersby stopped to notice. My eyes, which I hated. Eyes like an animal. Eyes so different, my Sioux friend called me Prairie Wolf.

Both Mother and Father died within view of Devil's Tower. I had escaped with my life.

For so long, I believed my father a model of perfection, an observation born from youth. Those who knew them told me otherwise. My mother had been the toast of Washington. My father was a cruel businessman.

The vision grew stronger.

Beside my mother's photo, my uncle John Maxwell. I'd had a run-in with him in Deadwood and learned only then he was my uncle, awakening new memories of my past. He was hung on Deadwood's gallows for unspeakable crimes.

Next to his photo was an older man in a fine suit, a bowler and cane by his side. My grandfather. I'd not thought of my grandfather in quite some time. He died before my parents and I left for the Dakota Territory.

A picture of me as a baby in a white gown anchored the five photos.

Those four were all the family I could remember. Four pictures on the mantel.

Perhaps I should have understood my troubled life long before. Families stand together in photographs. Not individual photos.

The past held me completely in its grasp, drawing me back to a time when I had been just as cold.

A warming fire, crisp and cheering. A hot drink thawing my frozen fingers. Sharp tingles on my skin. Drops of melted snow sliding down my eight-year-old skin.

I closed my eyes and basked in the warmth, the roar calming to crackling flames. Burning pine mixed with the aroma of warm tea. I tasted the creamy warmth. My mother's face beamed down at me. "Feeling better, Philip?"

I licked my lips. Father liked his coffee black and chided me for drinking tea with cream or milk, but I preferred the taste. And Mother made the drink perfectly.

She wrapped a blanket around my shoulders. "You were out there too long, silly. Sit by the fire for a bit, and you'll warm up." She gave me a squeeze, and I leaned my head against her shoulder and sighed. Her bun tickled my nose, and her earring pressed against my neck.

Mother stiffened, and she stood. Her bright eyes hardened as she looked past the couch, squinting as she always did when angry. Or protecting something. My heart sunk. A fight would ensue. A fight usually did with that look.

My father's voice came from behind. "It's done."

I threw my blanket off and jumped from the couch. "Father!" I bumped the short brass table beside the fire and almost spilled my tea. A few steps over the rug and I jumped.

He caught me and wrapped strong arms around me. "Whew, you smell like you played outside all day."

"Yup."

He held me at arm's length. "I've news for you."

"What is it?"

He set me down and rubbed his chin. "How would you like to go out West?"

My mother grabbed my hand and pulled me back. "Henry Anderson, not in front of Philip."

"Why not? It's done." My father removed his hat and tossed it toward the stand. The brim smacked the side and the hat fell to the floor. "Your father will be here in a moment to sign the papers."

My small, eight-year-old body suddenly turned cold, then

grew to a twenty-one-year-old man trudging through the snowstorm.

No, please no. Not this memory. Hadn't I suffered enough?

But I was back by the roaring fire, resting on the couch. I saw my father through the framed doorway, leaning over a table.

My grandfather, wearing the same suit as in the photograph, silver hair and well-trimmed goatee sharp in the lamplight, stood beside my father, pointing to a piece of paper. My father's voice drifted into the room, "Just sign here, Carl."

"Have you told John and Jacob what you're doing?" My grandfather's voice—the British accent that sounded so much like my mother's—was firm. He was a gentleman of the highest order, and at times I duplicated his accent instead of my normal West Virginian clip.

"There's no need."

"John is my son. At least tell him. He has a right to—"

"If you must, then you tell him. But I will not." My father held out a pen. "Sign the deed for the house. The place will be yours, a fine investment."

"And what of Jacob? He paid a heavy price for the map."

Father growled, not unlike a dog. "Let me handle him."

"And the map? You'll destroy it?"

"No. No, now that I have it—"

Grandfather pounded the table with a fist. "You promised, Henry."

"But now that we know it's real, we must use it."

Grandfather was shorter than Father but looked just as powerful as he pointed a finger in Father's face. "You promised. Tell John."

Father stormed into the parlor where I lay on the couch. As he reached for the family's wooden box on the mantel, the red of the fire cast a crimson glow against his skin. I drew back under the blanket. His eyes shone like a demon's.

The box snapped shut and as Father turned, Grandfather stepped close.

Father held up a yellowed piece of paper, curled his hands around both sides, and split it evenly with a soft tearing sound. "Here you are, Harry. Half of the map."

"And what is this for?"

"Half the secret."

Grandfather held out a shaking hand and grasped the page. "You . . . you would do this?"

"Tell John, if you like. Or Jacob. I don't care. But I'm going to find it."

"But Jacob is still out of the country."

"What do you want of me? Leave it with the monk who had the map. He seemed trustworthy."

They left the room.

I'd fallen asleep when my mother woke me. The fire had died to orange embers, lighting sorrow in her eyes.

Eyes so like mine.

"Philip, I've news, and not good news."

I rubbed my face.

"Dear . . ." Her voice caught. "Grandfather died tonight. His heart . . ."

The vision swirled into a mist, then a white fog that turned to snow.

My duster flapped in the wind, snapping violently behind me. With gloved fingers, I managed to fasten enough buttons to keep it from blowing off. The cloth whipped against my calves.

The visions had been worse of late. They corresponded with the physical world, drawing me back to a moment in time where my senses registered a similar sight, touch, or sound and brought me to a violently emotional memory.

I hadn't thought of my grandfather for quite some time.

He had been tied to the map. I hadn't known.

I couldn't think about having a portion of the map. I had to find those boys.

"Jake!"

I'd reached the end of the fence.

Just beyond, I knew the road rose out of my ravine, where the winds undoubtedly would be worse.

Weariness sapped my strength. What if they were already dead? What if I could save their lives by taking a few steps to the right?

Please, God!

"Jake!"

The echoing voice was distant, as if from miles away.

"Jake!"

Was that a voice on the wind? Maybe someone was calling out from downwind, across the lane.

I broke from my fervent hold on the fence and crossed.

Beside a mound of snow stood a dark figure. "Jake!"

The shadow waved.

I stumbled forward, perhaps ten feet. As I drew near, I made out the figure of a boy.

"Jake?" I yelled.

He wore a thin covering over his crossed arms, no hat, his dark hair blowing in the wind.

He nodded.

"We've got to get you inside. My place is that way." I pointed then started taking off my gloves. "Where are the other boys?"

"We made a cave." He took a step toward the mound then reached out to take the gloves I offered.

"Are you all able to make it to my barn? It isn't far."

"If we don't, we're going to freeze tonight." His voice was weak and high-pitched.

I followed Jake around the mound and saw a partial hollow carved in the drift. Four boys lay huddled in the small shelter.

I finished unbuttoning my duster as I dropped to a knee in front of the shivering bodies. I tossed my coat over them.

"I know it's cold, but you've got to get up. We're going to my barn."

None of them moved.

Jake leaned in beside me and moved the coat to one side. "Here you go, Andrew." He helped the smallest of the boys with a glove, tucking both the lad's hands into the leather.

All the boys shivered violently except Andrew. I moved closer to brush the snow from his pale face, and his head dropped to the side then jerked up. His eyelids sunk.

I looked at Jake and the rest of the boys. "Up, now!" I barked. "Let's go."

My fingers were nearly frozen as I snatched the duster off the others, wrapped Andrew in the cocoon, and lifted him into a tight embrace. I turned to see two of the boys struggling to their feet while Jake helped the third.

"Follow me! Stay close. We're not far, so give this walk all the strength you can."

I glanced behind me as we started for the barn. The wind nearly knocked them over. Regaining their balance, they trailed me through the snow.

My tracks were gone already and the fence was nearly covered now, but I kept my eyes focused on the half inch of rail that rose above the four feet of snow. Panic propelled me forward so that I barely noticed the winds that tore through my clothes.

One foot in front of the other. Then check behind. The boys followed, their arms clasped around their bodies, Jake following behind the rest. Another two steps.

Andrew's breath came in shallow gasps.

When were we going to get there?

"Hey, sir!"

I turned to see Jake on his knees beside a fallen boy.

Backtracking a few steps, I touched the boy's lips. My fingers were too frozen to feel his breath.

I looked into Jake's eyes, seeing a drowsy fear in the depths. "Walk along the fence line. Straight ahead. It runs to my barn. I'll come back for you."

He groaned but gave a single nod.

With Andrew tucked under my left arm, I scooped up the other boy with my right, then piled them like logs close to my chest.

I sprinted toward the barn, leaving the three behind in the cold.

My legs felt like I ran upriver in deep water.

I gulped for air, the cold wind pouring into my lungs. The pain didn't matter. These boys were dying.

What would I tell their parents, that their child was dead because I stopped to rest?

I almost plowed into the barn door. I dumped the boys in the snow and wrenched open the door. The wind knocked it shut, but I tugged it open again, braced my back against it, and pulled both boys by their ankles into the dark stillness.

Trevor barked and lunged toward the boys, his black-and-white fur matted with flecks of ice.

I gasped in a relatively warm breath, and the taste of manure and hay filled my senses. I patted his head. "It's okay, boy. I'll be back."

With all my strength, I pushed the door open into the wind. The violent, blowing gust almost sapped the rest of my strength.

My tracks were gone.

Jake had his arms under the other two boys' shoulders as they struggled along. Each one's head reached as high as my chest, but I picked up two and trotted back, so tired I nearly collapsed before reaching the barn. I dropped them in the snow.

While I held the door open against the wind, the three crawled in.

I let the door slam and slid the heavy bar to lock the doors closed.

Trevor stood beside the boys, his tail wagging. His nose lifted as he sniffed.

My breath came in heaving gasps as I stepped over the boys and grabbed a shovel. The fire in my blacksmith furnace was filled with orange embers from pine logs, but we needed more warmth. I crossed the barn to a stall near the door, thrust the shovel into a small pile of coal, and hefted the handle.

I rushed to the fire and tossed in the black chunks. I flung the shovel aside and lay down several horse blankets.

Jake pulled Andrew closer to the fire.

"Take your coats off." I grabbed the boy I'd carried first and lifted his lifeless body. His clothes were too thin, useless against the cold. I tugged off his jacket as I laid him beside the furnace.

I'd rescued the blacksmith forge from rust and decay years ago. A mobile Civil War piece, no one had use of it now. I prayed it would warm these boys. During the summer it produced incredible amounts of heat. But my barn was huge—two stories and eight stalls—with the hayloft filled with hay. And I had never felt this cold before.

The wind outside rattled the wood planks. The howl covered the sound of the horses in their stalls.

I stripped off the boy's boots and socks and flung them to the side. Trevor bounced toward them and sniffed.

One of the other boys was taking his jacket off as he tried to stand, but his shaking fingers wouldn't work. My hands, trembling as well, weren't quite as frozen, and soon he gave up and lay by the fire. I started on his shoes. His laces were frozen solid, and I snatched a knife and cut his boots.

"If you can, stand."

"I'm so sleepy," one muttered. His tongue sounded thick.

"Stay awake!" I snarled so loud Trevor turned and tucked his tail. "Don't sleep." None could stand.

Soon all five boys lay close to furnace as fire licked their skin, all wearing only pants and shirt. Jake rested on his knees close to Andrew, who hadn't stirred. I felt the small boy's chest. The heartbeat was faint, and his breaths were shallow and distant.

Please, God.

I had a lot on my conscience. This I didn't need to haunt me.

"Will he survive?"

I looked down into Jake's eyes, reflecting the yellow flames. His sandy hair was matted against his skin, and freckles stood out against pale, frostbitten cheeks. Despite his youth, his muscles under the thin cotton shirt were firm. "I think so."

One of the boys stirred.

I reached for a stack of horse blankets and wrapped them around each of their shoulders or lay them on their shivering bodies.

I brushed the melting snow from the stirring boy's dark hair. "What's your name?"

He opened his eyes. "John."

I looked at the boy beside him, who did his best to stay awake. "And your name?"

He'd been leaning on his elbow but now sat up. "Paul."

"And you?" The other lay with the blanket covering his torso. He sobbed. "Joseph."

"Boys, you're going to be okay." I set a pot of coffee on top of the furnace and settled beside them. "You're going to be okay." I was trying to convince myself. I sat next to Andrew again and watched his short breaths.

Trevor curled up at my feet, and I ran my fingers through his warm fur. My skin tingled.

I rubbed my hands together. In seconds, pain ripped through my bones.

How frozen had my fingers been?

Jake wrapped his arms across his body and tucked his hands in his armpits. His eyes closed and he leaned forward and groaned.

Joseph sniffed then coughed. "My hands hurt. Bad."

"It's going to. But that's a good sign."

Please God, let it be a good sign.

"Oh. Ow!" Paul sat up. Maybe the pain was exactly what they needed.

Over the next few minutes, the boys' groaning turned to sharp cries. Joseph rolled in front of the furnace, curled in a ball. I leaned over and set my hand on his back. He shivered as he rocked in pain.

Sobs and screams filled my barn as agony racked the boys' bodies.

And I was helpless to do a blessed thing.

"Hold on. Hold on." What else could be said? "It'll be better soon."

Three of the boys wailed, while Andrew lay unmoving. Jake stared at the fire, tears streaming down his face. His arms were still curled around his chest, his breath puffing out his cheeks as he let out the air slowly.

Through a crack in the door, time seemed to stand still, but as the snow continued to pile up outside darkness overtook day.

Their cries quieted into whimpers. Soon, as the fire roared, all five rested under their blankets. We lay in a semicircle around the fire, Jake and Andrew to my right, Paul, Joseph, and John to my left.

I sighed. "In the morning, if the snow stops, we'll get you home."

Joseph's voice was weak and sounded as if he spoke a foreign language.

Jake lifted his head and spoke past me. Then said in English, "He left his bag in the snow. I told him our parents will understand." He laid his head on the blanket. "I'm sorry. It's rude to speak in a language you don't understand."

The barn shook from the wind.

"Was the cave your idea, Jake?"

"Yes."

"You probably saved your friends' lives." I couldn't help constantly checking Andrew's torso. His chest rose, stronger this time.

The coffee was boiling, and I poured a cup and handed it to Jake. Joseph took one as well. "Anyone else?"

They shook their heads.

I sat down and stared into the flames.

After a sip Jake said, "You're him."

"Who?"

"Philip Anderson."

The boys sat up, all except Andrew.

"I can tell by your eyes." Jake set his cup down beside him. "They say they're wolf eyes."

"That's what they say." How old was this boy? Thirteen?

He kept talking. "They say you killed four men in the Badlands."

"Yeah."

"You outdueled John Maxwell. And fought off Jacob Wilkes in a swordfight."

"I did."

"And you're a deputy marshal."

"I'd forgotten about that, but yeah. I have a badge."

By now all the boys were leaning on their elbows, looking at me. All but Andrew.

"Is Raven in her stall?"

I glanced into the darkness, beyond the light cast by the fire. "She is."

"I saw her once," Joseph said from my left. "You were riding into town."

Paul moved to sit up. "I've never seen her."

"Stay by the fire," I said. "You'll see the horses in the morning."

No one spoke for some time, and Paul lay back down.

Jake finally said, "I read in the papers that the government wants to talk with you."

"Yeah." I rubbed my forehead and kept my hand over my eyes, as if hiding. "In Deadwood after the Maxwell Gang was broken up, the Senate wanted to hear about what happened."

"Why?"

"Because they make laws where they're needed after certain events, I think. They don't like gangs within their borders, and maybe they want to find a way to stop them." I leaned back and crossed my arms. "They didn't need to talk to me then but changed their minds."

"But the paper said you didn't go to Washington."

I'd decided to just stay put. I wasn't about to leave my land. "No. I didn't go."

"Can you get in trouble for that?"

"What are they going to do? They have all they need to understand what happened." I remembered these were just kids, and although they read the paper, they didn't need to know more than that. "It's okay. I've worked it all out." Which wasn't entirely true. I just hoped the whole situation would go away.

Jake took a sip of his coffee. "They say Jacob Wilkes is still roaming out there."

I grimaced as the idea rushed into the forefront of my mind. "Yeah, he is."

"You going to have to kill him?"

If I were a kid I suppose I'd ask the same question. I thought back on when I was that young. I probably peppered

the man who trained me to shoot a gun with a barrage of incessant requests for information about glorified violence.

The question was honest and deserved an honest answer.

"I hope it doesn't come to that."

2

Anna trudged through the snow. Wind picked up the white flakes and flung them into her eyes, the only part of her that was uncovered.

Doc Wilson had set aside time this morning to speak with her, and the worst storm she'd ever seen wasn't about to stop her. She tucked the small package deeper under her heavy long coat and approached the fence to his house.

She was in love. What of it? There was nothing she or Philip could do about the fact a blizzard kept them from seeing each other. It wouldn't change the longing in her heart to be with him. Even if he were by her side, there was only one thing that could assuage the passion that burned in her belly—a lifetime with him.

Many women had fallen in love—perhaps all of them—at one time. Her heart had simply chosen a wonderful man. Wonderful and filled with violence. So her love came with adventures of a life-threatening kind. Her favorite authors would be proud.

She pushed on the fence, shoving aside a fresh drift.

The overcast day was dark enough to allow the warm glow from the front window to cast light on the snow, giving the blanket a brighter hue. The window's curtain was swept to the side, and a small man peered through the glass. He let the cloth fall, and his shadow moved away.

Lifting her feet high to pass over the deep, suffocating snow, she approached the front of the house.

The door swung open. "My dear! Come in out of this cold! Quickly now."

She lost her footing on a step and caught herself on the door's frame. That was close.

"You really shouldn't be out in this."

"I know, but I had an appointment."

He grabbed her arm and led her inside. "I expected you to stay home."

In the entrance, she gently pulled her arm from his grasp and removed her hat. Snow fell to the thick rug. When he closed the door, the wind stopped as if a phonograph was shut off.

Silence rung in her ears.

Without speaking, she removed her scarf and coat. She breathed in a thick smell that seemed to shoot through her thoughts. She sniffed again.

"Ah, you smell alcohol. I use it to stop infection after a surgery." Doc Wilson pushed his thin, wire glasses farther up his nose and ran a hand over both sides of his hair. Anna tried not to look at the creamy bald patch in the center.

"It smells clean."

He rubbed his hands together and motioned to a door to the left. "Through there, where we can talk in private." He reached out, took her coat, and hung it on a wooden stand with three long prongs.

Down the hall was a room devoted to operations. To the

right, Rachel had a bed after Jeb had stabbed her. Upstairs, Doc Wilson lived with his wife.

Someday Mitchell would need a proper hospital. Doc Wilson was getting older, and while he took care of the patients like he would the children he didn't have, his aging body wouldn't be able to keep up with the rising demand of illness and injuries.

With the small package in her hand, she started toward his office door to the left but peeked into the opposite room.

Her stomach clenched as she saw a sleeping man lying in the bed wearing a robe. One leg was stretched out without a covering. The other was simply a stub capped with a red stained bandaged.

Doc Wilson again grabbed her arm and led her into his office.

"Frostbite," he whispered as he motioned to a seat. "I was forced to remove his leg." As he turned around the mahogany desk and sat, a look of pain filled his eyes. "Above the knee."

She rubbed her cold cheeks to keep her thoughts from her fluttering stomach.

A clock pealed to her right, and she glanced at the pendulum that rocked back and forth to the rhythm of her breath. The chimes, the hands declared, would ring eleven times.

Medical books filled two bookshelves behind him, and by the window on a low wooden bed designed for examinations lay three open tomes he'd been studying.

Before the last bell rang, he folded his hands in front of him. "So, my dear. What can I do for you?"

Anna set the package in front of her. Her hands shook from the cold, but she carefully tore off the brown paper.

She spun the novel around so Doc Wilson could see the cover.

He leaned forward and peered through his lenses. "Anderson's War. Interesting." He reached out. "May I?"

"Please."

He touched the vague imprint of a black horse, a shadow of a man with a gun, and a cabin with flames roaring from its collapsing roof. Drawing the book closer, he thumbed through the pages. "Does he know?"

"I haven't seen him for a month. He was called to Fort Randall to discuss horses with Captain Smith for two weeks, and now the storm." She leaned back into the cushions behind her. "So I doubt it, no."

He read several lines.

Would there be a moment she would forget the clock ticked? The tick-tock pounded in her mind.

"No," Doc Wilson said finally. "He's not going to like this. He didn't like the articles, did he?"

"If he knew I saved them in my diary, I'm sure he'd be angry."

Doc Wilson sighed and looked at the book as if it held a trapped mouse. "And now he's a dime novel hero. How much of the story does it cover?"

"Nothing of his trouble with Jacob. Just his fight against the Maxwell Gang."

His brow lifted. "You've read it? This looks new."

"I . . ." She looked at the snow-encrusted window, then at the table where the morning's sallow light fell. "I have another copy." She felt the red touch her cheeks.

He broke the book open with both thumbs. "Nothing to be ashamed of, my dear. He's a hero, whether he likes it or not." He looked into her eyes. "He's *your* hero."

Her cheeks burned now.

"You didn't come to me just to discuss a book." He took off his glasses. "What can I do for you?"

Where to begin? "This book, along with some other things . . . well, when Philip finds out about them, he's going to be upset."

"I agree. I don't know him well, but yes. I know him well enough to say he doesn't like to be noticed."

She swallowed and drew from a small reserve of courage. "A war rages inside him." She rubbed her temples, as if rubbing away pain. "Memories bombard him, triggered by . . . by little things. Memories so powerful it seems as if he's been transported back in time. He's there for minutes, sometimes longer. He'll move as if in that moment—actions that sometimes make no sense to the here and now. Every so often he breaks down after the memory—"

"Breaks down how?"

"In tears. He'll curl up on his side while holding his head, utterly without control." If telling Philip's secrets to the doctor was wrong, at the very least the release she felt at this moment was worth the cost. "He told me that before a gunfight, when he feels like he'll need to pull his gun, he sees the night his parents were murdered. In the vision, he is able to draw a gun faster than the outlaws and stop his parents from dying."

She rested against the arm of the chair, her energy spent.

Doc Wilson's contemplative gaze seemed to push past her into some realm of his own mind. He stood and approached the bookshelf to his right. "You're wondering if there's a tonic that might help."

"His mind must be clear in case Jacob returns."

He paused. "Jacob Wilkes." The venom in his voice was an echo to her own feelings. "Perhaps he's gone, never to return."

"You can believe that if you like," Anna said. "I'll prepare as best I can, just in case."

He ran a finger along the top shelf, then the one below it. He put a finger on the first book, a thick blue volume. Then the next, a faded red. The third was green. His finger pulled and the book slid easily into his hand. He turned and set the thin book on the table and pushed it toward her. "Orson Squire Fowler's new study on the human mind."

She read aloud the title. "Human Science of Phrenology."

"Parts of your brain have different functions." He returned to his seat. "The stronger part of your brain, the larger the protrusion, and there will be a bump on your head." He touched the center of his bald forehead. "If I'm shy, then the shy part of my brain will be larger."

"How will this help?"

"I must diagnose a patient who undoubtedly won't be coming in to see me. If you can tell me where the protrusions in his cranium are, I will know his temperament, his disposition. What is out of balance will be clearer, and then I'll be able to give him the tonic he needs."

"You believe those bumps on his head will tell you all you need to know?"

His shoulders squared, and he sat higher. "My dear, this is science. Not guesswork. Yes, I'll be able to help him once you map his head for me."

Something was unsettled in her stomach. But like he said, this was science. Did the answer lie in chemicals the powders could divine? Or was there other help for Philip?

She didn't want to lose him, especially if there was something she could do.

3

The view from the saddle was like nothing else. I sat higher, looking over the world as if a king—watching between two black, upright ears.

From where I sat atop Raven's back, the world was white. I looked into the valley where my land stretched along the frozen James River. One hundred sixty acres, with a copse of trees along the north and south edges, a field I planted in the spring to the north of my barn, and a one-hundred-acre horse pasture to the south. Between the two fields was a lane bordered by a split-rail fence, my favorite part of the land.

I wasn't ashamed to admit I was leaving my property and traveling five miles to Mitchell just so I could talk with Anna.

Or maybe it was the food. I was tired of beans. Beans and bacon.

Two weeks ago the boys had been reunited with their parents.

Andrew had survived the night and was hungry. I learned a few days later he lost two toes. Not important ones, I was told. They all seemed important to me.

The boys were lucky to be alive. Their fathers talked of children crawling home, their faces masked with ice, only a small hole visible for breathing. Most had made it home, all of them from the Hutterite school. Not all schools had been as fortunate.

In my barn, the fathers had thanked me for saving their boys' lives. We would talk about an option to buy the land on the other side of the river in the spring as a token of their appreciation.

The mothers had made me two pies each which made ten pies, a good portion of which were rhubarb. Pie. Ugh. Rhubarb especially. But I took them with all proper appreciation, and now they sat almost frozen in the tack stall. I sat up in the saddle. No, that's not true. I left Trevor in the barn.

I thought of going back. No. He earned himself a pie. Ten pies.

Spring couldn't get here soon enough. Horse training, wheat planting, land clearing, cabin building—I simply loved this land. The work, the animals, the river, the field filled with buffalo grass and blue grama so perfect for my horses. I couldn't wait to be back to it.

And now Anna would have a hand in building a cabin, a home she would live in someday.

Raven tapped the snow with her sock-covered front foot, feeling my surge of eager energy.

I tugged the reins toward Mitchell, and we started along the top of the ravine where the road to town should be.

Raven's hooves punched through the top layer of ice crusted snow. The sun was thinly veiled by a high layer of clouds, but I still squinted as the light reflected off an eternity of snow. Ice crystals fell, filling the air with a clean, frozen scent.

My Smith and Wesson bounced at my side under my duster. Behind me, saddle bags jostled as Raven pressed on. I'd decided to bring ammunition with me wherever I went, as well as a handy Colt .45 single action. My Winchester rested in its scabbard by my knee.

I wanted to add a tomahawk or bow and quiver of arrows, perhaps even a Gatling gun. At some point, I needed to trust God that my weapon at my hip was enough protection, so I drew the line. A rapid repeater Gatling gun was high on my purchase agenda though. When I bought it, I'd even let Anna shoot it.

Heavily armed as I was, I knew I was only as protected as my eyes and fingers were ready. I kept a steady lookout.

Raven recognized the buildings as we rode into town. She blew a long cloud of mist, then chomped on her bit.

She enjoyed the ride almost as much as I did.

Months ago I decided Raven wasn't to be tied outside a business. For a dime she could be housed in a livery for a few hours. The expense would not only keep her warm but keep her hidden. I didn't need everyone in town knowing my location.

I dismounted at the long barn and caught the reins. I pulled her to the sliding door and tugged. The rollers above gave way, and we slipped inside and closed the door. Several horses whinnied as I let my eyes adjust to the light.

"Mr. Anderson." The boy's voice came from a distance, and his footsteps padded across straw and dirt. "This snow."

"I know. It's been a while since I've made it to town."

"Glad to see Raven is well. Sir," he added quickly.

"Of course she is, Devin." With one hand I gave him a dime. With the other I gave him the reins. "Why?"

"Lot of people lost their cattle in the storm. Hooves froze to the ground. Then their legs just"—he dropped the reins and snapped his fingers—"broke right off." He picked up the leather strips.

I tried to hide my revulsion. "Awful. But no, my horses are in fine shape."

He led Raven toward the stall. The livery smelled a lot like my barn—straw and manure. Comforting, really.

"And Devin, last time I brought Raven in you gave her a rubdown. I hadn't paid for that. Here's a nickel."

"Please, sir, no. It's an honor. Really it is."

"An honor?"

He turned and looked around Raven's belly. "Since you've been bringing Raven here, our business has nearly doubled."

"Doubled? Why?"

"You're a hero, if you don't mind me saying, sir. Yes, a hero." He wiped his berry-red nose with his sleeve. "And if you bring the likes of Raven here, well then sir, we must be the best."

Raven whinnied, and the other horses answered as if there was some sort of joke. In the daylight that streamed through the cracks in the livery walls, I could see the admiration shining from the boy's face.

I should try and live up to his dreams. Instead I asked, "Devin, how old are you?"

"Twelve, sir."

"Well, it's time someone told you. There's no such thing as heroes." I reached into the saddlebag, pulled out a small leather pouch, and slid it into my duster pocket.

I vaguely recalled that if I were twelve and someone told me something so ludicrous, the comment would simply fly past my ears. As proof, his beaming face changed none at all.

I bit my irritation back like Raven chewed her bit.

"Have a good day, Devin." I tipped my hat.

"Wait. Wait! I forgot." He dropped Raven's reins and dashed off to a small office beside the sliding barn door. In two seconds he returned at a run with an envelope in his hand. "Colin said someone left this for you in case you came back into town." He held out the small rectangle-shaped paper.

Before I took it, I smelled perfume. "A woman?"

"He didn't say."

The letter wasn't sealed, so I lifted the flap. A small page was imprinted with flowers. In the center, scribbled in black ink, were the words *I'm sorry*. The writing looked like a child's handiwork. I turned the paper over but found no other words.

I stuffed the note in my pocket and nodded my thanks to Devin.

Who could have sent the letter? A man wouldn't send a note of apology. And Anna's handwriting was beautiful, not childish. I didn't know many more women, especially ones who would write me a note.

Beth, Anna's younger sister? What could Beth possibly be sorry for?

My steps in the snow crunched faster.

What about Becky, my best friend Scott's girl? Seemed unlikely.

Rachel? I'd helped her leave a life of prostitution, and she'd taken over Caroline's Kitchen just after Caroline died. Hadn't she come from a family that had supplied her with education enough for better handwriting?

Between the two best possibilities, Beth and Rachel, Rachel's past held the most to be sorry for. Anyway, pointless speculation. Time to move on. Hopefully the reason for the apology was simple, like she changed the name of Caroline's Kitchen or something.

I rushed across the packed snow of First Street, took a right past Wilkes Bank onto Main. The history I had with the Wilkes family made me shiver.

Every breath came in large puffs, and I stepped through the vapor. I hurried down the wide street then turned toward a side road until reaching the restaurant. The large, red sign had been swept free of snow. Caroline's Kitchen. Not a name change.

I stepped onto the brushed boardwalk and grasped the

knob. I pulled and was met by a blast of warmth and the smell of roasting chicken.

I took in the scene as I unbuttoned my duster. The orange glow of lamplight splashed against the wood-paneled walls and twelve tables—six on each side, two with families. I recognized both as acquaintances.

I scanned the back table where my old buddy Leroy always sat to the right of the door to the kitchen.

Scott's red hair caught my eye first, and his back was to the door. His girl Becky sat next to him, her blond hair bouncing as she turned to look at me. Leroy's grizzled face squeezed tight, and he squinted as I stepped in the door.

My gaze leveled at the man standing beside the table.

Ryan, one of Jacob Wilkes's chosen men.

At night as I lay down, my back still stung. My jaw twitched in every storm. The bruises on my stomach had taken six months to fade.

Ryan's face flashed through my mind every time my body ached. The beatings this man delivered could never be forgotten.

His massive form towered over my friends. He held a shotgun in both hands.

My hands were a blur as I leveled the Smith and Wesson at Ryan. "Drop the gun, now!"

Both families ducked under the table, their chairs falling over like trees in a tornado. Screams mixed with the crash of dishes.

Ryan turned toward me as slowly as the second hand of a clock.

I pulled back the hammer. "Drop the gun!"

His red lips—so thin I barely made them out—opened wide, his bottom jaw protruding just half an inch from his top lip. His tiny, dark brown eyes held a look of confusion.

City Marshal Stone had put out a warrant for Jacob, Ryan, and Jeb, insisting shoot on sight if armed.

If the muzzle of his shotgun moved one inch closer, I would fire. And not into his shoulders like I had John Maxwell. At this distance, I could send him to eternal judgment in the fiery pits of hell. Similar, no doubt, to the hell he'd made my life.

My finger twitched. Not enough to drop the hammer on his death.

Scott held out a hand. "Philip, no!"

Rachel stepped into the kitchen doorway in Ryan's shadow. He was a massive man, but I couldn't take the risk of firing now. A lesson from the man who taught me to shoot flashed through my mind. Bullets pass through men and kill what's beyond them. I kept my revolver pointed at his heart.

I held my fire.

"No, Philip, please!" Rachel sobbed. "Don't kill him!"

My gun quavered. What was this?

Scott stood slowly, both hands held out, palms forward. "Philip, he's one of ours."

I squeezed my lips together and stared down the sights of my revolver at Ryan. It wasn't often you had a mortal enemy facing the barrel of your gun and you didn't fire.

"Ryan," Scott said. "Lower the shotgun. Slowly."

Ryan's eyes, dull and unthinking, looked from my face to the Smith and Wesson. His mouth still hung open.

Rachel's voice was shrill. "Philip! I love him!"

The world swirled around me as I stood still. Love him? Jacob's second? Ridiculous.

Ryan stood unmoving, his features bulging, his idiot expression incapable of love.

Red curled around my mind as I pressed on the trigger. Ask forgiveness instead of permission. Deal with consequences later.

Danger always offered a vision. So why wasn't my mind filled with the vision of my parents' deaths?

I leveled my gaze into Ryan's eyes and saw nothing. No fear. Not even worry. "He stabbed you, Rachel."

"No, that was Jeb, remember?"

"Anna shot him!" I motioned with my left hand. "In self-defense!"

"Philip, please!" Rachel grasped Ryan's arm and pulled herself in front of him so that my aim was between her eyes. "Please, just listen."

I lifted the muzzle toward his forehead. "He must answer for his crimes."

Ryan moved almost imperceptibly toward the table. With a hand on the barrel and his other on Rachel's shoulder, he handed his shotgun to Scott.

A child at my feet whimpered.

I pointed my gun to the ceiling and slowly lowered the hammer.

Dear God. What have I done? What have I become?

While the families skirted past me as fast as they could, I holstered the gun. A burst of cold air hit my back as the frightened men and women escaped with their children.

Two emotions battled inside my gut. The first was shame. But more overpowering was the feeling I'd been stabbed in the back.

Betrayed.

I was about to turn and leave when Ryan finally opened his mouth. "Sent you a note." His voice was flat and a little scratchy.

"What are you talking about?" I returned with a snarl.

"A note." He nodded like a small child several times.

His clay-colored hair, thick sideburns, untrimmed brows, and neckless body made me shiver with revulsion. I knew—yes—the note, but I wouldn't acknowledge the two words he sent me. "You're a killer."

No one moved. I looked into their pleading eyes, first

Scott, then Becky, Leroy, and finally Rachel. Rachel, who had been a prostitute. And now it seemed she'd fallen into the same trap. "You love him? This . . . this killer?"

Her blotchy face didn't turn from mine, but her thick lips quivered. "Yes."

"Fine. He's yours."

As I turned to leave, I heard her burst into tears.

I heard boots come after me, not heavy like Ryan's, but the quick, light pad of Scott. I heard his order for Becky to find Anna before I slammed the door behind me.

Outside in the cold on the street, my best friend faced me. "You won't even give us a chance to explain."

"Explain?" His finger against my chest made me want to break his bones. "Scott, your loyalty is . . . is pathetic."

He pointed toward the restaurant. "You weren't here. You can't know."

"What is there to know? He's made his camp. He sits at Jacob's fire."

"He's misdirected."

"Has this whole town gone crazy? He's a murderer. He's supposed to be in jail," I yelled, but the snow around us muffled my voice.

"Or have you been on that farm too long?" Scott's face was bright with a mixture of anger and cold. "You won't let anyone explain!"

"I don't need anyone to explain." As soon as the words slipped from my mouth, I knew I was being thickheaded. But the fire in my brisket burned too hot for me to back down. He should be in jail! I looked away.

Scott took advantage of my averted gaze, obviously taking my embarrassment as a sign he was getting through to me. He stood on the boardwalk so that he was tall enough to look directly into my eyes. "Look, Philip, I'm not mad at you. I see your point. Yeah, things changed fast here. But you're not alone anymore, buddy. Remember when it was just you and me in the field shooting cans and talking about women? Those days are over. You're famous. And I'm involved in law. People look up to us now. We need to watch each other's backs like never before."

I grunted.

"Philip, you're a hero now." He patted my shoulder and grinned. "Not all are born heroes like me."

I set my boot on the boardwalk and leaned on the rail. I let loose a long breath, and the vapor looked like I just loosed a draw from a cigar.

With my boot I cleared snow from the edge. "Did I make a fool of myself?"

"Yeah, this time you did. The Jacksons and the Millers—"

"I'll buy them a month of meals." I leaned both arms on the rails and looked at the door of the restaurant.

"Good, good." Scott settled by my side. "And keep in mind, they weren't the only ones in there. I was a victim—"

"I'm not buying you free meals." But why not? I had money—lots of it—from hunting down the Maxwell Gang. "Perhaps one wouldn't hurt." I took another breath, pushing out the anger that had threatened to turn to violence. "This isn't easy, you know. I just want to be left alone."

"Maybe someday you will. But for now, you'll need everyone on your side. As many people as you can get." He nodded toward the restaurant's door. "It's not easy taking advice, especially when you're a leader who doesn't want to be in charge."

A leader who doesn't want to be. His words echoed through my mind.

Footsteps on the end of the boardwalk caught my attention. Not a man's, but a feminine, soft step. Anna.

She wore a tan coat that draped from her neck to her

boots. Long buttons closed the fabric across her chest, and a clasp lay close to her neck. A warm hat framed her wide cheeks, raven hair, and bright blue eyes.

Our gazes locked. "Philip, are you all right?"

"I am now." All my anger was gone, replaced with a desire to be with Anna. I was pathetic. In love and confused. "I . . ."

Down the street, five people walked into the empty lane. One man entered a store as I heard the sound of a bell. Across the street, an older woman and a tall, young man—probably her son—shuffled to Gale's Market. Another man marched down the street, his hands in his pockets.

None of them worried me.

What caught my eye was the thin man with his head wrapped in a linen cloth. His hat set atop, heavy coat wrapped loosely around him, and tattered pants hanging over his boots. His walk was direct, as if he were motivated for more than shopping.

His hand reached into his coat.

"Anna, Scott, inside now." I unbuttoned the bottom half buttons on my duster.

As I barked the order, both listened.

Anna was inside first, but Scott lingered. "What?"

"That man."

Scott glanced back. His voice was colder than the air. "Philip. That's Jeb."

Recognition filled me. With Ryan inside and Jeb outside, my trust wavered. I didn't want to take chances. "Jeb in love with anyone?"

"No, he's not ours."

"Keep an eye on Ryan."

"Yeah." The door closed.

Was Jeb returning to kill Rachel? Or perhaps to find me? Everyone knew I loved hanging out at Caroline's.

Jeb and Ryan. All we needed was Jacob and the reunion would be complete.

I took a step away from the restaurant, my Smith and Wesson within easy reach.

Jeb slowed.

The high clouds, the snowy streets, the muffled sounds of distant horses and wagons moved to the recesses of my mind. Night pushed into my head, a familiar vision. My father sat reading by the fire while my mother cooked. I could smell the food on the warm, gentle wind.

Three outlaws entered our camp.

Jeb took a few steps closer, this time halting then moving closer.

The robber asked for the box.

My fingers tingled. Buffalo grass swayed around me as the moon's light bathed the covered wagon in a silver glow to my left.

"We've no money," my father replied.

Almost time to pull my gun.

"Anderson!" Jeb's voice cut through the vision. "Philip Anderson!"

The snow-covered street with the lone figure of Jeb filled my vision. His hand was still in his coat pocket.

My fingers hovered over my gun.

He was close now, and I made out his gray, oily hair. Thick wrinkles ran contrary to laugh lines, and tobacco stained his scraggly beard.

The frigid air was still, but the ten feet between Jeb and me felt like a whirlwind of snow and fire.

I took a few steps to my left, each stride crunching under my boots, and stopped in the middle of the street. Bullets that passed by me might hit someone. But I hoped it wouldn't come to that.

A few onlookers paused on the boardwalk.

My hips shifted so my gun was visible.

I was lean, my eyes the color of a wolf's, and I was five

inches taller than Jeb. I used all of it to intimidate him. "Come down to the jail house."

His eye twitched. "Been doing some thinking." He shook his head slightly. "They're going to hang me if I come with you."

"Probably."

"I don't see any other way."

"You don't have to do this, Jeb."

"I'm open for suggestions."

In the cold light of reason, Ryan could be on the streets as a citizen. His crimes were typical of a brawler. But Jeb had brutally stabbed Rachel. And I believed he shot and killed the security guard in the Wilkes Bank. The man would hang.

"See," he said in a slow drawl. "There's nothing for it 'cept going down into history."

His hand twitched and his coat moved at the pocket. I almost drew.

A figure appeared to the right, just inside the window of the mercantile. The only man I knew who could be that big was Ryan. In the shimmer of the reflected light, I made out his shotgun. The barrel was pointed at Jeb. He must have gone around through the alley to flank Jeb.

The door opened without a sound, and Ryan stepped onto the boardwalk.

Was I facing two men? Or was Jeb?

Ryan started for Jeb across the snow. The big man was quiet, his feet barely making a sound. I had to give him some credit.

Jeb turned to see what I glanced at.

"Jeb," I said quickly before he saw Ryan. "Take your chances in the courts."

He turned his attention back to me. "I'll hang."

"I stood before a judge and didn't hang."

Ryan moved closer.

My hand hovered so close to my gun, I could almost feel the grip. "Give it a chance. Choose honor."

Jeb stared at me for a moment, then burst into laughter. "Honor?"

Ryan lifted his shotgun and brought the stock down. Jeb crumpled in a heap.

Fire burned in Ryan's eyes, but his face remain placid.

"Ryan, do me a favor and lay your shotgun down."

He looked at me then took off his coat, shifting the shotgun from one hand to the other. He wrapped the gun and set it in the snow. "They say . . ." He licked his lips. "They say you can't get a gun wet."

"They also say don't wet your lips in freezing weather." With Smith and Wesson in hand, I pushed Jeb's shoulder, and he slumped back. His head rolled to the side.

With my left hand, I searched his coat pocket. Empty. Interesting.

I felt around his waist, his chest, his legs. Nothing.

I looked up at Ryan, who seemed to watch with interest. "He's unarmed."

"Sometimes. He keeps a knife. In his boot." He pointed. "That one."

After finding nothing, I rocked back on my heels. "I don't get it."

"He never went without a gun. Never."

Still hunched, I said, "I can imagine." With the barrel of my gun, I pushed my hat back so I could get a better look at Ryan. "I've got to tell you, I don't trust you. I don't *want* to trust you. You and this guy," I motioned to Jeb, "go together in my mind. If I ever, ever get a whiff that you might hurt one of my friends, even if you say something to hurt their feelings, I'll kill you. You said you were sorry. Well, I *don't* forgive you. I want to kill you."

"You didn't kill Jeb."

46

I opened my mouth to respond to such a bland, stupid statement, then shut my mouth. "Yeah. I didn't kill Jeb."

What was going on? Why would Jeb face me unarmed, as if he wanted me to shoot him? What kind of man walked to his death so that another simply looks guilty?

4

I had imagined having life-changing conversations with Anna in the small library of her home. Instead we sat in Caroline's Kitchen.

Anna sat across from me. Rachel next to her. Leroy next to me.

Ryan and Scott had taken Jeb to Marshal Stone's office. I expected to see Marshal Stone show up in ten minutes with his bulldog face demanding to be told what happened. Odds were split he would swear.

As Anna spoke her hands waved one direction then swirled in a circle, a mesmerizing dance. "The first rose came just before the statehood party in Yankton, right after Rachel was stabbed. When I visited Rachel, I went up Doc Wilson's step and found a single rose propped against the door." Her brow lifted, as if she spoke of a mystery. "Since she moved back into Caroline's house, she's gotten a rose twice a week." She lowered her voice. "Despite the snow."

I wasn't quite as enthralled. "Ryan?"

Anna ignored me. "A week before the snowstorm, Ryan walked into Marshal Stone's office and turned himself in. The marshal kept him overnight, and the next day they met with the judge. Ryan simply kept repeating, 'what can I do to make this right?'"

Leroy snorted and coughed, as if still trying to clear the gun smoke of Civil War battles from his lungs. "Judges love that kind of thing."

Anna's eyes flashed. "Ryan and Marshal Stone have been close to each other ever since. As a child, no one taught Ryan what was right and wrong."

I must have grunted too loud, because Anna stiffened. "Look," she said, "He's not bright. But he's honest. He apologized to me right away." She crossed her arms. "I forgave him."

"If he's not bright, why did you choose to love him, Rachel?" As soon as the words slipped from my mouth, I regretted them.

Rachel's hands were shaking, and when she spoke it was through clenched teeth. "Why did you trust me so long ago, and yet you don't trust Ryan?" If she could flip the table and smash the heavy wood over my head, her eyes told me she would. "I did far worse things than Ryan, so why did you give me a chance? Because you're big and strong and could subdue me? You've got a gun, Philip. Guns are levelers. Are you afraid of him?"

I opened my mouth, but she spoke quickly. "You were nicer to me because I'm pretty. Give him the same opportunity as you did me."

She erupted into tears. She'd been holding that in for a while.

The only sound was her weeping. I stared at the table, searching my heart for an answer. "I'm struggling with the fact that he can go from lawless to . . . to *this* in one month." I motioned to her.

Instead of firing back, she looked into my eyes. Did she see I earnestly tried to understand? She lifted her apron and wiped at her face. "I know men. With every beat of my heart, I choose kindness over the frills and foibles any man can offer." Through her tears she said, "Ryan brought me a rose." Her hands covered her eyes and she sobbed.

What did it all mean? I had been kind to her. But kindness can be faked.

Kindness itself doesn't matter, but the feelings behind the kindness. "He loves you."

"He's honest. That's new to me."

I looked at Leroy.

"I like him," he said.

My gaze met Anna's. She said, "I . . . I guess, Rachel, I'll speak openly in front of you. Philip, she's happy. And she respects your opinion this much." Anna put an arm around Rachel. "Enough this rips her apart."

Rachel put her head on Anna's shoulder.

This was my fault?

Yeah, Philip. This is your fault.

But I so wanted to hang on to my anger.

I still didn't trust Ryan. But I said, "I'm sorry, Rachel." I reached out and touched her hand. "Ryan threw punches, I threw punches. In the end, we've all been caught up in Jacob's brutality."

Rachel sniffed and wiped her nose. She actually looked at me. "This is hard on you, I realize that. But . . . I . . . he made me smile." She reached into her apron pocket and pulled out a piece of paper. "Look at this."

She unfolded a newspaper clipping and slid it across the table. In the center of a long list of sales in a border with large, bold print were the words *I'm sorry*. Nothing else.

Rachel returned the paper to her pocket. "His letter to the city."

I pulled out the note. "I'm guessing this is from him."

"That's my stationary." She smiled as she read the note. "He means well."

When I had reached for the note, my hand had touched the leather pouch. The map.

Ignoring the pressing thought, I said, "What does Scott say?" I offered the question to Leroy.

"If there's a fist fight in the court room, it's Ryan he'd want in there with him." Leroy patted his fingers against the table. "Ain't gonna ask how Becky feels?"

"Sure, how does she feel?"

"'Cause she wouldn't like being excluded from being asked. 'Cause Becky's opinion's the most important, you know."

"Leroy!" Anna looked at him in a warning I'd seen a few times before.

After a few seconds of silence I ventured, "Trouble?"

"Becky is . . . is a little possessive," Anna said carefully. "Nothing but a stage in their relationship." She let go of Rachel. "You've got something bothering you. What is it?"

She'd noticed my reaction when I touched the pouch. And now my hesitation. I shook my head.

In the awkward silence I glanced at the planking, the four hanging oil lamps, the empty tables, the two windows out the front, and then back to the four of them. "I wish Scott were here." I would talk, then.

The moment was like wondering when the train would arrive and then you see smoke billowing off in the distance. Scott's red hair bounced by the front window. Then the door swung open.

The blast abruptly stopped as he slammed the door shut and blustered to the bench beside Leroy. "What'd I miss?"

"You get him put away?"

"Yep, Jeb's in jail, and Ryan's taking the first watch."

He paused, perhaps feeling the tension inside me. But then kept talking. "Becky must have taken my headache. She went home."

More tension, but Scott didn't let that stop him. "Marshal Stone said he had some news and wanted to talk to you about what happened here, so stay." He made the same signal I used when making Trevor halt. "Stay."

Anna caught my gaze and made a tiny motion with her head, as if wondering if I was okay. Should this stay between us? I touched the pouch again.

No. These were my friends. They deserved to know. "Look, can I just talk for a minute?"

While they gave me their consent with nods and 'sure things', I unbuckled my gun belt and laid the leather on the table. I took a deep breath, gathering my thoughts. My past was usually privileged information, but I was learning to trust my friends.

Where to start? "Wasn't 'til fourteen when I put this on. This very one."

Their wide eyes watched my every move. I was, after all, a gunman.

"I walked into a shop and asked for a Colt."

"Here here," Scott muttered.

"And he said I would like a Smith and Wesson better." I twisted the belt so the holster lay on top. The cartridges in the loops tapped the table. "While I practiced, an old man started training me."

I rubbed my head and brought forward the past. So loath was I to tell people about my life, I found it difficult to proceed. "I've been dreaming a lot of those days again. I was shooting into a stump with the old man by my side when a cavalry officer rode up. He had yellow hair and was full of energy. I had to . . ." The memory took hold of me and I stood on a grassy hill in Iowa.

The old man was beside me, and the massive stump rested on the side of the hill. In his shaky voice, the old man told me I couldn't marry a horse, but I *could* marry a girl who's just as faithful as a horse.

"Any other advice?" I set my gun belt on the stump and hitched up my pants over my skinny hips.

The old man shielded his eyes from the brilliant sun. "Speak your mind, but make sure your horse is fast."

I laughed. "I suppose."

"When you're older, you'll understand. It helps if you don't mess with things that don't bother you."

A man galloping on a horse drew my attention away. His blue officer's uniform was visible from this distance. As he rode closer, I could just make out the yellow curls that poured from under his hat. Golden tassels on the brim danced with every step the horse took. He stopped just short of the stump.

The old man looked up. "What do you want?" he spat.

"Just a chat." The officer rested his forearms on the saddle horn so his white-gloved hands dangled on either side of the saddle. "I have a right to chat with him, don't I?"

"No."

"Well, Philip. Tell me. How have you fared?"

"Surviving."

"Good. Good. Life's been hard for you, eh boy?"

I remained silent.

"Well, nothing like getting straight to the point. You didn't happen upon a map, did you?"

I pushed the memory away as I finished the story.

"Map?" Anna asked. "What map?"

I stretched out my legs and brushed hers. The touch lingered, and for a moment I was distracted. "Well, I've Trevor to thank for that." I reached into my pocket and set the leather pouch on the table. "He broke my family's box. This was in the lid."

I opened the pouch and carefully pulled out the yellowed paper.

"What is that?" Scott asked. "A treasure map?"

Anna slid her fingers under the paper and studied it under the lamplight. "Rachel, do you mind?"

Rachel slid off the bench, and Anna followed.

"Is that the cure for my stomachaches?" Scott elbowed Leroy.

"Stop that." Leroy pushed Scott.

Anna held the map closer to the light, her lids squinting. "Philip."

The banter quieted.

She didn't look up. "Philip, would you like to discuss this in private?"

"No, I trust them."

"Because the implications are . . ."

So she understood. "I wanted to burn it."

She winced and looked at me. "Because?"

"My uncle John Maxwell died taking this secret to his grave. A man as bad as he trying to protect me?" I said, shaking my head. "I want no part of this."

"So why *didn't* you burn it?"

I reached back into the pouch and pulled out the necklace. Diamonds and emeralds encased in gold shimmered in the lamplight.

Rachel gasped. Scott stiffened. Leroy whistled.

Anna marched straight for the front door. She grasped the bar and slid the lock across the door until it smacked the edge. Her boots punched the wood floor and she slid across the bench, slapped the map on the table, and crossed her arms.

Scott whispered, "Maybe we should leave."

Anna ignored him. "Was this a detail you should have told me about?"

I met her gaze. "I just want it to go away."

Her shoulders squared then finally dropped. "You really feel that way."

"Jewels or secrets." I gripped my arms lightly together. "Simply not worth a life."

Scott leaned his elbow on the table and looked past Leroy and into my eyes. "I hate when he's noble." He rested his forehead on his fist and shook his head. "Honestly noble."

"Anna?" Leroy's voice was softer. "You feelin' ill?"

"This is a letter," she whispered. "A letter on one side. A map on the back." She licked her lips, her dry mouth making it difficult for words to come out. "Scott, you may be right."

"I think it's Devil's Tower."

She didn't look at me but nodded. "1650."

"How can you tell?"

"It's in French." She read, "Andrew, he is in control of Parliament. Ireland is no longer safe. Please, my love. Flee to the colonies. Tarry no longer."

"Wait," Scott said. "You speak French?"

"*Oui.*" Anna ran a finger down the letter. "*Ainsi que je parle anglais.*"

I couldn't hold back a shiver and a smile at the sound of her accent.

She said quickly, "English courts spoke French in the 1600s. But farther down the page is English. *Constance, I leave this note in the hands of a monk traveling to the abbey near Martha's Vineyards. He is Josh MacDougal, and I trust him. I will also leave with him news to tell you, as the ship is near departing, and I must away this letter. May our fortunes return soon.*"

Silence fell over the table. With the snow outside deadening sound, no noise filtered from the streets. Leroy's breathing however, was steady and growing louder.

Finally I leaned back, an arm on the table, and said, "Constance. My mother." I snatched the map from under

Anna's fingers and held it high. "I should burn this. Look at us. I'm twenty-one. Anna, you're nineteen. Rachel?"

"Eighteen."

Scott folded his hands together. "I'm twelve."

"You're twenty-two." I lifted the note higher. "We're children! Just children to be entrusted with such a secret."

"Age hasn't a blasted thing to do with it," Leroy said with a snarl. "You just want to live on your little farm with your horses and not think of nothing bigger than you."

"Is that so wrong?"

Anna held the necklace in her hand and traced the gems with a finger. "This is history." Her voice cut through my swirling mind. "Don't destroy the map. If you must, give it to someone who cares. But don't destroy it."

I lowered my hand, took one last glance at the map, the small thimble labeled Devil's Tower, and I held it out to Anna. As if moving through water, she reached up, took it, and slipped the page into her back pocket.

She lifted the necklace. "And this?"

"Keep it too."

Rachel rubbed her forehead. "Oh, Philip, you could have made this somewhat romantic."

Anna lifted the gems closer. "Unimportant, Rachel. I've nothing to wear with it anyway." She closed one eye. "The history here. 1650 was the English Civil War. Roundheads and Cavaliers. King Charles and Oliver Cromwell. To say England was in disarray at the time is an understatement." She offered a tentative laugh that sounded like she was making light of the moment to keep from bursting into tears.

"My uncle spent his entire life looking for what this map points to. But it's incomplete."

Anna held it up to the light again. "Yes, the paper looks as if it were torn. Here, along this edge."

"I remembered my father tearing the map in two. This

map points to Devil's Tower, but where at Devil's Tower? It's a big place."

"What do you think it is?" Rachel said. "This *X*, I mean. What's there? Treasure? A body?"

Scott tapped the table. "A book on understanding women?" When everyone glared at him, he shrugged. "Who wouldn't spend their life looking for that book?"

I lifted both hands. "Does it matter what the *X* is? My uncle spent his life looking for it, and my father and mother died for it. They believed this *X* led to something worth risking their lives for. Are we willing to do the same?"

"No." Anna's voice was like a tap on a drum. "Besides, we don't have the second half of the map."

I didn't like the way she said the word *we*. This was my family's secret. Not hers. A moment later, I almost slapped myself. I'd given this secret to them. All my life, I'd lived thinking information about my personal life was for the privileged. Well, if anyone in my life deserved the honor, it was these.

As if reading my mind, Scott said, "Talking about this can't be easy, buddy. Thanks. Hey, there's a little something more we need to talk over with you."

Anna's transformation from thoughtful, intelligent beauty to terrified rabbit was palpable. Her ears were straight up and her nose was twitching.

"Anna?"

"I . . ."

I raised a brow.

She took several deep breaths through her nose, keeping her lips squeezed tight, then tighter. I didn't think they could disappear, but they did. Then she reached down into a small carpetbag and pulled out a book.

With both hands gripping the cover, she held up the novel.

Orange shaded the exterior, a putrid color. A black American saddled horse, a Kentucky Saddler, was drawn with thin lines. Beside the horse, a shadow of a man with a Colt revolver pointed toward a burning cabin.

In green letters splashed across the top was the title. I whispered the words aloud. "Anderson's War."

Anna winced.

I stared at the dime novel, searching my feelings. By all rights, I should fling the book across the room and put a bullet through the thin pages.

Who was more surprised when I started laughing—my friends or me? Tears poured from my eyes. "Look," I managed. "The author's name isn't even on the cover."

Anna's grin was unsure. "They don't have anything about Jacob in here."

"Good." My heart calmed. "Good. No need him getting a big head."

"Glad you find it so blamed funny," Leroy said. "'Cause I don't."

"I know. I know. I really shouldn't. But how many people can say they have a book written about them? Look at this!" I held the novel up. "Wrong horse, wrong gun, and the gunman even has a mustache." I looked closer. "I don't even recognize the kind of grass around the cabin!"

Anna kept the map in her pocket and the necklace in her bag as we left Caroline's Kitchen. I gripped her hand firmly.

"Why are you grabbing my hand so tight?" she asked.

"If you go down on the ice, we both go down."

Her laughter was lost in winter day.

The sun's rays did very little to warm my face, but the yellow light was welcome all the same. As we walked toward Anna's house, women smiled our way—a knowing smile that I did not understand. The men's nods and hat tips were far more understandable.

"How many people read dime novels?" I asked.

"Everyone on Earth who can read is my guess." She

squeezed my hand. "You really are brave to take it the way you are."

"How many people are novelized?" With my free hand I tightened my collar. "I suppose there's an element of me that believes it's all over. I can settle down now."

"What about the map?"

"Not much can be done without the second half."

"And your family history?"

"I think I've reached a dead end."

"But your dreams of General Custer. Don't they give you any insight?"

"I suppose." We turned the street corner and walked past a stone building. "But he's not around to explain, is he?"

"He seems like he knew you, Philip. Knew about the map."

"My Sioux friend Running Deer was at Little Big Horn, but he wasn't there when Custer died."

"Surely there are other Indians you can ask." Anna stopped and pulled her hand away.

"Perhaps," I said, turning to look at her. "Please, Anna. Give me time. For ten years I believed myself all alone in this world. And then in a few months I've learned my past isn't what I believed it to be. These visions are very specific and they recast my past. When there are new memories injected, my mind takes time to work through it all."

I winced and rubbed my head. "I had a grandfather who died when I was young. Almost forgot about him until I saw him in a dream. So please, give me time."

She looked over my shoulder toward her house. "Yes, you're right, Philip. I'm sorry. It's just a mystery. I want to discover everything about it. I'd love to hear what your grandfather was like."

I swept her up into my arms, and she giggled. "You know," I whispered. "Sometimes I think that's why you love me. I'm a mystery."

She drew back a bit and gazed into my eyes. "And your horses. I like horses."

I leaned close and felt her smooth skin against mine. Her lips were cold but quickly warmed. Finally, we drew away and she leaned her head on my chest.

"As much as I would love to uncover this mystery," she said, "I'm afraid we're not done with Jacob yet. And I'm worried about the Senate meeting you didn't attend in Washington."

I imagined Jacob holed up in a cabin somewhere with one novel to read.

A novel about Philip Anderson killing the entire Maxwell Gang.

"Don't worry about the Senate. They'll leave me alone."

She drew up on tiptoes and kissed my cheek. "Philip, be careful. I feel a storm coming."

I held her in my arms for a moment, looking in her eyes and knowing she didn't mean snow.

Her hands reached my head, and her fingers started massaging my scalp. "Now, this is a little test. I'm looking for bumps."

"Bumps?" Her touch felt too good to protest.

"We're going to learn your personality."

5

The next morning I opened the barn's side door and the horses wandered slowly into the corral, testing the deep snow with one hoof like a cat's paw. As the horses milled about, the white blanket was tramped down and mixed with the dirt below.

Ice crusted the river behind the barn, and drifts lined the rail fence that edged my land. A few charred poles of my burned cabin shot up from the snow like obelisks marking the history of the last year.

The windswept wheat field showed frozen dirt. Grass in the horse pasture held to large clumps of snow.

Spring was coming. I could feel it in my bones. And the bump on my head that said I was domestic.

I crossed the corral and stopped at the gate leading to the horse pasture. Franklin, the Belgian draft horse, thumped a massive hoof against the ground. His side quivered, and the soft breeze rippled his golden mane and tail. I reached up to pat his neck.

The Arabian stud Solomon walked past me in a manner befitting his name, his chocolate flanks shimmering in the cold sun. He thundered off in a gallop deep into the pasture. Too wild to ride, he'd been in the barn far too long for his restless nature.

Raven, my jet barren mare, trotted into the pasture but didn't stray far. She pawed at the ground looking for grass, while keeping half a mind on what happened in the corral.

The breeding mares, Desert Sand and Sheba, started into the pasture behind Raven. But before their foals could follow, I closed the gate.

The mothers whinnied and pressed against the corral fence.

"Not today, ladies. Today we halter break your babies."

When the snow forced us inside, I'd done little things like work with their hooves, filing the edges and tapping the heel and toe. Despite their youth, the two foals trusted me.

The filly's twin had been brought to me dead last year. Jacob's fault. Jacob, Jeb, and Ryan. Blast it all, why was Ryan so trusted by everyone? I swallowed the feelings.

I slid a halter off the rail and spoke gently to the filly I called Patience as I walked her direction. Teaching her to fear me would destroy our relationship, for to whom would she turn when she was afraid? I hoped to be her first choice.

Patience stood without moving, looking up with chocolate brown eyes. "Such a pretty girl, Patience, so pretty. And smart too." Her muzzle felt like cloud and feather as my fingers slipped the leather around her face.

She snorted but stood still.

I took a step back. No need to pressure her more today. One trick at a time.

The second halter was laced in my fingers as I crossed the corral toward Mustard. The colt boasted an odd mix of his father's reddish black and his mother's creamy butternut.

He also boasted his sire's ornery nature. One step away, and he bolted around the corral, circling me with his immature mane bouncing to the rhythm of his hooves. He kept a sideways gaze on me.

When he stopped, I approached again. "Hey, boy, you'll learn I don't want to hurt you. Just keep you safe. Useful is safe, 'cause then people will want to keep you alive."

The idea sounded sardonic in my own ears, and Mustard must have agreed as he galloped around me again.

I set a boot on the bottom rail and watched him run.

Would a child be running in this corral someday as well? I let the comforting idea of raising a family on this land settle over me, and the warmth lingered.

I spun.

South of the horse pasture, the bare branches were rocking as if someone were there. The entire copse of trees seemed to move of its own accord, bending back and forth.

I reached for the Smith and Wesson.

Ghosts in blue emerged from the distant thicket.

On horseback, a long row of perhaps two hundred men stretched the entire length of the valley. Their uniforms were dulled in the hazy sun, looking almost gray.

Several men jumped from their saddles, grasped the rails lining the horse pasture, and tugged them away from the posts.

I pulled my gun. "Hey!"

Solomon, standing on the small knoll in the center of the pasture, whinnied. His wide eyes and flaring nostrils told me all I needed to know. He was about to bolt. I opened the corral gate and whistled.

Raven was the first to thunder into the enclosure, followed by the mares and last, Solomon.

Trevor trotted from inside the barn, stretched, and sniffed the air. He noticed the approaching cavalry and barked. With a hand signal, I silenced him.

Along the river rode an officer I recognized—Captain Smith from Fort Randall.

I holstered my revolver.

The sound of boots on gravel behind me made me spin. Marshal Stone from Mitchell sauntered my way, his large eyes watching the oncoming soldiers. He swore and I cringed. "I hoped to get here before they came."

I motioned with my thumb. "You know about them?"

He ducked under the top rail and lifted his leg over the bottom. Inside the corral, he adjusted his hat as he straightened. "Grab Raven. Come with me before they get here."

They were less than a minute away, and I would never have Raven saddled in time. "What's going on?"

"You're being summoned."

"What?" I closed the pasture fence, grabbed Raven's bridle, and pulled her toward the barn's side door.

"Remember that Senate meeting you decided to skip?" He held a hand toward the oncoming soldiers.

The mares followed, along with Patience. Mustard stood by Franklin, looking up at the Belgian draft horse's massive head. Solomon followed his dams, snorted, and Mustard leapt into the air and followed his father into the barn.

Marshal Stone had kept quiet.

"I trust Captain Smith," I said, but the look in the marshal's eye made me pause. "You have more."

He glanced at the oncoming horses then gave a single nod.

Mustard's head peeped from inside. "Get in there," I snapped and stormed into barn behind the colt. "What is it?"

"Jacob's been reported in the area. He's subpoenaed too."

"Of course." I hurried past him.

"I'm worried."

I paused. "Me too."

"I had all the girls spend the night at Anna's. Leroy, Scott, and a couple deputies are watching the house."

"Who's watching Jeb?"

Marshal Stone tipped back his hat so the shadow over his face disappeared. "Tom."

"That's it?"

"Ryan."

"You're joking."

He didn't respond right away. Finally, he said, "Someone's waiting for you. Back in town, at the Dakota University."

I snatched Raven's saddle and flung it over her back. With practiced hands, I cinched the belts under her and tugged down the stirrups. "Students still meeting there in the evening, right? I haven't been through that side of town for a while."

"New building. Can't miss it. Near the church, three-story stone building." He started for the front doors. "I'll take care of your horses."

I pulled back my duster and mounted as I heard hooves beside my barn. "Who is it? Who's meeting me there?"

He tugged on the door and it pushed away on its hinges. "You may not like it."

Raven pranced impatiently, reflecting my own mood. Her hooves clacked on the hard packed dirt. I looked down at the marshal.

He turned away then gazed back at me.

When he didn't answer I tapped Raven's flank, and she burst out of the barn and into the wintry afternoon. The cavalry had just reached the corral. To his credit, Captain Smith had held his men from firing.

Who was waiting for me?

Raven was in a full gallop when I heard Marshal Stone's voice following me, as if he couldn't contain the secret a moment longer. Or that he was out of my firing range.

"Libbie Custer!"

6

Dakota University was etched into the sky as a shadow against the stars, a castle on the prairie. Had I expected the stone building to be desolate at this time of night? Haunted? A trap?

Most of the windows in the towering building glowed. Horses and carriages lined the hitches along the front.

Raven sped along the road like a train barreling down a track. I kept my head low so the wind wouldn't blow away my hat, but I lifted my gaze as we slowed in front of the building. Through the windows, I saw people in chairs crowding a room, their attention turned to a speaker in front of a chalkboard.

A single image slammed into my brain like a boot to the temple.

Tall grass waved in an Iowa wind. A stump filled with holes rested on a grassy hill, tiny pricks I'd put there with my Smith and Wesson. My fourteen-year-old hand held the heavy revolver. Riding toward us, the frozen horse in midstep, came a cavalry officer. His golden curls flowed back in the wind, and his smile rivaled the sun's gleam off his golden buttons. But the person at the bottom of the hill caught my attention.

She was beautiful. Filled with youth, energy, life, as if the sunlight flowed from her eyes.

The same woman spoke to the people inside the building. Older now—I could see through the window as I approached the front doors—but this woman had seen me as I worked to learn the craft of gunplay. She knew me.

I needed to know how and why.

I would wear my guns, hat, and duster inside.

My boots tapped against the marble floor, and the air was cool and stale as I took a breath. Perfume hung like a cloud in the darkness, a smell mixed with a strange whiff of formaldehyde.

To the right the door was open, casting a bright rectangular glow into the hallway. Libbie Custer's voice drifted from the classroom into the hallway, echoing away into eternity.

I stepped toward the door. Instantly two men blocked me and pushed me back into the hall.

One man's hand reached for my gun. I caught his wrist in an iron grip. "No need for that, my friend," I whispered. Even in the stone lobby my soft voice carried.

"Who are you?" the other man asked, his hand on his hip, probably near a gun covered by his fine, black jacket.

"Philip Anderson."

The man I gripped yanked his hand back. He rubbed his arm. "Doesn't . . . doesn't matter who you are." He tugged on his tie, checking the knot and the loose ends that hung over his chest. "Can't let you in there."

"Why not? She knows me."

The other man choked, looked back toward the room, and leaned toward me. "Sir, she speaks with no one." He touched his nose. "No one."

"Why not?"

"Dedicated to her dead husband, she is. Won't ever be seen talking to another man alone, no matter how famous."

I rubbed my jaw and considered the two barrel-chested men. Hired for the evening, they were simply thugs to deter people from bothering Mrs. Custer, no doubt. "I'll just stand in the back and listen."

The men exchanged glances then nodded. "You'll stand between us."

We filed into the room, silently standing by the door.

I decided to leave my hat low on my head.

In front of the fifty or so people sitting on benches, Libbie Custer stood. Her back was straight, her chin high, her hands gesturing slowly as she spoke. Her long, blue dress swished as she paced slowly back and forth. White ruffles encircled her neck, where dark hair that had slipped from her bun tickled her neck.

My mother would be her age.

Her eyes showed the vitality of youth, but the wrinkles around her eyes, forehead, and mouth told of experience and wisdom.

My brain churned like a steam engine. Libbie Custer might connect so many strange problems of my past, and living on the edge of this moment was intoxicating.

She didn't notice me as she spoke.

"Twelve years of my life with my husband, I wouldn't trade for the world." Her voice was surprisingly strong. "I met Autie—that's what we called him—at a party." She folded her hands in front of her. "He was home from the Great Rebellion for just a short time."

She rested an arm on a podium to her right. "Let me tell you about Autie. Handsome. Action was his love. Goals drove him on, and love gave him purpose. He dearly loved his siblings. He was never sick, never laid up. He was, though, rather evil."

Nervous laughter filled the room.

"Since I'm speaking to writers, I'll explain. Injecting a twist, a word change quickly, is jarring. The surprise can be fun, interesting, or off-putting. But proceed carefully when playing with words." Her lips lifted into a warm smile as the small crowd murmured.

She paced again, lifting a hand and then a finger, which silenced the crowd. I studied her leadership quality with keen interest as she continued. "Autie was a prankster. In West Point during a language class he asked the professor to translate a sentence of Spanish. Obliging, the professor read the paper provided. *Class dismissed.* My Autie stood and marched out of the room."

I smiled as the others chuckled.

"I met Autie in 1862 after I graduated from seminary." A year after I was born. "He was on a short reprieve from his war duties as a cavalry officer. Our budding courtship ended as Autie tottered down the street in a fit of drunken reverie. My father forbade me to see him again."

She crossed the front of the room as she spoke. "But please understand why he remained the love of my life." She held both hands in a prayerful pose and brought them to her lips. "*He looked such things at me.*" After the laughter died down, she said, "He staggered home, and his sister dragged him into a study and said something to him that I to this day do not know. But from that day, General George Armstrong Custer never took a drink, never swore, and his pranks were only at his own expense. He was a different man."

Libbie Custer reached across a table and took up a piece of paper. "Autie returned to the war and wrote my father of his exploits. So reckless and bold, so brave." She swallowed the look of anguish that crossed her face. "His charges at Gettysburg, at Brandy Station—Autie even routed Jeb Stuart's cavalry."

Returning to the podium, she picked up a pencil. "After some time of correspondence with Autie and no small amount of pressure from his daughter . . ." She grinned. "I finally convinced my father by helping him understand what it was like to be a girl. I was in love. Autie was in love. We were the perfect match."

She touched the pencil to her chin and looked to the white molded ceiling. "I wore a dress of mist green trimmed with a yellow cavalry braid. Autie wore his blue dress uniform, chevrons gleaming as bright as his smile. Many claimed the wedding was the most magnificent they'd ever seen.

"Autie and I toured Washington. As a war hero, he was invited to the gayest dances, the most important socials, and simply splendid receptions. But soon it was back to war, and I moved to the front, staying in his quarters." She set the paper on the podium, and even from the back row I heard the scratching as she wrote. "He fought in Virginia, and I saw the long rows of men with caps in the air, voices ringing with the sound of my husband's name." She paused her writing and closed her eyes. "Glorious."

After a moment of writing, she set down the pencil and continued. "I was invited to Washington to the grandest balls, simply to toast my husband." With her back straight and manner calm and reserved, she walked down the center aisle made between benches. "Near the end of the war, General Sheridan claimed my husband was the single most important soldier who contributed to the winning of the war."

She marched straight toward me and held out her hand. Between her middle finger and ring finger was the folded piece of paper. As if in a dream, my hand reached out and took it. Everyone in the classroom had turned to watch the exchange, eyeing me with curiosity. She simply continued speaking.

"Autie gave me a present offered by the generals—the table the war's surrender conditions were written on."

I glanced down at the paper as she returned to the front of the room. She was explaining to the students in the classroom how General Custer was now a fixture in the military. He wanted to do something else with his life like work business opportunities but felt compelled to continue with the cavalry.

With a quick flick of my thumb I opened the paper.

Philip Anderson, please stay afterward.

My heart pounded in my ears.

7

Eyes open or closed, the darkness was the same for Anna. She listened to the soft snores that filled her room and guessed which raucous sound belonged to which girl. The game would keep her worried mind busy.

Anna tipped her head back against the wall and shifted in the wooden rocker. The creaking chair didn't seem to bother anyone. She unhooked the top button of her shirt and took a calming breath. They decided this first night together everyone would wear riding clothes, just in case. No one felt it necessary to explain what the case was.

Rachel slept to the right of Anna's bed. The thought felt rude, but the former prostitute's soft snores were delicate and appealing. Did she teach herself to be attractive even when asleep?

With every breath, Becky clicked. Would the sound remind Scott of a spinning chamber on a gun when the two were married?

The trouble was Beth. Her ten-year-old sister slept on the bed and competed with the distant train rolling into town with a high whistle. Then inhaling, she growled like a cougar. Beth snored in a steady rhythm, so Anna's mind fell into the pattern. Whistle, growl. Whistle, growl. Then stopped. Anna opened an eye, panic rising in her chest. Had her sister stopped breathing?

Beth whistled again, and relief flooded Anna.

After a deep breath, Anna curled around the feather pillow on the side of the rocker. She flipped her hair past her neck and resettled.

Sometimes having an imagination is a curse. In her mind she saw the stars beyond the walls, the moon shining bright on the stone building across the lane. How could she feel safe this night? Jacob was returning. Even if the marshal hadn't warned them, she would know. She could sense it in her bones.

Evil was coming.

The distant sound of the train's steam escaping as it pulled into the station was somewhat comforting. People going about their nightly tasks meant life was normal for some.

All that stood between her and the vile darkness of Jacob's soul was a thin pane of glass. That and she was on the second floor. Her fingers gripped the pillow until they felt numb.

Father was downstairs, sitting in the parlor, shotgun in hand. Mother slept across the way.

Was Philip in his barn, nestled in the straw, guns close by?

Why couldn't he be here? She would feel safe if Philip were near.

She trusted God. But Philip made her feel safe too. Perhaps she should trust only God? Don't be silly, Anna. What else were men good for? Isn't that why God made men? To help her feel safe?

Thoughts of Philip were always on her mind, always ripping a hole through her very existence. Did he know how much she suffered, just for him? She didn't want him to know, but yet in some small way she wished he would suffer her pain as well. There was small comfort in the fact that she knew he wanted nothing more in life than to settle down on his farm with her and to be held back was driving him mad.

Footsteps on the gravel road pricked her senses. She recognized the gait. Leroy. The old man insisted on taking a watch. Scott waited with Deputy Boothe in the stone building across the way. Marshal Stone had ridden to talk to Philip and should be back in town soon. Ryan was watching Jeb.

Was that a good idea?

She felt like she could trust Ryan. Philip did not.

Time to focus on sleep.

How to sleep when she knew with every fiber of her being that Jacob was coming to kill them all?

She patted her waistline to feel the small derringer against her skin. Then she recited a Longfellow poem in her mind.

For I am weary, and am overwrought
With too much toil, with too much care distraught.
And with the iron crown of anguish crowned.
Lay thy soft hand upon my brow and cheek,
O peaceful Sleep!

She must have drifted, because the sound of thunder brought her wide-awake.

The long, continuous roar continued.

He was here. This was the end. Death had arrived on the sound of horse hooves.

For the end to be coming, she was surprisingly calm. Perhaps she didn't really believe Jacob had come for them.

Perhaps the thunder wasn't the sound of hooves.

The first gunshot she heard rattled any illusion the riders were peaceful. Her mouth went dry, and her heart thumped in her chest.

Beth's scream was short. "What was that?"

"Don't light a match," Anna said as she heard someone fumbling in the darkness.

"What's going on?" came Becky's sleepy voice.

Anna couldn't say it, couldn't admit it aloud.

Rachel could, and her gravelly voice filled the room. "He's here."

Beth scrambled out of bed and threw herself in Anna's arms. "No! Please no!" Her fingernails bit into Anna's shoulders.

A roar of gunfire shook Anna's soul. Did all she loved and cared for just die?

Jacob's hatred knew no end. Nothing she had known could cure his indefatigable cruelty. This was inevitable. Why hadn't they prepared more?

Because they had harbored some hope he would run to a distant country, never to return. Because somewhere in her dreams she saw Jacob losing interest in Philip.

Windows shattering and the shouts of men and the screams of horses ended the illusion.

Sounds of Becky and Rachel shuffling through the room brought her to her senses. "Stop. Stop moving." She hugged Beth tight then gave a push, and Beth slid off her lap. "Barricade the door with anything you can find. Here, Beth, help me with the dresser."

Despite the darkness, the girls got to work. Doing something helped stop the shakes.

Becky burst into tears. "I don't want to die!"

"If we can hold them off for a bit, help will come," Anna said.

The gunshots reverberated in the night, sending waves of fear through her. Philip would know what guns were used, maybe even whose guns the shots belonged to.

But Philip was far away.

One heavy blast echoed, and all was silent.

"Is it . . . is it over?"

Anna reached toward her sister, where she'd heard her voice. "Time to be quiet." She dared not open the curtains.

The sounds of horses again, more individuals speaking below, and then the crash of wood. The house shook.

The front door hadn't held them long.

Which meant the guard outside was dead. Scott and Leroy were dead. The deputy, dead.

God, please!

A shotgun blast—her father's—then more gunfire and crashing glass.

Anna closed her eyes as Beth screamed.

Philip, will you come save us? Anyone?

"Anna!" Beth's voice, the terror. "Anna!" Beth's fingers tore into Anna's skin.

Heavy boots on the stairs pounded.

The other two women moved close to Anna.

The room opposite hers was their first target. The door smashed in.

Swearing filled the hallway. The door on the far end of the hall crashed as well.

Her door rattled as someone tried to break through.

"This one's got stuff behind it." The voice was a country drawl.

"Perhaps you are a little girl," said another in a similar accent.

The door again.

"Idiots." This voice had a much different accent. From another country she didn't recognize. "They wait behind this door." She heard a tap, as if a pistol were used on the wood. "Señorita, come out. It's time for you to go."

Anna surprised herself by returning his request in a calm voice, "No, not today. Perhaps another time."

Rough laughter was her reward.

"Señorita? You are brave, but we must take you with us."

"Don't come in. I have a Gatling gun." She sounded more like Scott than herself. But what else could she say?

Silence from the other side of the door. On this side, Beth gasped for air.

A wicked smack, and the doorknob fell with a thud.

The door scooted an inch, and a sliver of light drove through the door and split the black. The beam drew a yellow line down Rachel's face and flannel shirt.

Anna jammed her shoulder against the dresser. "Help me!"

Another smack against the door and the crack grew an inch wider.

Rachel braced her back against the dresser as Becky pushed with both arms.

Anna had only one bullet. One bullet against the many men beyond this door. What could she do?

If they had wanted the girls dead, the door would be riddled by now. She and her sister and friends would be bleeding out on her bedroom floor.

The door seemed to explode as she flew backwards, tangled with Rachel and Becky's arms and legs. Beth's scream shattered her ears.

A massive shadow filled the doorway, the man's hat so round, the brim almost touched both sides of the frame. "Which Señorita is Anna?" There was no mistaking the outline of a pistol in his hand.

"I'm Anna." Rachel pushed away from Anna's body and groaned as she stood, hunched. "I'm Anna. Let the rest go."

Anna couldn't stop trembling, and blood roared in her ears. She leapt toward the man. "You killed my father!"

His gloved hand caught her throat and stopped her cold. His laughter ripped through her body as he squeezed. Air. She needed air, and her lungs had just exhaled. Her lungs pumped as if they were about to burst.

"This is her. A wildcat."

He brought her close, lifting her toes off the floor, so that his unshaven cheek brushed her skin.

She needed a breath now.

He squeezed tighter.

Air. Please.

Her eyes felt like were about to pop out.

Rachel and Beth's voices echoed through a tunnel. Just in her view, Beth's small fists pummeled the man's stomach.

A man with what would be white skin if he washed reached past Anna's captor and slapped Beth. She flew to the side and slammed against the hallway wall.

This was a nightmare. A dream would explain the fog that clouded her eyes.

Finally, it came to her. This man was Mexican. The other men beyond were a mixture of white or tan skinned.

These were mercenaries. Jacob hired men to do his dirty work.

Why not just shoot her?

The grip shifted to the back of her neck, and as cool air filled her lungs, the grasp straightened her spine as the man dragged her to the stairs. They marched down and her legs thumped on every step.

The scenes came in flashes as she struggled for breath through her bruised throat. Rachel pulled by her hair. Beth squirmed in the thick arms of a gunman. Becky was prodded in the back by a shotgun.

At the foot of the stairs, the dining room smelled of gunpowder. The table where her family had spent so many happy hours, so many precious moments with Philip, so much laughter and joy now acted as a shroud for her father's body. The carpet beneath was stained in red.

Before she was hauled through the front door, she thought his chest rose and fell. Please! Let it be real.

An ancient Conestoga wagon waited with four horses stamping in their tresses. Nearly a dozen men, some with lamps, stood guard on the street, pistols held high.

The night air brought her mind to life.

"What took so long?" a man with wizened face asked. As the struggling girls were brought up, he reached out, grabbed Beth's wrists, and bound them as quickly as a cowpoke would tie up a calf. He gagged her, grabbed her collar and back of her pants and picked her up like a bag of flour. He chucked her into wagon, and she landed with a loud thump.

Another horse thundered through the night, and Anna had a vision of Raven bursting from the darkness, Philip in the saddle with his pistol ending these men's reign of terror.

She almost laughed, thinking of the revenge God had planned for these villains.

"You better run," she said in a low voice to the men nearby. "If that's Philip, you're all dead."

The horse that burst into the lamplight wasn't black, and the rider wasn't her hero.

Jeb rode high on the back of Alita, her horse.

She stared up at him, the light deepening the grooves in his demon face. "Get off my horse."

"Now Anna, aren't you lookin' pretty this fine evening."

"How did you escape the—"

He grinned, and his mouth opened into a wide, toothless cave. "Pick in my false teeth."

She shook her head.

"What are you all waiting for? Load these darlings." He turned his eyes to her. "Marshal Stone's dead. Had to take him down or this wasn't going to work."

She pushed the image of Marshal Stone's bulldog face covered in blood out of her mind. Her world was changing too fast.

Becky was tussled and tossed into the wagon's covered bed. If only Anna had taught Alita to leap at a whistle as Philip's horses could.

Anna looked up at him in defiance. "What are you going to do with us?"

Instead of answering, he pointed an arm toward the house. "No. Not her. I said kill 'em."

Anna spun to see her mother in the grasp of two Mexican men.

"Amigo. She cooks."

"But we won't get a dime for her. Kill 'er and let's go. We're outta time."

"No!" Anna broke from the grip on her wrists and dashed toward her mother.

In the five seconds it took for her to reach the front gate, Anna heard a click behind her. "Stop."

The tone was so powerful it acted as an arm that wrenched her around.

Jeb had Beth's hair clasped in one hand, a gun in the other. This was too much.

Too much. She turned away as the hammer fell with a loud snap. There was no bullet in the chamber.

Jeb burst out laughing then stopped. In the following silence, he offered one word. "Behave."

He shoved Beth under the canopy, then motioned his pistol inside the wagon. "Load 'em all, quickly."

Anna was the last in the wagon. The word *behave* pulsed in her mind like a heartbeat in her head.

She would most certainly not behave.

Before they gagged her, she looked into Jeb's flakey eyes. "You know he'll follow. He'll hunt you down and justice will be served."

The gag was shoved into her mouth.

He and another man grasped her legs and tossed her onto Rachel, Becky, her mother, and a sobbing Beth.

Jeb's face appeared in the small opening. "Dearie, you're putting your hopes in a dead man."

Anna tried to respond, but he simply laughed.

Did he mean Philip was dead?

She laid her head back and shut her eyes as the tears trickled down her temples and into her hair.

The wagon jerked, and her body bounced as they left her father bleeding under the kitchen table.

8

Libbie Custer, I learned as she spoke, wanted to honor her husband's memory. So after he died she took up writing and speaking—writing about her husband and speaking about writing.

I studied her as she answered writing questions, simply the most boring subject I'd ever come across. My mind wandered, and I kept thinking back to my discussion with Captain Smith when I sold him Tucker.

I appreciated the officer, and no doubt I would apologize for running from him this afternoon, but a thorn of bitterness still caught in my heart. He'd known my parents but waited until a chance meeting to inform me? Intolerable.

Libbie Custer also knew me by sight, so why had she waited so long to contact me?

Her excuse would be similar to Captain Smith's, no doubt. Everyone believed me to be dead.

After she answered questions and the students were dismissed, I waited at the back of the room with my arms crossed. Mrs. Custer spoke with several people who lingered, and as each left and passed by me they met my gaze and nodded hello. I returned the gesture.

Finally only a few people remained. Some talked in a group, others rearranged the classroom.

She danced between the clusters, her hoop skirt swaying as she weaved past.

I'd expected pleasantries, chitchat about weather or the train ride. Instead, as she approached she said, "You look like your mother. Your eyes."

"I've questions," I said, motioning to chairs in the corner. I tossed my hat on a desk.

"I will answer them." She took a seat, and I sat across from her. Nothing was between us but years of history. The air was electric. "Your voice is like your father's."

I rested my elbows on my knees and wrung my hands together.

She sat straight, hands folded on her dress. "I thought you dead, Philip, or I would have found you. It wasn't until I read the dime novel that I knew you were alive."

There was my answer. But I had a memory to bring to her attention. "That's not entirely true. You visited me after I supposedly died."

She cocked her head to the side, her earring dangling against her shoulder. "Did I?"

"Sioux City. I was shooting at a stump."

She brought a finger to her lips. "I remember. That was you? Autie was visiting Dave Mather—"

"The old man?"

"You were the boy with him." She rubbed her forehead and closed her eyes. "Oh God, I'm sorry." Her gaze rose to the ceiling then back at me. "I'm sorry, Philip. I want to do right by you. Please believe me."

Dave Mather. The man hadn't told me his name. I'd just known him as the old man. "Tell me about Mather."

"Autie fought with Dave against the Sioux, but then Dave left the cavalry to become a lawman. That's all I know about him."

A stabbing pain shot from the front to the back of my mind, but I'd known the agony was coming. My past was written in concrete across my mind, and new information was a sledgehammer to my brain, as well as a chisel to the wall of my understanding.

"I don't remember much of the past." I rubbed my fingers together and wouldn't meet her gaze. "For some reason, I don't remember much."

Libbie pressed her lips together. "You were young. And your parents were very busy."

I eyed several glasses and a pitcher of water. "I need a drink." Without waiting for a reply, I stood and crossed the room. My hand felt weak as I picked up the blown-glass pitcher and tilted the handle. Water streamed into the tumbler, the familiar sloshing a comfort. I took a sip as I filled a second cup, letting the cool drink trickle down my throat. I took them both back to our seats. I handed her a cup.

In the time I'd taken to fill our glasses I decided to trust her, and when I did my irritation vanished.

I leaned my elbows on my knees again, the cup of water grasped in both hands. "When my parents died, everyone else simply disappeared out of my life. I should have known of their friends."

"You were young. You're not to blame."

"But my image of my parents has been so wrong. Captain Smith at Fort Randall told me he knew my parents and changed everything I thought of them."

Her gaze was sad and generous. "There are many, just like Randolph Smith who could tell you of your parents."

"How close were you to them?"

She set her glass on the nearby desk without taking a drink.

"Some people use closeness, or perceived closeness to a person, to garner sympathy when tragedy strikes. I will be honest with you, and you can guess if I'm trying to gain your attention. Your mother and I were close."

She struggled to gain control over her quivering lips.

I waited.

"I loved her like a sister. And when I heard she died . . ." A tear trickled down her cheek. "I hated her husband. I hated him." More tears, and her voice was choked. "And I need forgiveness, because it has eaten at my soul."

I realized she was asking me for forgiveness. From what I was learning, along with my awakening memories, she was one of many who didn't think of my father as the hero I'd believed him to be. My first inclination was to ignore her request since it seemed such a silly emotion to hold on to. Instead I said, "Thank you. You have my forgiveness." I couldn't hold back the ironic laugh. "I suppose I'm the only person on Earth who can offer what you ask."

She looked at me through crying eyes. "You have the best traits of your mother, Philip."

I turned my head so I wouldn't see her tears.

"Oh, Philip," she said. Her voice was calm again. "If you only knew me better. I haven't cried for quite some time."

Was it safe to look at her? When I did, she'd finished brushing her nose with a white handkerchief. She returned the lacy cloth to a pocket or some other hidden hole in her dress just under her neck.

My duster had fallen open, revealing the gun belt. She gazed at it. "So it's true. You are a gunman."

"Not by choice," I said, throwing the flap closed and buttoning. "I've an enemy."

"John Maxwell is dead."

"Another." I hoped she would drop the subject, but she kept her eyes on me. I said, "One hundred sixty acres with

Arabian horses and a log home. That's all I want. But I've found love, and love always comes with a price."

"A rival?"

"Bitter. Angry. There's nothing that holds him back. No conscience. Not even God seems to be able to stop him." I pushed Jacob from my mind and shook my head. "That's not fair, what I said about God. But this is not an enemy I chose."

"Autie had no enemies. Not really. Everyone loved him. So after the Confederates made peace, he decided the Indians were his enemies."

"I would prefer to lock this away in a chest and throw it into the sea." I tapped my hip. "I would live peaceably with everyone."

"Like your mother." The wrinkles around her mouth deepened as she smiled. "You may not believe me, but Constance—your mother—made me your godmother." She held up a hand. "Again, no one is forcing you to believe me. I must, I feel, give you an explanation of my feelings."

I wasn't good with emotions, so I asked, "Which are . . ."

"I've a strong sense of loyalty to you, Philip. To explain, I say no to presidents, I ignore the notes from Mark Twain, but if you ask something of me I will do it."

"I have no memory of you." When she looked hurt, I explained. "Like I said, I have perhaps nine or ten memories of my childhood up to the point my parents were killed."

"There's an explanation, I believe, but I'll have to start with when I first met your parents. The Southern Rebellion was a boon for Autie. He took advantage of the war, gaining prestige and honor. Your father was in business overseeing several blacksmith shops and a factory."

"My father didn't fight?"

Her smile was gentle. "He had the money to buy himself out of the war."

"Three hundred dollars."

"Yes, to buy a substitute to fight in his stead. Many men, especially businessmen, took advantage of the offer."

I couldn't fault him. If I could pay one thousand to sit out any of the fights I'd suffered, I would. But that would mean destroying the cause, no doubt, and my cause was Anna. No, there wasn't a penny I'd pay to miss out on my cause.

My back was to the chalkboards, and I watched the doorway into the room as well as the black windows along the front. I took a second glance, just to be sure, even though the ghosts I looked for didn't appear. For some reason, I was feeling unsettled.

"Perhaps you have so few memories of your parents because of your father's work and your mother's parties." She put a hand to her heart. "Oh, your mother was a delight. Now understand, parties in Washington and other high society cities are for social elites. Autie was new to the life and I was only a small town judge's daughter, but Autie found himself General George Armstrong Custer and a famous man. He was a dandy, and oh, the fun we had. But your mother was . . . simply your mother, and the most incredible person I have ever met."

Captain Smith had said the same. "All my memories were of my father." I looked at her and said carefully, "Sometimes I wonder if I'm like her or him."

"You were a boy child, and boys always look up to their fathers and despise the women who birthed them." She offered a wry smile. "At least children feel that way when they're told to go to bed."

"You've no children."

She shook her head. "No."

I glanced at the door again. No one had left, and no one had entered. Why the growing apprehension? "You believe I have so few memories of my parents because they weren't home often."

"You were in the care of a nurse, and sometimes your

grandfather watched you." She adjusted her dress and leaned back. "I remember the first time I met your mother. We were at a party with several senators, and one kept asking me if I worried Autie would be killed in a reckless charge. I assured him I was ready to sacrifice those I loved most for the cause, but he would not stop his badgering." She set a hand on her hip. "I retired for fresh air and to clear the tears, because he was starting to pry open the fears I bottled, and behind me came the soft English accent of your mother."

Mrs. Custer lifted a brow. "'Reckless men on the battlefield,' your mother said, 'are safer than a loose tongue in Washington.' She had come up beside me with her dazzling smile, your smile. And her eyes, Philip. Oh, her eyes. She said, 'There is a man who will not be voted into the Senate again.'"

I couldn't hold back a smile as Mrs. Custer attempted an English accent.

"Constance grabbed both my arms and looked into my eyes. I couldn't help but believe every word she said. 'He is safe now. He will be safe. He will return to you, more heroic and more dashing than ever before. And his devotion for you grows with every beat of his heart. How could it not?'"

Hearing my mother's words soothed my own aching heart.

"Philip, if you could have seen the colors of that evening, the swirling dancers, the laughing officers, the chatting women, you would understand the magic of Washington. Lamps lit the large ballroom. The air was warm and intoxicating as your mother and I returned to the party. The evening wore on and feelings were intense and passionate as only a war can bring. As if this could be our last night. Music ran around us like a river of light, coaxing inhibitions from our souls. I must admit, I danced with a young officer, believing it might help Autie. Another young man, very handsome, asked your mother to dance.

"Your father had shown no interest in your mother the

entire evening until the officer took Constance's hand. I've never seen a man in such a fury. He wrenched her arm from the socket as they left. I visited the next day, and only on my insistence was I allowed in. The servant was very reluctant to announce me."

I didn't remember a servant.

"Makeup on your mother's face, thick." She touched her cheek. "He'd slapped her so hard, she bruised."

I leaned back and crossed my arms.

She must have noticed my irritation, because she said carefully, "Philip, please understand. I tell you the truth because you've earned that of me. Every story has a point of view. This is my perspective. But how I saw events unfold is as important as anyone else." She held both hands up. "The facts as I understand them are yours to do with as you see fit. I can only tell you my perspective. Would you like me to stop?"

"No," I said, almost growling. "Please, go on."

"You were her life," she continued. "She loved you more than life itself. When she found herself pregnant and still your father did not want to marry her—"

I slammed my fist down. "Don't say such a thing."

She jumped. "I thought you wanted the truth." Her brows creased as if she was hurt. "Philip." She looked away for a moment, then back into my eyes. "Their decisions weren't yours. You're not accountable."

"But yet my father's decision to leave our home cost my mother's life, and now I must piece together a world that's forced upon me." My mind flashed back to the map and the reasons my father abandoned a comfortable life in the East. "My parents' decision has sent me on a journey so horrible, so evil, I cannot sleep at night. There's no peace. Never. And I chose none of it." I clamped my jaw tightly as feelings burned in my chest.

Mrs. Custer stared to the side at the desk, then picked up

her water and took a sip. Finally she said, "God chose to let Indians kill my husband. Chose to let your mother and father die." She rubbed her head. "Perhaps Autie dying caused peace to come between the soldiers and the Sioux faster. Perhaps his death kept every American Indian from being wiped out. What do we know of such things?"

"So the death of my parents was to bring about something else?"

She shrugged, an awkward movement in her constricting dress. But her smile was genuine. "What do we know of such things?"

"And where my life is leading . . . You would say—"

"What do we know of such things? All we have is a compass to point our way." She touched her heart.

I took a deep breath, calming my heart as I leaned toward her. "I think I understand you better." My mother was the care-free sort, happy to be with those she loved. She spent time at parties but followed the man she loved into the frontier. Mother would have liked Libbie Custer. Loved her. If I was honest, I liked her. "What do we know of such things? Thank you."

"What is the name of your girl?" The playful look, similar to the one she wore on her face during her speech, returned. "The one you love?"

"Anna. Anna Johnston."

"I'm sure she's beautiful."

Anna's image came to mind. "Dark hair, blue eyes, soft cheeks. I like the way her smile is like the sun on a cool day." I looked away.

"Be careful, Philip," Mrs. Custer said, laughing. "You sound like a poet."

I balled my hands together. "Our lives would be perfect, if only it wasn't for Jacob Wilkes."

Mrs. Custer straightened. "What did you say?"

"My horses, the farm, Anna—"

"No, the name."

"Jacob Wilkes?"

Her face was pale and she took another drink. "Lord, have mercy." A few drops of water trickled down her chin, and she absentmindedly rubbed the moisture away with her fingers.

"You know something." I studied her expression, full of fear and of confusion.

"Your father had three friends, all very close, very secretive." She spoke quickly. "Of course, he had business dealings with other men, but these were his inner circle. One was your grandfather. Another was your uncle, John Maxwell. Both men were your mother's family. And there was a reason why."

The map. My father was close to my mother's family because he knew of the map. Did Libbie know?

The fear in her voice floated like a cloud between us. "The third friend—Jacob Wilkes."

I held up my hand. "Jacob Wilkes is my age."

Her lips squeezed tight before she said, "He was your father's age. They were close, from long before I knew them. Aggressive businessmen. And Jacob, a banker, financed your father's factory." She pressed a hand against her forehead. "There was some map that your father found, something that held his attention. He split the map in two and kept one half. The other, he gave to a Catholic priest to hold for Jacob Wilkes to retrieve when he returned to the States. That I learned from Constance before she left."

She looked up at the men who washed the blackboard, then turned her gaze back to me. "Your family had been gone a month on your move to the Dakota Territory when Jacob Wilkes arrived back in town. What I tell you now is simply a rumor. One, I must admit, I pressed from a monk. The monk would not hand over the map unless Jacob Wilkes adopted a child."

"That doesn't make sense."

"The boy was new to the convent and needed fed. Needed a future. He was too old for most families to adopt. And what's more, Jacob Wilkes had a reputation as a ruthless businessman that a frail wife couldn't tame. So I believe the monk hoped a child would give Wilkes a better sense of purpose, of direction and honesty."

"He named the boy after himself."

"Yes, even though the boy was ten."

That was ten years ago. "Did Mr. Wilkes get the map?"

"I don't know. I believe so."

Had the banker moved to the Dakota Territory to watch me? Did he think I had the second half of the map?

How had he known I survived?

I had the second half of the map. Could there be anything on this planet worth destroying my peace and the blossoming love in my heart? Love, above all, is worth fighting for.

My head ached.

This minute I would march to Mr. Wilkes's front door and hand him my portion of the mystery and be done with it all. The map led to such wonton destruction that I couldn't in good conscious keep the blasted thing. What could be worth all that these men attributed to it? I said aloud, "What could the map point to?"

Her chin thrust out as her head lifted and eyes widened. "Must you be like your father?"

I pulled my chair forward. "Now it is I who would like to be understood. There is nothing I can think of that could possibly entice a treasure hunt or convince me that anything of physical value could be worth a life." I pointed toward the West. "How many lives had John Maxwell taken in his search for the treasure? How devastating is my mother's death on you, on me, all because my father was driven by greed?" I lowered my hand. "No, I'm giving away my half of the map to Wilkes.

95

And then they can do as they see fit. I'll end this once and for all. And there will be peace."

Instead of the relief I expected to see in her eyes, her brows furrowed. "You have it? There's no need to hand over the map, Philip, surely. Your parents did die for it."

Didn't she just ask if I was acting like my father? And I knew in that moment she could no longer help me. There was nothing more I could learn, nothing more she could advise that would change my course. Even before I reached out to take her hand, a wall was building around the gunman part of my life. I grasped her fingers. "I feel like my mother and you were sisters." As I said the words, the darkness inside was pushed to another part of my heart. "Just talking to you makes me feel as if you're family."

Her shoulders slumped and her fingers went limp in my hand. As if she knew she was being dismissed. As if her life of celebrity was nothing compared to mine. "Thank you, Philip. For coming to see me."

"How long are you in Mitchell? I must introduce you to Anna."

"I leave on tonight's train."

I let go of her hand and stood. "I've business I must see to, but now that we've met, surely we can write?"

"Your future adventures will be in a novel as well, no doubt," she said as she stood. "Philip, please, with the map—"

"I had to shoot my mother's brother. The path of destruction that piece of paper sent the world on . . . intolerable."

"Just be careful."

Of the two kinds of people—those who acted and those who told everyone to be careful—I was glad to be a man of action. But what could she do? Strap on a gun and fight beside me? I'd welcome the help, no doubt, but in the end this entire affair was my problem. I truly felt it a shame to lose this new-found connection to my past. "I'm serious about writing. Please."

She stepped past me, walked up to the podium, and scratched out a few words on a paper. "My address," she said, handing it to me.

I tucked away her note in my vest pocket. Something wasn't right, and I realized the feeling didn't come from my conversation with Mrs. Custer. I looked out at the blackness. Something was going on that needed my attention.

"Autie had that look sometimes," she said. "You're troubled. Follow the feeling. Trust it to the point you feel better. I wonder if Autie had the feeling the day he died and ignored it."

I didn't say that he surely had the feeling as he saw Sioux surrounding the 7th Cavalry, but the thought spurred me to action. "Thank you."

In four bounds I was out the door and down the hall. I slammed the door behind me as I dashed for Raven. The cool night air touched my skin. The only welcome sounds were Raven's snort when I lifted into the saddle and the comforting squeak of leather.

"C'mon, girl." I tugged on the reins, and she pulled away from the school and shot like a star into the night.

We passed under a tree, the frogs calling as we thundered down the country lane. Wind whistled in my ears, and the thrill of Raven's night run coursed through my body.

Dark windows stood empty as we sped by empty businesses. Main Street's wide stretch seemed vast without the daily bustle, and the length stretched before us in the starlight and disappeared in darkness.

One window light shone like the moon—a lighthouse on the rocky shore. I slowed Raven as we approached the Wilkes Bank and Loan.

We stopped under the light and I looked up. The window overlooking the street belonged to the office of Mr. Wilkes, and I pictured him sitting behind the desk. Time for some questions to be answered, as well as a peace to be bought. I'd offer the map.

I spun Raven's rein around the hitching post and tried the bank door. It opened without a squeak.

Before stepping in, I unbuttoned my duster and felt for the handle of my gun. The hair on the back of my neck prickled. No sound came from inside, and the smell was of gold bricks. At least, the metallic smell was what I thought gold bricks would smell like.

The cavernous main room was pitch dark. I stepped inside and clicked the door shut.

To call out? Or not call out?

No. Tonight, *I* was the phantom in the darkness.

I strode to the vague, shadowy steps and saw the upstairs office light reflecting off the brass banister.

He'd offered me a cabin to pay for his son's sins.

He moved here, simply to follow me. What had he said after offering me a drink? *I'd like you to keep an eye out for my son.* I groaned. Only now did I understand he meant to pull me closer. How had he known so many intimate details about me? Now I knew why.

He'd been watching me.

One step, then another, my left hand on the banister and my right ready to draw. I ascended.

My boots made very little noise on the hard planks.

Near the top of the stairs, I heard shuffling papers. I stepped onto the second story balcony and started for the office. A shadow to the right looked human.

I froze and nearly pulled my gun.

A half-lit tree stood sentinel, and I watched the leaves, expecting a branch to pull a revolver.

Taking a breath, I kept walking.

Four more steps, and I leaned into the light to gaze into the office.

Mr. Wilkes stood facing the door, both fists pressing against his desktop. He looked down, his substantial weight forcing him to peer over his belly. Lamplight shone off his head, the glow dimmed only by the long strands combed over his bald skull.

The shepherd and sheep painting that had hung on the wall was missing, exposing an open safe. Behind him, the black expanse of a window overlooking the street gave the sense of an endless tunnel.

He shifted the page he was looking at then flipped the paper over.

My breath caught. The yellow sheet looked identical to the map.

I stepped into the room, my hand over my gun.

He glanced up, and his widening eyes held a moment of recognition and surprise. In the next breath, he regained control. "Philip Anderson. We're closed, son. You'll need to come back during banking hours."

"What can we do to end Anderson's War?"

He feigned confusion, though he wasn't nearly convincing enough. "Well, Philip, I'm not sure why you'd ask me." Without looking down he slid the paper to the side, lifting another stack with his thumb. The rest of him remained unmoved.

I didn't like this. None of it. Why was he looking at the map now, of all nights? Why catch him on this one night of hundreds?

Because he looked at his half of the map every night.

Are men so easily bored with the conventions of a normal life that the promise of mystery and the hope of a gigantic reward was enough to control lives?

"You knew my parents and didn't tell me." My anger propelled me a step forward. "Five years in Mitchell and you never said a word."

SHADOW OF DEVIL'S TOWER

"I've known a lot of people." He lifted a hand. "And I don't like your tone. You're upsetting me, Philip, and I'd like you to leave."

"You moved here right after me. Followed me here."

"You're bordering on the absurd. No, you *are* absurd. This interview is over. Leave immediately."

"But if you knew I was alive . . . knew where I was . . ."

The image flashed in my mind, the nearby river, the monolithic tower in the night, the gunshot that killed my father.

I looked into Mr. Wilkes's heavy face. "You had my parents killed?"

I heard a click behind me.

I froze.

"Well, well. What have we here?" came the mellow voice of young Jacob Wilkes.

9

Jacob chuckled as he circled me, a cane in his left hand, the Colt grasped in his right. His white suit, even as a criminal on the run, shone like the moon in the lamp's glow. "Have I prevented a bank robbery, Father?"

The mirth on Jacob's face didn't hide the dead calm in his eyes. The gun pointed at my head didn't move.

"Your father isn't all he seems, Jacob."

Jacob's brow rose. "Fascinating," he said, his tone light. "As lovely as this is, I must tell you, Father, I'm leaving now. Cavalry are on the streets tonight." He shook his head as he looked at me. "Both Philip and I have been subpoenaed to testify before the Senate. Seems the Dakota Territory wants to be a state, and they think we're a bit rowdy to let into the Union. Philip's little novel has caused quite a stir, and they're considering the matter. And somehow they believe I might not be as guilty as first thought." His eyes narrowed and a grin crossed his lips.

Mr. Wilkes waved a hand as if dismissing the Senate issue and sounded worried as he asked, "Is it done?"

Without taking his eyes off me, Jacob nodded once. "But it wasn't in the house."

"Philip," Mr. Wilkes said as he took his hands off the desk and stepped close to me. "A clear proposition. Anna back, for a little piece of paper you have in your possession. A letter."

The room swirled around me as red filled my vision, and if it weren't for a gun pointed at my temple, I would pull my revolver. My voice was a whisper. "What have you done?"

"Jeb and his men killed them all." Jacob's voice almost held regret. "Everyone at her house is dead. Anna, however, is alive."

"Jeb's in prison." I struggled to remain standing. The girls . . . Becky, Rachel, Beth, Mrs. Johnston. "Jacob, what have you done?"

Mr. Wilkes stood directly in front of me while Jacob pressed the revolver against my ear. The older man's breath was tainted with sweet whiskey. "If you want her back alive, then the map."

"You knew my father."

"Henry wasn't about to share his secrets with the likes of me." Mr. Wilkes thrust his jaw out. "I paid for that map. I paid for it! Bought it from the monk. Paid a dear price. Then your father ran from me."

So transformed was the man, I would have taken a step back had it not been for the gun pressing on my ear.

His eyes flashed lightning. Where was the banker? Who was this new man?

"Jeb killed Marshal Stone." Jacob's smooth voice ripped at my heart.

"Marshal Stone?" My throat closed. Please be lies. "And with cavalry in the city?"

"Father, let me kill him."

Mr. Wilkes shook his head. "I need the map."

"After, then. I'll kill him when you have it."

I winced. "What did I do to you, Jacob? Why do you hate me so much?"

Jacob's breath seemed to sizzle in my ear as he spoke. "I loathe you. I've wanted you dead since the day I came to this God-forsaken territory. You think you're someone, believe you're important. But you're nothing. Do you hear me? Nothing! You're vile, and I will have your heart on a plate."

I didn't respond, but the waves of hatred washed from him like lava pouring from a volcano.

Mr. Wilkes chuckled. "We know he has the map." He moved close enough to step on my toe. "I'm not entirely sure I need him to tell us."

Jacob pulled the gun back, but from the corner of my eye I saw he kept it leveled at my head. "You know where it is?"

Mr. Wilkes studied my face. I stared into his eyes. Finally he said, "Philip knows of the map. His house burned, so he won't trust it in the barn." He rubbed his jaw. "The map is with someone in his confidences. Not someone he cares for but trusts. Scott Ladd has the map."

"Jeb said Scott's body wasn't among those at the Johnston house." Jacob adjusted his grip. "What if he gave it to Anna?"

Mr. Wilkes took a deep breath through his nose. "No. Anna's just a woman. She wouldn't know what to do with the map even if Philip did tell her. You searched her? Well, then no, she doesn't have it. We'll search Scott's home before we leave, and if it's not there we'll find him."

Jacob's laugh was genuine. "How hard can it be to find his glowing red hair? It's a constant sunrise."

My desire to kill him grew even stronger. First for their offense to Anna's intelligence. And I'd always liked Scott's red hair. The insult was small, but the ire made my heart race. I wasn't fast enough to beat Jacob. In front of me, maybe. Not to the side. He had the drop on me.

Mr. Wilkes considered me a moment longer, his thumb

playing against his forefinger. He rubbed his chin, looked at my chest for a moment, and turned away. "Jacob," he said over his shoulder. "Kill him."

Without hesitating, Jacob squared his shoulders and tilted his head a fraction.

His finger tugged on the trigger.

Behind me, I heard the hammer click on a shotgun.

Jacob didn't fire. Instead he turned to look.

I twisted to see a massive form behind me with a shotgun. Ryan.

Jacob must have known Ryan would fire, because instead of pulling the trigger he lurched back, away from the view of the door.

Both barrels blasted in the confines of the bank's office. Tiny balls ripped through space where Jacob had been a second before.

I spun away and dropped to a knee, reaching for my revolver.

Jacob dove behind a rocker, and as I lifted my gun he slipped through a waist-high door in the wall.

A loud crash filled the room and I spun to where Mr. Wilkes had been. The window was shattered, and he was gone.

"Ryan! Go after Mr. Wilkes!" As I dashed toward the short door, I felt his heavy bulk on the planks as he passed behind me.

About four inches taller than Jacob, ducking into the dark passageway was far more difficult. Papers in large, messy stacks lay on either side.

A few feet away, another small door stood open. I cautiously stepped into the next room, gun ready.

A single lamp on the center desk lit the empty office. I started for the open door—Jacob must be stopped at all costs. But what the light reflected made me pause.

Over the mantel hung a full-length portrait of Anna. She

wore a revealing dress of blue, the wind blowing back her hair and tugging at the flaps of her skirt. While the representations of her blue eyes and generous cheeks and dark hair were accurate, I didn't remember Anna's body being so sumptuous.

Did Anna know he had it commissioned? The painting must have cost a fortune.

Below were another dozen paintings and photographs of women. I took a step closer.

Anna was in every one.

Some paintings were crude, as if a child had done them, as if Jacob had attempted using a brush. Others were detailed, no doubt done by an artist. I counted six photographs, most blurry, and Anna never looked at the camera. In fact, she was walking on the street in most.

On his desk was a faded blue bonnet. Anna's.

With my revolver in hand, I cross the room and glanced behind the desk. A chest lay open. With my left hand I shifted the lamp so I could peer inside. Women's clothing.

With my boot, I shifted the dress. Anna's.

Under the dress were several intimate pieces of clothing. With a growl, I kicked over the chest and stormed from the office.

I stopped again. Hanging by the door was a necklace with bear claws. The same necklace Running Deer had given me.

I ripped the sacred piece from the wall and slung it over my neck, promising never to remove it again.

What kind of monster was Jacob?

Ignoring Ryan in the office and Mr. Wilkes who was surely dead from his fall from the second story, I charged through the darkness and down the stairs.

The door was open. I sprinted through, gun ready for the challenge from Jacob Wilkes.

Instead the kerosene lamps shimmered off the brass

buttons of several dozen cavalry marching down Main Street. They lifted their rifles and pointed at me.

"Halt! Throw down the gun," an officer barked.

"There's no time for this—"

A rifle shot reverberated through the business fronts as a bullet smacked the stone above my head. As I dropped my gun and ducked, I shouted, "You're shooting in town? You're shooting against rock? Idiot!"

As soldiers fanned out, I lifted my arms and stepped toward them. My boots crunched broken glass. "There's no time! You fools, Jacob's escaping!"

"Running down the street with a revolver pointed at cavalry's not on my list of innocent activities, me boy." The officer's shadowed face was nearly invisible as he lowered his rifle. His Irish accent cut through the night. "Now, you'll be explaining yourself in a moment as soon as the captain arrives."

"Didn't you see Mr. Wilkes fall from the window?" I pointed up.

"Another reason you're detained."

I gripped both sides of my hat, looking over the ground where Mr. Wilkes should be lying. "Did you take his body?"

"He marched away to the doctor, laddie. Now, enough—"

The soldiers spun toward the door, rifles lifted. Ryan stepped out. "You better let Philip Anderson go," he said in his deep, guttural voice. His shotgun was pointed at the officer's head.

This was getting us nowhere. "Ryan, it's okay. Lower your gun." The last thing I wanted was a conversation with Rachel about Ryan's death.

As he complied, a handful of soldiers jumped onto the boardwalk and took our weapons.

Rough hands grasped my arms and tugged me to the center of the road. "You've put us through a great deal of trouble tonight, boyo."

"Trouble?" I tried to pull away. "Let go. I'm not going anywhere. I must speak with Captain Smith." How could Jacob pull off the kidnapping with so many cavalry in town? Rays of hope that he lied pushed my impatience to new heights. "I'm leaving. Now. Shoot me or let me go."

"Capt'n will be here soon enough. He's checking on a disturbance on the east side of town."

Anna's side of town. A ringing burst in my ears. "What disturbance?"

He didn't answer, and this time I managed to wrench from their grasp. "What disturbance?"

"Form up!" A sharp voice echoed between the buildings despite the wide street. "Columns of two."

The thin figure of Captain Smith was a welcome sight. Even in the faded kerosene lamplight, his white pencil mustache was the first noticeable trait of the gentleman soldier.

"Capt'n." The Irish sergeant kept a weapon leveled at me. "We've got him."

"Columns of two!" Captain Smith barked as he approached, pointing at the end of the forming column.

The officer hesitated, and I wondered if he would ignore orders. Instead he straightened and lowered his rifle. He saluted and jogged down the line.

Captain Smith turned to me, and the look in his dark eyes made my soul cry in anguish.

I nearly grabbed the lapels on his uniform. "What happened?"

He swept off his cavalry Stetson and fiddled with the golden cord. "Interviewed a few locals. Seems a band attacked the Johnston house. Made off with her."

My mind went blank as my emotions turned cold. I started for her home.

Captain Smith grasped my arm. "Wait a moment, Philip. March with us. We're returning to the house."

"Why?"

"They may still be here." He let go. "Or they may have marksmen. You're someone I need to protect."

"No, Anna's someone you need to protect." I looked toward the boardwalk. "Where's my gun? Give me my gun!" This wasn't happening.

Dust filled the air as soldiers ran past, nearly stretched in a perfect line.

"My gun! Give it to me." My mind held one image. The death of Jacob. I would hunt him down and save Anna.

A large man stood in front of me. What was his name? He held out my gun belt.

Ryan. "Thanks." I snatched the leather from him and strapped it on in a practiced motion. "Let's go."

Captain Smith kept pace and called, "Lieutenant, follow with the men." He pointed toward the bank's broken window as we jogged. "What happened?"

"Jacob got the drop on me." I lifted a thumb to Ryan on my left, his breath already coming in gasps. "He saved me." It reminded me of something Ryan had said, and I slowed, suddenly unsure. "They told me Marshal Stone was dead."

Ryan nodded, wiping his wet lips. "Got him in the heart. Jeb. That's why he went in jail, I think. Why he wanted caught. Cause he had a lock pick." He pointed under his tongue. "Here."

"If Jeb had the drop on you, how'd you escape?" I growled, picking up speed again.

He turned so I could see the back of his head. A knot the size of my fist was a shadow in the dim light. "Saw him pull the pick out of his mouth. But when I started to get the marshal there was an iron bar right there when I woke up."

I wanted to blame him for letting Jeb get away, but the mound on his head reminded me of the size of the cursed Devil's Tower.

We stormed past shops—once familiar in the light, now stark and strange in the darkness. Recognizable in the calm of my life, they now mocked me as I neared Anna's house. My gut told me what I found there would change my life. I would never view this lane the same.

We passed the last kerosene lamp, and at the end of the city street the Johnston house stood forlorn, a lonely shadow against the stars. Every window glowed with candlelight.

A dozen men moved in the front yard, lamps held high. The stone building across the way, windows all broken, was lit as well.

I sprinted to the front gate, leapt the white fence, and passed several soldiers looking over the yard. Just inside, I yelled, "Anna!"

I heard a cry to my left, the parlor. "Anna?"

Beside the cold fire grate, Mr. Johnston lay in his chair. Three men in blue leaned over him, one with scissors cutting his pant leg. A wicked gash in his upper thigh gushed blood. His left sleeve had already been stripped away, blood oozing from his biceps.

"You could be a little gentler!" Mr. Johnston yelled.

I wanted to turn and vomit but instead forced my legs to stop at his side. Normally in absolute control, the man's wounds tore at his soul. "Anna?" I managed. "The girls?" I pictured a slaughter upstairs.

"Took them." He released the grip on his arm and held out a bloody hand. "Philip, find them. Find my girls." He fell back.

I stared at him, hand on my Smith and Wesson. I took off my hat with my left and held it to my head. This was my fault. "I'll find them. Or die trying."

He let out a deep breath, a rattle from his lungs escaping, and he closed his eyes. "Thank you, Philip."

I glanced at the soldier I guessed was the company's surgeon and nodded toward the leg.

"It'll cost him a leg," he said. "Shattered bone. We don't take chances with gangrene."

I needed to find the doctor for confirmation. Where was Scott? Was Leroy okay? Questions needed answered before riding for Anna. "I've got to go."

I stormed up the stairs and glanced through the bedrooms. The Dakota Territory was known for its tornados, and one must have visited the bedrooms. Papers were flung across the plank floor, beds were turned over, dressers ripped apart, mirrors shattered, and porcelain broken.

A soldier was working in the hallway, clearing debris.

One step into Anna's room, and I sensed her presence was but a vapor. I held out a hand, trying to catch her soul as if she were a ghost. Instead I felt my heart rip into pieces. How could I let this happen? How could I be so stupid?

I'd given her the map. And they hadn't found it. Was it here?

My gut told me she had the map on her person. She was in far more danger than just a kidnapping.

I took another step and my foot crunched on glass and wood. Below my boot was a broken photograph. I reached down and picked up the fresh picture, thinking back to when it was taken. I'd been busy, and she pleaded for a photo of the both of us—had made an appointment, even. I stood behind the park bench in a fake setting, leaving my gun and duster on. Anna's dress was . . . I didn't remember the color. Dark, according to the picture. My hand was on her shoulder, and she smiled. I was serious.

I pocketed the memory of the only woman I'd ever loved, the lone person on this massive Earth I knew my compass pointed toward, and lit out to make good my promises. I repeated it to myself as I charged into the night.

Find Anna or die trying.

10

As I left the house and stormed across the street, all but President Grover Cleveland arrived. Riding out of town wasn't possible—not with such chaos, both around me and in my mind.

I answered a few questions thrown my way. "I'm not in charge here," I muttered. If Marshal Stone was dead, who was in charge?

I was no leader.

His death was a spear through my heart. He'd done his best to fight for me the past year against Jacob. A mutual respect, then a friendship had grown, especially since Marshal Raymond Hill deputized me as a U.S. Deputy Marshal.

Where was Scott? I checked for his body across the way and couldn't find him. Lots of blood on the rough-planked floor though. Was it Scott's?

I couldn't imagine a worse moment—checking for my best friend's corpse.

The crossroads at the edge of town was lit at the corners

by four kerosene lamps. Cavalrymen walked toward the center, then left, as if getting orders and rushing to carry them out. I looked into the sky, viewed vague points of light. I rubbed my face. When would I wake from the nightmare? I started for the middle of the street.

I slowed as I approached. I stopped in my tracks, stunned.

U.S. Marshal Raymond Hill and his deputy Running Deer had ridden into town. They argued with Captain Smith.

I pushed through a small knot of men and nearly grabbed Marshal Hill's collar with both hands. He looked at me as I felt the words explode from my throat. "All we've been through," I said, "Deadwood and the Badlands and the Black Hills, and you chose now to show up? Just after I needed you most?"

His brow furrowed. "Been tracking Jacob," he said.

"Pretty poor job of it, I'd say." I let go and stepped back. He said nothing. Was it hurt that filled his eyes?

Marshal Hill and his intolerably bushy mustache stood off to my right, while Captain Smith, directly in front of me, rubbed his tiny mustache with a finger. I was a good half foot taller than the stocky marshal, only a few inches above the thin officer. Behind him, Running Deer was nearly my height.

I didn't need these men. I felt Anna slowly pulling away from me across the prairie. "Find Scott. Or somebody. Have them care for the horses."

Running Deer looked into my eyes for a moment, and an eternity passed between us—when he found me under the hateful presence of Devil's Tower, burying my parents, the visit to an Indian agent, good-bye at the edge of Sioux City, and then reunited at Devil's Tower during the Ghost Dance. His gaze lowered to the bear claws he'd given me so long ago. He took a step backward, and like a ghost disappeared into the night.

My heart surged until Captain Smith grabbed my shoulder. "You can't just ride off. We *must* plan. We'll need men.

Supplies." Even in the darkness, Captain Smith's small eyes shone. "You're to come with me to Washington D.C. to testify before Congress."

"Are you serious?" I turned all my anger and fear onto him. "And Jacob too, I heard."

"I can arrest you."

"Arrest Jacob! What kind of justice is this?"

"Philip," Marshal Hill snapped. "He's got a point. A posse don't up and ride the same night. Not if they want to be on the trail for more'n a week."

I hated everything about this. My single-minded drive to find Anna and the girls didn't seem to matter to these men.

If I wanted Anna back, I must be calm. But a visit to Washington was nonsense. No need to think about anything other than Anna. I took a deep breath, took off my hat, and said a prayer. Best get God's attention. I calmed some.

God. Help us.

I turned to see Doc Wilson step up. He wiped his forehead with a handkerchief. "Cavalry surgeon's right, Philip," he said over the thump of soldiers running by. "Mr. Johnston's leg is going to be infected, sure as you're standing there." He tucked the handkerchief into his chest pocket. "Leg's gotta go."

"Thanks, Doc," I said in a grumble. "Sure you did all you could do."

"Mr. Johnston's in good hands, Philip."

"I know."

"Then give him to God and us."

"Sure thing." I tried to put him out of my mind, but first said another little prayer for his healing.

He looked at the ground and shuffled his feet.

I tried to stay patient. "Doc. I don't have time. Tell me."

"Leroy probably won't make the night. They shot him up pretty bad. He's lost a lot of blood. The deputy in the storehouse across the way died right away." He pulled the handkerchief out and wiped his forehead again. "Went by Marshal Stone's office. Reminded me of Rachel. Blood everywhere. Stone's dead. Jeb used a knife on him."

My fingers wrapped around the handle of my revolver as I looked toward the marshal's office, as if I could see through the buildings.

Revenge, God. Grant me revenge. I closed my eyes.

"Remember," Marshal Hill said in a quiet voice. "Revenge isn't justice."

Did they always have to read my mind? "All right. I'll ride with the men." Until I grew weary of the company. Then I was off.

Captain Smith straightened his collar. "Marshal Hill's on the trail, Philip. You're coming to the District. With me."

"If you say that one more time, I will declare war on the United States." I held myself back from shoving him. "Get some perspective. I'm going after Anna."

"Think carefully," Marshal Hill said. "If you ignore the United States Senate, the price might be high. Very high."

I glanced at Captain Smith, throwing him a questioning look.

"The hearing is in two weeks." He rubbed his jaw. "Jail time, Philip, if you're not there. They'd make an example of you, a dime novel hero. Power over the popular."

Marshal Hill stepped closer to Captain Smith as if I weren't there. In a low voice he asked, "Anything you can do? Postpone?" I barely heard his next words. "I really could use him."

Captain Smith looked over Marshal Hill's shoulder at me as if contemplating whether I was worth the trouble.

Finally Captain Smith stepped back and lowered his shoulders. "I've wronged him enough. I owe him at least this. I may lose my career, but go ahead. I'll postpone the hearing for a while. There are a few favors I can call in."

"Wait," I said, pushing my way past Marshal Hill to look into Captain Smith's eyes. "It's me who's leaving. My responsibility. No need for you to land in trouble over this." Why did everything have to be so complicated?

He lifted his chin and sniffed. "Surely you've felt it, Philip, or at least thought it. Why was I living so close to you without revealing myself? Well, if I waited it was for all the wrong reasons. I'll make my decisions by proceeding as I see fit."

I started to speak when he held up a hand. "Philip. As my conscience dictates, let me act."

I imagined a long train of soldiers slowly snaking along Jacob's trail. "And your men?"

"Sending U.S. Cavalry across the country in search of missing girls isn't my mission." He straightened and shook his head. "Perhaps we'd be better for it if duties included such rescues." He gave a short bow and said in a clipped voice, "I leave you and Marshal Hill to it. I best know nothing about it." But the look in his eye spoke of how badly he wanted to ride.

"Thanks. For all you do."

"When this is over, find me stationed here in Mitchell or find the commanding officer at Fort Randall."

He walked away, tugging a piece of my heart with him. I didn't want to leave it like this. Especially with his career on the line. But there was nothing for it. I lowered my voice as he barked orders. "We'll all make heavy sacrifices before this is over."

"None of this is your fault." Marshal Hill wrapped his dark duster close around him.

I gave him a nod. "Time to put evil in the grave." Raven whinnied as I started for her. "I'll find a grocer for provisions." It was settling in that their start was now too far ahead, and we might be in for a long ride.

"I've money." He tightened his hat and mounted the Morgan next to Raven. "My orders have been to follow Jacob Wilkes, like I said. Tracked him here."

"You were a bit late," I said as I settled into the saddle.

He lifted his aging body and gave the house a grim look. With a pull on the reins, he tugged his horse's head around. "I'll find Running Deer and then send a message to my superiors. Maybe they can help Captain Smith hold off Washington. But he's right. I'd rather face Jacob's new gang than the mess in the Capitol."

"One enemy at a time." Raven sensed I was ready to go, and she turned.

Marshal Hill's attention was focused on a fight in the crossroads, the raised voices filling the square.

I moved Raven closer to see.

Captain Smith was saying, "If you feel that strongly about it, go. But send me reports. If I don't receive a telegram once every three days with an update, I will report your desertion. You understand? Both of you?"

An officer with a ruddy complexion visible even in the soft light stood immediately in front of Captain Smith. The red faced officer turned toward me.

Corporal Jackson. At Fort Randall when I'd sold Tucker to Captain Smith, the corporal had tried to put me in my place. He'd been a two-stripe officer when we had a run-in, and his words rung in my head—*Horses are like women. Have to show 'em who's boss.* He'd gone after my horse with a stick, and Tucker had chased him away.

He wore three stripes now and a diamond, a first sergeant. Impressive promotions over the winter.

As he approached, the pock marks on his face grew pronounced. I gripped the reins tighter.

He stood at attention before Raven and offered me a salute. "Permission to join the expedition, sir."

What? I bit my tongue not to say it aloud.

I slid from the saddle and stood in front of him. "Last time we met, you weren't keen on me being at the fort."

"I'd like to apologize." His tone seemed sincere. "Reckon I can be a help." He jutted out his chin but kept his eyes down.

I looked over his head toward Captain Smith, who'd gone back to giving out orders for positioning the men around town. "All right, Sergeant. I'm in a hurry. You have one minute to convince me."

He brushed away a strand of hair that had fallen off his brow and into his eyes, and he licked his lips. "Been thinking on things," he said. He looked at the dirt below his boots, and he rubbed his hands together. "Lots of things."

"You've been thinking about things," I snapped, grabbing Raven's reins in my left hand, preparing to mount.

"Wait. Please."

His tone was so impassioned I was drawn back. The pleading in his eyes gave me pause. "Speak your piece."

"Mr. Anderson, I feel . . . First, I gotta say I'm sorry 'bout the way I treated you. You were in the right, and I was in the wrong." His shoulders lowered. "Raven," he said to my Arabian. "I'm sorry to you too. For treating your master wrong."

Did this man just apologize to my horse? There was no doubt, however, the distress he was under. Despite the cool night, sweat poured down his temples. Momentarily setting aside my own despair, I gave him my full attention.

"I wanted to kill you." He sniffed. "Kill you dead. But there comes a time in every man's life when he's faced with exactly who he is, and what . . . I mean, whether he wants to be remembered and mourned when he's passed. And I got to figuring what people would say if you died and what they'd be thinking if I died. Mighty sad for your passing, mighty relieved with mine. And if I was mad before, that made me the maddest of all."

He held up the back of his hand and studied the rough skin. "I was standing on two sides of a window lookin' at myself. The man to the right was in sharp clothes, a clean uniform, you see. An eagle eye, a clean gun, and a quick heart to help. On the left, yeah, you can imagine. Me. Scruffy uniform. Nothing but trouble to alls who knew him. I made a fist—the real scruffy me—and crashed it through that glass. None of this is for real, now, but just in my head. And I crawled through the window and found that I could just . . . become him. I felt if I just tried a might harder every day and do what the Good Book told me, I'd be like the fellow in the window. So I crawled through the frame."

His brow furled. "I've been working on my speaking lately, to sound smarter. But I ain't got it right yet."

Was he putting me on? But he was so passionate.

"The men watched you ridin' away—doggone, if you weren't the topic of every meal. And I wanted them to talk about me. But you see, people can talk good or bad about you. Getting them to talk bad is easy. But people talking good about you is hard. You've got to earn it. I decided to earn it, like you. By being that man in the window."

He shook his head. "I know my minute's up, but lemme tell you one last thing. I made new friends. Practiced with my colt. Worked my Winchester. I rode twice as much as anyone else all winter. Why? 'Cause just now I realized something when I looked at you. I don't care if the men respect me the way they do you. I'm thinking that it was the work that made me a better man—not some fight or some fancy riding or shooting. And now I don't care a lick for what they think of me. The work's what I'm in for, and if you can use me, then here I am. My gun's yours."

I opened my mouth but no words came out.

From a distance, Captain Smith paused long enough to nod at me. So Jackson was sincere. "And you're willing to take the consequences?" I pointed to the center of the lane.

Jackson looked back at the cavalry, some scurrying away, others pausing near their commander. "Aye. I'd follow you, Mr. Anderson. Anywhere."

A burden, a tangible weight, settled on my shoulders. The thought of leading men made my stomach churn. In his eye was a look of unwavering devotion, and I wanted to hate him for it. I wasn't the one who deserved his admiration. God, surely, and a few great men. But not me.

"I don't like this. But you can come."

"You won't regret it." Jackson motioned toward a man behind him. As the black man stepped close he said, "Matt, we can go."

How did a man with colored skin get into the cavalry regulars? There was a contingent of buffalo soldiers—freed slaves and other black men formed a regiment—but they weren't allowed to ride side-by-side with the whites. Many believed morale in the cavalry would suffer. Others thought black men simply couldn't, or wouldn't, fight.

As I listened to Jackson explain how Matt was a protégé and a test case riding with the regulars, I stopped him. "Jackson, was this your idea? Having a black man in a white regiment?"

Jackson's reply was sharp. "Yessir. Which makes him my responsibility."

Maybe there was more to Jackson than met the eye.

Well, with all the opinions about blacks in the newspapers, pamphlets, and talk on street corners and in parlors, I was now forced to come to a decision myself.

Opinions. Mine mattered most. The only part of all this that gave me pause was what Jackson had said. Responsibility. Taking care of myself was what I was best at. Taking care of others was a heavy weight.

But I was beginning to see we needed men. And a black man in a white regiment would probably be worth twice his weight. He would have to be good. "You can ride with us."

Running Deer stepped from a nearby shadow, and I did a double take. How did he sneak up on us like that? He turned and motioned backward.

At the edge of the light further down the street, I spotted bright, red hair bouncing above the heads of cavalrymen. A small part of my heart felt relief, but the feeling was quickly swallowed by fear.

Scott's white face shone pale, and his eyes searched among the men. His gaze finally settled on me.

He rushed past a group of soldiers and grabbed the front edges of my collar in his fists. "They got her, Philip." His voice was strangled. "Got her. Got Anna. Got Rachel. Got Beth."

I tried to hold firm, but he shook me. "I know, buddy. We're going to go get them."

He didn't let go. "We've got to go get them."

"We're going."

Dirt stained his face, tracks from sweat lining his smooth cheeks. "Escaped out the back." He pointed to the stone building. "After they got the girls, I started after them alone. The deputy was dead. But I decided to get Marshal Stone and went to the jail to get him, but he's dead. Came back here but everyone here was dead. Then I remembered Anna's horse Alita and remembered how Jacob had stolen her once, and I thought he might be there to steal her, and I started for the mill where Anna had her pastured."

I reached up to loosen his grip, but his hands wouldn't budge.

"The other horses were dead. Got Alita. Got Becky. Got Anna. Got Mrs. Johnson—"

"Scott." He was nearing hysterics. "Scott, keep your head. We're going—"

A roar erupted from behind, and two massive arms wrapped around Scott then flung him to the ground.

Ryan stood over Scott and roared again. The words barely intelligible, he said, "Don't touch Philip."

I tried to grasp his arm, but even my large hands couldn't surround his bulging muscle. "Hold back, Ryan. He wasn't trying to hurt me."

"Save Rachel!" His voice was pitiful. He turned his bulk toward me, towered over my head by nearly a foot. "Find Rachel!"

I reached down and grabbed Scott's arm as he held my wrist. "We'll find them." I pulled Scott to his feet. "We'll find them."

Scott straightened his shirt, pulling on the cuffs. "Yeah. We'll find them. Let's go."

"Provisions, first," Marshal Hill said from behind. "I just talked to Captain Smith. He says he can keep your horses at the fort."

"Will you speak with him? There's a young boy and his friends across the river who owe me. They would watch the horses." Safer with Jake than at the fort.

Marshal Hill left to finish the task.

"Scott, you think I can count on you to find the store-keep?"

He wiped his nose with a sleeve. "You can, Philip." He looked up at Ryan then back at me. "I'm sorry."

"We're all on edge," I said, keeping my voice calm despite the volcano inside. "There's bound to be tension. Be patient with each other, and we'll get the girls."

But as I mounted Raven and looked back at the small cluster of men, I tried to swallow my rising doubts.

I counted up the posse in my head.

An aging Marshal Hill. Could he endure the rigors of the trail?

Running Deer, my Sioux companion. He was still in prime physical condition, sharp as an eagle, sly and skilled as a fox, and a fierce fighter. But our reliance on a single man might put too much strain on him. Besides, he didn't seem as if he worked well in a group.

Ryan was strong, but could I trust the big man?

Could Scott fight? I loved him like a brother, and I was afraid to put him in danger.

What of Jackson? And Matt? The odd pair had surprised me. At least I knew they were trained to fight. But what if we had to ride for more than a day? A week? Perhaps longer? Their careers would be in jeopardy.

The posse stood like a knot in a sea of activity, talking, and I searched for the strength to lead them. Leadership comes from the heart. And my heart ached.

Would this ragtag bunch be enough to find Anna?

Captain Smith in the distance offered a vague salute and turned his back. Would his loyalty to my cause be stretched too thin? And what of the Senate? Despite my rebellion, I knew the implications of ignoring their beckoning. Jail, at best. But my compass pointed only toward Anna.

Would Anna be harmed? What would happen if Jacob decided the girls weren't necessary?

And Mr. Wilkes and Jacob—my family's history coming back to haunt an orphaned son.

So many questions, and as the men scattered and I reined Raven back toward Anna's house for one more search, I thought of one last pressing matter.

What of the map?

Some secrets won't remain hidden forever.

11

As the Conestoga wagon thundered on day after day, Anna's fear turned into a murderous rage.

Not all was fair in love and war. Jacob's villainy surpassed anything her imagination could devise. Although in the heat of the enclosed wagon, her creativity expanded daily.

How many ways could she kill Jacob?

The games of love were gone. The war had escalated.

They had courted for a short time before she knew Philip wasn't the kind to grow jealous. But Jacob believed her acceptance to a dinner was approval for marriage. And he took control of her life, her family's lives, until Philip found a way to chase Jacob away, at great cost to himself.

She looked across the dusty interior through the canvas-diffused light and into Beth's eyes. Her listless head shook with every jolt. Beth was only ten, and it took two dozen men to escort her south?

Slippery trails oozed below Beth's nose. Poor girl. She, most of all, hated the gag. But despite threats and a good beating, they yelled at the top of their lungs the first day of capture, so they'd been gagged for weeks. All their lips were chapped and raw.

Anna reached out her bound hands and touched the girl's fingers. Beth curled against their mother's breast and looked away.

She suspected Beth blamed her for the kidnapping.

Her mother's hands brushed Beth's cheeks, but the awkward position was difficult for her to maintain. Her mother lowered her hands and looked at Anna, a depth that swallowed the world in sorrow.

The tiny hole in the canvas opening allowed a token of fresh air. The farther south they traveled, and as April surged into May, heat drained their souls of hope and energy. They were let out once in the morning and once at night. Both times meant water, a bit of food and a chance to find a private bush or, as they entered the desert, a rock.

They were unmolested, and she'd found out why. They would be worth more money in Mexico.

The thought made her shiver despite the confined heat. This was hell, surely.

Next to Anna, Rachel focused on the tiny portal to the outside as if the bit of blue was a sapphire of hope. Did she wish she were back in Deadwood plying her old trade? No, that wasn't the Rachel she knew. Rachel was surviving, something she did best. These shackles were as intolerable for Rachel as they were for Anna, both free spirits.

She rubbed her forehead against her soaked shoulder.

Becky lay curled in a ball at the wagon's front. The only time she stopped sobbing was when she slept.

Thunder of hooves day and night. Sobs, woeful glances. Stolen whispers and rough hands pulling them from the back of the wagon capsulated their lives.

Philip was coming. Philip would follow.

She guessed the kidnapping had been in the works for months. Fresh horses and the animals' caretakers had been waiting for them at almost every stop, adding an additional member to the guards.

Numbers didn't matter. Philip wasn't simply a man. He was a whirlwind. And whirlwinds left a wide path of destruction.

Oh, if she could lay eyes on her whirlwind!

Jacob didn't ride with them. She debated putting a bullet through his heart the moment she saw him, the Derringer she hid in her shirtsleeve still undiscovered, but she decided against his murder. Jacob's warnings kept the guards civil, and they needed some semblance of peace for now.

Any hotter and she would melt into the thin blanket, then pass through the planked wagon bed into the sandy desert.

She closed her eyes and dreamed of the night in Branson, Missouri. It was a cool spring evening, when fireflies scurried across the cropped grass underhanging lanterns. On the dais, four violins and two cellos hummed, a tour from Washington. They lifted their magic into the night, capturing a young girl's imagination. The milling crowds around her swirled into a distant, colorful fantasy so that the only reality was the melody coming from fireflies. Stars had descended to listen as well. Bach's continuo in D minor vivace lifted her, along with the fireflies, into the skies to float on a bed of starlight.

The wagon jarred, and she opened her eyes. What a lovely dream. Her white dress and small body blossomed into the shape of a woman, trapped in jeans and a stained flannel shirt. She laid her head back and stared at the canvas tarp overhead.

Oh, if only something would happen. Anything! But she didn't want to wish too hard.

She sat up. Was that a dog barking? She could barely hear the sound over the horses.

Suddenly the nearby horses seemed to peel away, leaving

the beasts that pulled the wagon. After weeks of incessant horseshoes clapping against stones, thudding against sand, and kicking up dust that seemed to filter through the canvas, the silence was deafening.

Was she hearing the clucking of chickens?

The wagon slowed, and this time she was sure she heard the screech of a burro. She'd heard it once before in a traveling show in Branson. It continued to bray as they passed.

Women's voices sounded like tinkling water.

They were in a town.

They had all sat up now, leaning toward the wagon's end. She could just see through the slit in the canvas at the back. Small shacks lined the edge of town. Miserable lean-tos covered anvils, large clay ovens, and waiting burros. Few people were out. All were dark-skinned and wore colorful clothing. Everyone remained focused on their tasks.

In the distance, a bell rang.

Beth turned to their mother, and she tried to speak through the gag. "Uh shink were 'n a kown."

Her mother looked down and nodded.

The wagon stopped.

After jiggling in the wagon for so long, tingles ran through Anna's body like little bugs, and she squirmed.

There was the doleful ring of a bell, closer now.

A man's voice said, "You fool, take them around back."

The wagon jerked and they were on the move again.

They rocked back and forth until the wagon stopped again. This time the end canvas widened, and the hinges on the back flap squeaked as it dropped. A filthy hand reached inside and grasped Anna's leg. She screamed as it tugged her to the edge. She tipped, falling in a heap in the dust.

Anna brought both hands over her eyes as the sun beat down.

A body thumped next to her, and Anna reached out. Rachel.

Soon they all lay on the ground. A hand untied her gag.

"Up," said a familiar voice.

Through the tears, she saw Jeb. "You." Beyond him stood her horse Alita, worn, ragged, but alive.

He snatched the front of her shirt and jerked her to her feet. He looked at her as she stared back. She was too terrified to speak.

With a nearly toothless grin, he yanked her close and she felt his hot, slimy flesh against her neck. He was licking her skin.

She screamed, and he flung her to the ground.

Deep, scratchy laughter from several dry throats filled the small lot.

The men grasped the girls and hauled them into a shadow and then in the building, but they left her outside.

Gasping for air and rubbing her collar against her neck, she turned and looked up.

An adobe church filled her vision. A small bell tower topped with a cross threw the symbol's shadow at her feet.

"Lord," she whispered. "Help us."

The shuffling of feet brought her attention to a small wooden door cut into the adobe wall. Was it a friar walking toward her? A monk? A priest? She didn't know. Her Protestant beliefs were showing now. He wore a long, brown, home-spun tunic that brushed against the sand as he walked. A hood covered his head and face. His hands were folded in large sleeves, in pious devotion.

Her heart cried out to him for mercy. In all her books, those who had taken the cloth or taken vows of obedience or chastity had been kind and passionate. Monks and nuns, devoted to Christ, helped the poor, the needy, and the oppressed.

She was all three.

He stopped in front of her, his sandals just visible from

under the robe. The straps were elegant, smooth leather. The buckles were bright gold.

She looked up.

The man brought his hands up, the smooth, ivory skin of his fingers so familiar, the unwanted caresses still locked in her nightmares. His thumbs grasped the outside of his hood, his fingers wrapping inside, and he pushed back the head covering.

Jacob's blond hair was matted against his forehead with sweat. His bright, blue eyes—the color of the sky—met her gaze. His teeth, so perfect, were visible in his false smile.

"Hello, Anna," he said, extending a hand. "I'm pleased you can join me."

12

Two weeks of crossing the prairie, and I confirmed that I preferred the company of horses over men.

I rode in the middle of the group with Ryan by my side. Jackson was ahead and Matt beside him. Marshal Hill and Scott followed behind. Running Deer scouted somewhere nearby, as usual.

A few days after leaving the Dakota Territory, it seemed the sky no longer cared to offer rain to the Plains. Despite the warm spring, the normal thunderstorms around Mitchell simply didn't appear in Nebraska, then Kansas, and now Colorado. Granted, there were a few that caught my eye, but the black clouds that streamed like thread from the skies seemed to keep their distance from our small posse.

The horses loved the grass, as if the buffalo of centuries or millennia had prepared the vast, treeless stretch of land for us.

We'd crossed a shallow, wide riverbed, and the sparse grass stretched as far as I could see. To our right, a long line of dark blue jagged mountains rose from the earth like teeth in a long saw. Yucca plants dotted the dry ground.

"Should have stopped at the river," Scott muttered.

Scott had been asking for extra breaks the last few days. Truth be told, I was exhausted as well. But the passion inside drove me forward without complaint. I didn't respond.

Marshal Hill, however, said, "Give your flapper a rest."

While Jackson and Matt went to the left around a large patch of cactus, Raven chose her own path and stepped around to the right.

"Even a blind man could see there's no grass out here." The whine in Scott's voice scared away the prairie dogs. "We should have stopped by the river to graze."

"There's a few hours of sunlight left," Marshal Hill growled. "Can't waste the light. And there's plenty of grass."

"But horses can't go on forever without rest." He sighed so loud, his horse neighed. "*I* can't go on without a rest."

"Fine," Marshal Hill said. "We'll stop and let Jacob just take the girls all the way to Mexico."

I was surprised Marshal Hill was arguing with him but even more shocked when he added, "Anyone would guess you don't want your girl back."

I looked off at the vast expanse toward the left and wondered how far away I would have to ride before the two voices couldn't be heard.

"At least I go after my girl." Scott's voice was angry. "You've a wife and kids in the East and you could visit them anytime. They could be kidnapped for all you care."

Oh Scott, I thought. Shut your trap. You've gone too far.

I remained quiet but half expected to hear Marshal Hill defend his honor with a gunshot.

Instead Jackson turned and said, "Quiet in the ranks. The commander ordered us to move on. So we move on. Even if we die."

"Dying of starvation won't help the girls," Scott said.

"Ain't for us to decide," Jackson said.

Jackson defended my honor, so I kept quiet. As quiet as Ryan, but even the big man wilted under the heavy sun.

My Arabian was the only one who acted as if the ride was a grand adventure.

With closed eyes I recalled Anna's dark hair and pretty face. I could be in paradise with Anna right now under the shade of a cottonwood beside the James River. Instead I rode with a crew of misfits.

Every step Raven took, my shoulders bounced, and I swayed like a sullen plant with no water. Sweat trickled down my back, and I imagined the cool river we just passed, slipping off Raven and plunging into the water.

I took a swig from my canteen.

"What I don't understand," Matt said, turning his head toward me, "is why we're so dead set on following their tracks. It'd be faster if we took up the trail south. That's Pueblo, right over there. Santa Fe Railway runs to all points south. Why not head to Albuquerque or El Paso? Maybe San Anton—"

"We'd never find them then," Marshal Hill snapped.

"Besides," Scott said, his voice filled with energy again. "They've left the perfect trail. Alita, Anna's horse. Philip can sniff out her trail anywhere."

Why was his tone accusatory?

I glanced past Raven's tracks and saw the distinct mark of Alita's horseshoe.

"Look at that," Jackson said, watching me. "He kin spot the treck from up atop the saddle." He whistled.

"Philip," Scott said. "Matt's got a point. Let's break trail and ride to Pueblo."

I kept my eyes focused on the trail.

Marshal Hill answered. "Do you understand how big Texas is? Never find them. We've a sure thing here. Follow the trail."

Scott seemed to flip-flop his opinion. "Yeah, and when they get to Mexico, we've lost them. I'm not letting Becky go so easy."

Jackson rubbed a thick handkerchief over his face. "If Philip crosses the border, I'm crossing the border."

Matt nearly shouted at him. "Ain't no way we can cross the border."

"If they cross the border," Marshal Hill growled, "we cross legally. I'll wire Washington—"

"I told you!" Scott nearly squealed. "I told you, Philip. I told you! We lost them. We lost them!"

Had heat touched their minds? They were idiots. I'd swim to England if it meant saving Anna. Besides, borders were simply arbitrary lines on maps.

"Philip will lead us right," Jackson said.

"What are you thinking?" Matt asked, his eyes wide. "We following some dime novel hero across the territory? And what happens when some desperado in Mexico catches us and holds us ransom? Ain't no way the cavalry's going to pony a single penny for us." He grunted. "Might even lead to war."

"We're already in a war," Scott said. "*Anderson's* War. That's what Becky and me are caught up in. His war."

I turned to him, stunned. Our gazes met, and I knew he regretted the words. He opened his mouth, but before he could speak I flipped Raven's reins to the left, and I touched her flank. She was off like a bullet.

We raced ahead for a knoll.

How could he say such a thing?

Perhaps I was thin-skinned, but what really went on in his head? This wasn't my war, no matter what some dime novelist wrote about me. Had he lost his focus on what we were about—what we were after? How was any of Jacob's hatred my fault? Place fault where the trouble springs. Not at me.

As I topped the hill, I slowed and stopped between a

scraggly yucca and a gray bush. The strong sage tickled my nose.

I dropped from Raven and stared at the scene below.

Two dozen buffalo stood scattered within a rock's throw. Their heads bobbed as they searched for scarce grass, accompanied by the slow plod of their heavy feet and the mournful crunching.

Something to the right caught my attention. Running Deer.

He stood with his back to me about thirty yards away, his head turned so I could see his profile. His left hand held a bow. His right pulled back an arrow on the string. With legs spread wide, he almost looked like a star drawn by a child. He had changed to traditional buckskin.

Holding the bow steady, he glanced to the side as if looking at me. He refocused on a cow. She grazed quite some distance from him.

Running Deer let go the arrow. As the deadly point hissed toward its target, he reached back, snatched another from the quiver on his back, and notched the arrow. He drew back, wood scraping wood, and let loose the string.

In a blur he fired another, then another. And as the fifth arrow left the bow, the first smacked into the target's side.

All five hit the buffalo's heart before the animal dropped to the ground. Dust billowed around the carcass as the other buffalo trotted away.

I held tight Raven's reins as I neared Running Deer. He set his bow over his shoulder and pulled a long Bowie knife.

"Incredible," I said, tying Raven next to his bay. "I didn't know you could shoot like that."

He grunted as he started for the downed animal.

I followed. But as he leaned over the massive carcass, my ire had returned. We didn't have time for games. We had to ride on.

He grabbed the beast's shaggy head and, grunting, straight-ened the thick neck. With knife hovering over the back, he finally said, "Sometimes Sioux can shoot more arrows before the first hits."

I stared at the five arrows protruding from the side.

"I am nearly fifty summers." He held up his hand, fingers extended in the air. "All I can shoot is five."

He gripped the knife and made his first cuts between the shoulders.

"But the first would have killed it," I said.

"You must know what I can do."

"Why?"

He paused at the blades and looked up. "A chief knows his warriors." He contemplated briefly then returned to the work.

The sage scent had gone, and now I smelled the great beast's wild sweat, as well as fur and blood.

I saw the warriors halt at the top of the knoll I'd just left. I grunted. Warriors. More like a Barnum and Bailey Circus.

He continued the cut along the spine. "A Sioux chief is not like your president. The chief does not give laws. He does not force warriors to go to war." He pointed the knife at me and in a fierce Sioux tone said, "He leads by example. They follow him because he is worthy of being followed."

"What does this have to do with me?" I felt the lump growing in my throat, something that had started in the pit of my stomach days ago and was working its way to my brain. I wasn't in the right. I was missing something.

"*Miya Ca*, Prairie Wolf, you know here," he said, pointing to his head with his clean hand, "but you must know here." He pointed to his heart.

I glanced again at the group behind me. They watched, as if they understood something monumental went on below.

He was right. I knew I was a leader—I just didn't want any

134

of the responsibility. As I lowered to a knee, to his level, I felt like the young boy again, saved from outlaws and on the way to the orphanage. But the same words kept rushing through my brain, *I don't want to, I don't want to.* Running back to the farm like a child wasn't an option. However, going after Anna alone still seemed like the best idea.

"I'm no leader."

He grasped either side of the thick fur that shrouded the shoulder blades and tugged, peeling away the skin from the fat. He paused, catching his breath. "You tether your pony to the wrong tree, *Miya Ca.*"

"What do you mean?"

"You fear sending the men to their deaths."

I crossed my arms. "Won't deny that."

He tugged again. The two halves continued to pull away from the body. The thought to help finally dawned on me, and I grasped one edge. Looking at the vast, blue sky, I tugged. The hide didn't pull away, so I reached into my boot, snatched a knife from the sheath, and cut between the leathery skin and fatty meat.

Running Deer hadn't said anything, so I continued talking. "I know my duty. Anna. But where does duty end and surplus responsibility begin? I know I've been running toward Anna, my duty. But these guys," I said, pointing over my shoulder with the knife.

"I shoot my bow." He matched my speed skinning the buffalo. "What do the others do?"

"Argue."

He didn't look up, didn't even pause.

I set my knife down and looked toward the mountains. "Scott is average with the rifle. But up to now, I would have said his best gift was his wit. The way he speaks. He'll make a great lawyer."

Running Deer grunted but kept silent.

"Marshal Hill is a wealth of experience. Good with a gun, calm under pressure, a steady hand." I rubbed my jaw. "I suppose I envy his mustache."

The buffalo's flesh lay exposed to the sunlight, and Running Deer cut at the flanks, his head cocked to the side, listening.

"Ryan is big, strong, and silent. I like that." After thinking, I said, "I was wrong about him. He's loyal. He just needed to be on the right side." I almost added he needed to be led in the right direction but didn't want to admit I was a leader.

"Jackson and Matt are both fine riders. Probably shoot well too. Under fire, I guess they'd be fine." I touched my sharp knife against the beast's rib and cut along the edge. "Jackson isn't the man I remember. He's changed." I looked at Running Deer and I said, "He's changed because of my example."

Was that a hint of a smile in Running Deer's dark eyes?

After cutting away a large chunk of meat he said, "Anyone can lead today. It is tomorrow—after his will has been tested—which makes a man. Red Cloud was a great warrior, day after day. He was followed by all. He had blood on his hands, but he led well."

The thought hit me like a stampede. Blood on my hands. By the end of this, my friends will be dead. They would follow me to their ruin.

The knife slipped from my fingers as the full weight of what I must do crushed my heart. I stood and backed away, holding my hands in front of me. I stared at the buffalo gore that soaked my skin. My hands shook without control.

Send them to their deaths.

I took several steps backward, paused at the edge of a patch of cactus, then walked away.

With every step a voice threw commands at me, a voice that told me what I was, a voice from outside my head reshaping who I was. *Philip, they will follow you to their deaths.*

From somewhere else—*You cannot carry on.*

Every man has a breaking point. But yours is on another horizon. You will carry on.

Anna is lost. You cannot reach her. It is already too late.

I grasped my head as I walked.

You're the best with a gun. No one else can save her.

But you've already failed. You're too far behind.

As I neared a depression filled with trees, death seemed better than the voices. Storms ripped my heart and mind apart. What was wrong with me?

I wiped tears from my cheeks. Crying?

See? You are far weaker than you thought.

A man cries.

I walked into the trees, the shade a blessed relief from the scorching sun. A muddy stream, thick and barely moving, hosted millions of insects hovering over the water, ignoring me. Birds chirped their accusations at the intruder, as if they sensed my fear and confusion.

Too many considerations. Too many possibilities. Too many instances my actions might send people into the afterlife.

You've too much failure in your lineage to believe you can lead men.

Lead men by being a leader.

An image of General Custer riding into battle—his men slaughtered by the hundreds—passed through my mind. My breath caught. And the strangest sound burst from my lips.

Laughter.

The billowing clouds in my soul cleared with every burst from my lungs. I leaned over the water, clutched my stomach with one hand, and wiped the tears with my other hand.

What was I worried about? "I'm sorry, Mrs. Custer," I whispered as a thought entered my mind.

General Custer was a jackass.

Recognizing the fact was important. Why? Because I wasn't quite as foolish as many leaders. Scott Ladd and Marshal

Hill and the rest could be in worse hands. No, more accurately, they could follow a worse man.

I stood and turned away from the stream. With hands on my hips and feet spread wide, I looked past the trees, past the men standing around the buffalo's carcass, and studied the dark mountains. Yes. Recognizing the failures of others is the first step in becoming a leader. I would start by studying others.

Maybe, just maybe, I knew what I was doing.

I looked into the sky. "God, you and me, we're a long way from finished with this war. I'm in a predicament. I'm far from the man I need to be to save the girls." I wiped the last vestiges of fear and laughter from my face. I opened my mouth to say something more but realized there wasn't much left to say. I was a praying man. I'd read my Bible well enough for the truths to settle in my heart. I knew God, and He knew me.

The voices in my head weren't mine. Maybe they weren't God's. Some were common sense.

Follow what I felt was right and trust God that He would direct me.

All I had left to say was simple, and the words felt as if God said them at the same time.

"Let's go."

I returned to the dead buffalo, and all the men looked at me as I returned. Their conversation hung thick in the air. Scott looked away.

Should I explain the transformation from a only moment ago?

No, that didn't feel right. Instead I stood straight, chest out, hand on my gun. I eyed each man. Even Running Deer.

Action. Spur them to action.

I looked at the carcass and knew what I wanted. So simple, so temporary. So needed. "We spend the night here. Plenty of meat." I motioned to the stream. "Water there. Scott, bring up a couple buckets then bring up some wood. Jackson, you've cooked pretty well, you can start on some steaks. Matt, water the horses. Ryan, I want you to scout past that hill. I want to know what's ahead a bit. Marshal Hill, I thought I saw a well-established road on the other side of the stream. You mind scouting it out?"

They studied me for a moment.

Oh, please, move.

Then Scott, rubbing his backside after the long day's ride, started for the thicket. "Always knew I'd be wasted on the worst tasks."

Jackson took the horses' reins and headed for the water. The rest gave words of agreement and began their tasks.

Marshal Hill offered a nod as he passed by.

Running Deer, it struck me, was a man who worked best without orders. Something good would happen just by letting him do what he did best—whatever he wanted. To his credit, any cracks left open he would fill. And lately, that was leadership.

"Thank you," I said as soon as the Sioux and I were alone.

He kept cutting away meat from bone without acknowledging I'd said a word.

That night, as the sun settled behind the mountains in an array of blues, oranges, and reds, Scott apologized for the things he said. He whistled a tune I couldn't make out. Jackson had an extra spring in his step. Matt told stories of life as child on a plantation in Georgia. Marshal Hill laughed when Scott was worried his health would fail from desert dust coating his lungs, and Ryan watched me with interested eyes. Running Deer slipped away with a mostly raw steak.

The smell of roasted meat flavored with sage couldn't assuage the burning in my soul to keep riding after Anna. But I'd asked much of these men, and they needed a break.

Loud frogs overshadowed the horses chewing grass, and when they stopped we heard the horses again. Jackson had to speak over the din as he lifted a hunk of meat. "More tender after leaving a steak under the saddle all day, but this'll do."

As we ate, I kept the conversation light. And after cleaning up, we laid out bedrolls under the canopy of stars.

"Tomorrow we'll make progress," I said. "The road Marshal Hill scouted sounds like the old Santa Fe Trail. May be the shortcut. My gut says that's the route they took."

I settled on my back, lay my head on the saddle, and felt a few wayward rocks under my blanket. After shifting, they seemed to disappear. I looked up at the band of stars overhead.

Many times hope leads to disappointment, but I allowed myself a fraction of optimism. The satisfaction of bringing the men together gave me strength. We might—just might—pull off the impossible. But if we had to cross the border, Scott was right. We may be in trouble.

The one thing I clung to above all else—I was finding Anna.

And stopping Jacob once and for all.

I adjusted the Smith and Wesson under the saddle.

I'm coming, Anna.

13

Anna shivered in the cold crawlspace. Accustomed to the heat, any chill drove straight to the bone. She rubbed her wrists together, but the ropes crossed her arms and kept her from touching her fingers.

Three days ago after halting at the church, Jacob had thrown the girls in the church's cellar. Jacob's haunting, blue eyes from under the hood were the last she remembered of him as he left them in the dark prison. Jeb did the dirty work now— food, water, and sometimes cleaning out their bucket.

Today was Sunday Mass, and she guessed Jacob couldn't risk the echo from their cries. Gags only held back the voice of a woman so far, and since only their hands were tied they kicked at the thick wooden door until their legs were numb. How many thumps echoing through the building could a priest endure? Jacob had too little patience with such simple tortures. No, he wasn't anywhere near the chapel.

In the middle of the night the girls had been moved to a saloon crawlspace.

The girls were lying around her, shivering. She huddled with Becky, and Beth curled around her mother. Rachel lay near the trap door.

With the ceiling just inches above them, their legs were tied so they couldn't kick the wood panels and thick supports. The smell of smoke and alcohol from the saloon drifted through the tight cracks above and weren't a fair tradeoff for the putrid conditions of the church basement.

Soon there would be a ruckus above, but in the early morning the only muffled voices sounded like a saloonkeeper and bartender. "Last night's total was eighty-two dollars."

"Slow night."

"Some high-end drinkers, though. I'll need more scotch."

"All right. Shipment will take a week."

The voices were so similar she couldn't tell which was the owner.

She heard footsteps behind her near the trap door. Why, with each thump, did she feel her doom approaching?

"They're coming. Back room."

After a few seconds, two new voices.

"Now lad, they're unharmed?"

She didn't recognize the voice.

The second, however, she knew. "Unspoiled." Jacob.

Anna closed her eyes and wished the men away. She wasn't Philip. She wasn't brave.

Was it the confines of the tight space that made her mind spin? Or had her energy given way? Panic just wasn't part of her nature.

The trap door opened, but Anna kept her eyes shut.

She heard a cough. "Surely, bathing wouldn't cause harm."

"More than you might expect," Jacob said. "That one. Anna. She will escape if she can." His voice rose. "I know you're awake, Anna."

"Close it. Quickly."

The trap door shut.

She didn't hear them again for a moment. Above in the bar, their conversation resumed.

The man was saying, "And you're aware how dangerous Anderson is?"

"I've dealt with him before."

"He is angry now."

Jacob laughed. "His anger is nothing. I've seen him angry."

The man's voice was muffled. "You've seen him disturbed before. Now he is angry."

"I know how he thinks," Jacob said.

Fire burned in Anna's chest. Jacob knew nothing of the honor and courage Philip possessed. The banker's son couldn't begin to understand Philip's mind. *She'd* barely scratched the surface.

"My good fellow," the man said. "He is a horse you've saddled. If you can ride him, do your worst. Until then, you know why I'm here."

"I don't have it. Yet."

The man's voice turned into a growl. "I grow impatient."

"Well, wait a little longer."

"Jacob." The man cleared his throat. "I've been a gentleman thus far. Do not make me change my ways."

"You promised a pardon. And seventy-five thousand. Perhaps those were idle boasts?"

There was something tickling the back of Anna's mind, something forgotten that she shouldn't have forgotten, but a wall of fear stood in the way of her seeing clearly.

What was wrong with her?

The derringer was small comfort. The prospects of escape for them all were abysmal.

The floor above seemed to creep closer. Closer. Smothering. Choking.

Philip? Where are you? Please don't fail me. Please, God, send Philip.

Where was her hero when she needed him?

She's so resourceful, Mr. and Mrs. Johnston, friends had said. But now there was nothing she could do.

There were times, she realized, she depended on others. When the trouble is daunting, no one can accomplish what must be done alone.

"Are you aware," the man said, "of Philip's heritage?"

"Heritage? Philip is an orphan. He has no heritage."

"You are frightfully wrong, my young fellow. Philip doesn't need to know his heritage. He's living it, my dear boy. He is a Maxwell."

Please, Philip. Please.

What if he never came?

14

I held out my hand, and Marshal Hill placed the binoculars in my grasp. When I pressed them against my eyes, the world was blurry. "How do you see through these?"

"Here." He took them. "Press here to move the lenses. The world will come into focus."

We lay in a row at the edge of a modest ravine, looking into the valley. Everyone wore denim pants except Ryan, who wore cotton. Marshal Hill and I wore a vest over our shirts. Scott's red button-up was rolled at the sleeves. Jackson and Matt both having discarded their uniforms long before, wore thin white homespun we purchased on the trail. We were dressed for the desert.

Running Deer roamed on the other side of town.

I tried the binoculars again, and this time the village popped into view, as if jumping at me. I tried not to jerk back.

The adobe buildings below were crowded together and almost looked like buttons on a ragged quilt blanket. Although several hundred yards away, the binoculars were magic—as if I could reach out and touch the hovels.

As I looked I asked, "He said the name of the town was..."

"Lajitas," Marshal Hill said.

"And how many people live there?"

I looked toward him. I lay on my belly atop a stone shelf above the valley, and to my right Marshal Hill rested on his stomach and elbows. Beyond him was a local farmer and then the rest of the posse, all positioned like me.

Marshal Hill turned to the local man. "Cuántas personas viven ahi?"

"Alrededor de doscientos cincuenta personas. Pero muchos más cercana en las granjas." His accent was crisp, and I wanted to understand him without a translator.

"He says about two hundred and fifty people, but there's more on nearby farms." Marshal Hill leaned forward, groaning. "Getting old." He pointed. "There. Town's big enough to bring in the railroad." He motioned to the train.

I looked through the binoculars again, this time pointed at the train. Three yellow passenger cars and two goods cars waited on a sidetrack, while the engine broke away and steamed toward a turntable. People rushed around the train, and the incredible binoculars brought them close, as if I was waiting nearby and watching them work. An unsettled feeling lodged in my gut. Did they know they were being watched?

Down the center of the village ran a wide road, splitting the settlement in two. At the opposite end a chapel stood as sentinel to the edge of town, its tall front spanning the width of the building, a cross gleaming from the center. A steeple rose high with a bell hanging inside, swinging side-to-side. I turned my head and caught the faint sound of ringing.

"And he says he saw several women?"

After translating and listening to the reply, Marshal Hill brought a hand up to his mustache and smoothed the edges. "He saw bound women being led into the saloon. But he also heard they were being held in the church. Maybe the black-smith shop too." He looked down at the city, his dark eyes surveying the valley. He blew, and tiny bits of his mustache stuck out. "Don't like it. Not a bit."

"Is no one in . . . in . . . what's the name of this city?"

"Lajitas."

"Does no one in this village care women are being held captive against their will?"

Marshal Hill hesitated before asking. When the Mexican man was finished, Marshal Hill didn't look pleased. "He said this happens often."

"What?" I dropped the binoculars and reached over Marshal Hill, grasping the man's collar and pulling him over the marshal's prone form. I pressed the farmer into the dust. "How can you just let this happen? What are you people, idiots? Are all Mexicans as evil as—"

"Philip, stop!" Marshal Hill's strong hands pulled us apart, and the choking Mexican man backed away, grasping his throat.

"How can he let this happen?"

Marshal Hill struggled to pull me back, but with us still on the ground he found it difficult to get traction. "Stop! Too much dust. They'll see you."

Ryan's hand spun me over and pressed down on my chest. I struggled to escape. "Get off me!"

"Not until you listen to sense." Marshal Hill's aging face hovered over mine. "Don't you dare say a word about these people, you understand me? Ever. They scratch an existence from dust and sand without water and love more than anyone I've ever met. Remember the city on *your* watch? Mitchell? Any better?"

His words felt like a slap in the face.

Marshal Hill continued. "Think long and hard about how you allowed Mitchell to be controlled by Jacob before con-demning what happens in another village."

Shame made me want to continue the fight, but I leaned back and Ryan let go of my chest. Had the desert heat addled my mind?

Then I realized.

Marshal Hill's Spanish was excellent.

I groaned as I leaned back. "Your wife is Mexican."

"And I don't like hearing her race talked bad about, especially when there's not a lot to be proud of among our own."

"You lied. She's not from the East."

"I lied because of men like you."

I sat on that but couldn't collect my thoughts. Finally I answered his stinging retort. "Marshal," I said, not meeting his gaze. "Sorry."

He grunted, a sound I took as apology accepted. "So, what's your plan?"

"We're going to have to scout the town." But how best to proceed?

I glanced over at Scott, who was scanning the sky. "Gonna rain, Scott?"

"Just checking for buzzards."

Jackson reached for his canteen. "Buzzards?" He twisted cork and took a swig.

"Smart birds," Scott said, grabbing at his side for his own canteen. "They know when a fight's coming."

"Scott," Marshal Hill snapped, his voice tight. He looked back at the town. "It doesn't work that way."

Matt couldn't stop laughing. "Prophets, every one. Them buzzards got names like Moses and Elijah."

I shook my gaze from the pointless search of the skies. "All right, here's what we do." I pointed to the far edge of town. "Jackson, Matt, you two take the church. Marshal Hill, Scott, the blacksmith. Ryan and I will take the train." Below, men leaned on hitches and stacks of rails, casually watching the engine and cars. Too casually. Maybe they guarded something.

Marshal Hill lowered his voice. "We should ride into town together. We can cover each other that way."

I remembered how we took the cabin in the Black Hills. We surrounded the log home, but we'd ridden together until the last minute before fanning out. Even then one of the men escaped and I had to ride him down. Fodder for the dime novel, no doubt.

Here we had no idea where the girls were locked up.

"No need to let them know we're here," I said, sitting up. "Just walk into town and look around. Start running toward the sound of gunfire."

Matt stopped laughing. "We're gonna be outnumbered. Like a rooster in a hen house." He whistled and pointed at my gun. "You better be as good as they say, mister."

"He's still alive," Marshal Hill said in a calm voice. "That's saying something."

As we broke apart to secure our horses and gear away from the cliff's edge, I felt a hand on my shoulder.

"Hey, hey," came Scott's soft voice. "Is there a reason you and I aren't working together?"

"Yeah," I said, reaching for my saddlebag. "The train's tight. Small gun work. You're best with a rifle, so the black-smith is your mission." I hefted a box of ammunition.

He nodded, a grim look of determination on his face. "I won't let you down."

I grabbed his shoulder with my other hand. "Be careful, buddy."

He offered the smile I remembered, the one that won Becky's heart. "We'll get the girls back."

"That's right." Ryan came up from behind. Hearing him speak was rare, so we both gave him our full attention. "We gotta get these guys. Then you can step back into oblivion."

Scott spoke from the side of his mouth. "You mean obscurity, I hope."

Ryan nodded and reached for his quarter horse.

We'd ridden far together. There had been fights between us, but the tension that pushed us forward now seemed to draw us together. I'd not been a perfect leader. But we worked to get this far. Now could we fight together?

I was proud. But more. I was eager.

I drew the duster over my clothes.

"Obscurity. You're right, Scott. Hey. Remember target practice over the James River?"

"The way we spared the can's life by shooting around it?"

"I can't wait to get back there, you and me."

"You know," he said, leveling his gaze with wide eyes, a look I recognized as anticipating action. "Anna's not one to sit out target practice. She'll join us in that field."

"You okay with that?"

He pointed with a thumb to the valley. "Let's get the girls and find out."

Jackson and Matt walked down a narrow path leading to the valley floor. Before Marshal Hill and Scott followed, the marshal paused. "What about young Miguel here?"

"What of him?"

"He'd be an asset in town."

I considered the Mexican for a moment. His dark skin and black eyes were so foreign to me, I couldn't tell what he was thinking. "I'd rather he not."

"Why?" Marshal Hill motioned toward the village. "You blame them for this trouble and then won't let him join us?"

"We can't trust him."

"Because he's Mexican?"

The rocks under my boots bit into the bottom of my feet, and the heat scorched my duster, creating a mobile oven I sat inside. I didn't reply.

"Can't believe you, Philip."

"He hasn't ridden the trail with us."

"Sad excuse. If he's willing to take a bullet for the cause of freeing the girls, don't stand in his way."

I didn't care one way or the other if the kid died. But if he got one of my men killed . . .

Marshal Hill spat. "You're just scared of him. Well, there's only one way to get to know him. Ride into town with him by your side."

But he was so foreign. At least the people in Mitchell, I could guess what they were thinking. Miguel looked at me intensely, as if hating every bit of my presence on his land. "No. Tell him to go home."

"Don't be a fool—"

"Casa! Or whatever word they say for go home." I spun on a heel. "Come on, Ryan."

Ryan and I started for the train.

I let my anger simmer. This was our problem. Ours. We would solve the issue and maybe fix theirs as well. Ridiculous.

The sun baked the desert around us, and I appreciated the wide-brimmed hat. Ryan trudged close behind.

The path dropped to the desert floor, and I led Ryan toward the depot. Shimmering in a mirage, the western road that led into Lajitas had been covered by nearly a dozen men, ready for an ambush. That morning, we scouted the area from a distance and spotted the waiting men.

No one in town would guess we'd slip inside. Surely we could walk the streets without harassment, until we came across Jacob or Jeb. Then I would exact justice with the Smith and Wesson. Eager anticipation surged through my body, giving me a sense of invincibility.

As we drew closer to town, the chapel bell stopped ringing.

The desert sand and rock made for easy paths, so Ryan's long legs matched my stride. I glanced at him. "Thanks. For what you said back there." He thought of someone more than himself. A good-natured man should be appreciated.

I smiled, despite myself. I was thinking like a leader.

When he didn't say anything, I decided to cut directly to the question I needed answered. "You kill a man before?"

He wiped his sweaty face with his sleeve then shook his head.

"Could you?"

"For Rachel." He took a sloppy breath through his nose. "For Rachel." He lifted his shotgun.

The earnest look in his small eyes convinced me.

Smoke billowed from the distant engine as the massive beast moved along the second rail to the front of the cars. The long compartments hid our movements from the station.

"I don't think we'll have to fight. But if we do, stay close."

He was silent and we still had about half a mile to walk, so I asked, "How did you and Rachel start courting?"

He shrugged. "Just kinda happened."

Not an answer, but then again I might have answered the same if someone asked me about Anna. "What do you like about her?"

He stopped and looked at the village. I turned.

"Smart," he said. "Smart. Don't know how she got so clever. And she don't lie. And she done things in her past, but so did I. She said we don't need to talk about it, just start new." He smiled. "That's smart. Mighty smart. No one ever cared for me before, and she does." His voice dropped to a whisper, and his gaze grew distant. "And she does."

He was hard to hate.

"Ryan," I said, getting his attention. "Let's go find her."

Side by side, we marched to the train. I could smell the coal smoke and steam as the engine backed closer to the cars, and I eyed the wheels coasting so smoothly over the iron tracks until the cars shook with a loud crack.

We kept moving.

The train blocked our view of the station but covered our approach.

The engineers glanced our way, but returned to securing the engine to the cars.

With my left hand I grasped the first car's rail and pulled myself up, keeping my right hand free. I tugged the knob and the door opened easily.

The smell of fresh paint hit me as I took a step inside the empty passenger car. Seats and tables lined the center aisle. Sun streamed through a bank of windows atop the ridged ceiling, casting a warm glow about the room. Despite my heightened senses, keen for danger, I suddenly felt a strong desire to travel with Anna by my side. We'd roll the miles away with books in one hand, holding the other hand as we read. Something I would keep in mind when I finished this trouble.

Behind me, Ryan's presence filled the narrow room, dispelling the distracting thoughts.

"It's empty," I said to Ryan and I started down the aisle, hand close to the Smith and Wesson.

Through the window to our right, the vast expanse of empty desert stretched toward the cliff we'd just descended. On our left, the edge of the railway station filled the view. No one was in sight.

"This feels like a trap," I said to Ryan. "But we can't chance missing the girls if they're here. Be ready."

He nodded.

The next carriage was linked with a plank over the couplers, a sliding door with window blocked our way. I peered through the glass into the empty car.

I slid the door opened and in a few long strides reached the opposite door. On the station platform, I saw the waiting men. This close, I made out their heavy weapons.

"I bet the sun's keeping them from spotting us in here," I

said to Ryan. "They'll see us for sure when we cross to the next car. Should we see what happens?"

He shrugged.

"All right then, let's make it quick." I swallowed my growing apprehension and despite losing nerve, I slid open the door and stepped into the space between cars.

I couldn't resist a glance at the men.

And they looked at me. Into my eyes.

My wolf eyes.

Recognition filled their faces.

They drew.

I was faster.

There were four in my narrow view.

No visions, no pictures from the past entered my mind as one man crumpled from my bullet. I pulled back the hammer for another shot as I dove to the right, lowering my shoulder and crashing into the last car.

I tumbled and rolled to my feet but couldn't keep back images of the gunfight in the Badlands.

And another thought—Anna must be in Lajitas, or they wouldn't be putting up a fight.

A barrage of gunfire exploded outside the car, and glass fell like hail around me. I felt an odd sensation of peace. Of floating on mist and darkness.

How did I get outside the car? Why was Ryan standing over me, shotgun pointed toward the sunset?

And why couldn't I move?

The chapel bell rang again.

15

Anna closed her eyes and faced the morning sun, the warmth descending on her like a welcome peace.

The chapel courtyard was silent except for the ringing bell. The air was delicious, and she breathed in a soft scent of flowers she didn't know.

She tugged at the ropes that bound her wrists. The habit had ringed callusses around her arms, but she relished the small attempt of rebellion.

Don't open your eyes. Reality is in the mind, the truth created in the kindness of the sun. After the dank basement night after night, the rays gave her renewed life.

She could almost feel Philip's touch on her cheek, his lips on hers. Her heart fluttered as she sensed his need for her.

The chapel bells stopped. The sound of horses approaching caught her attention.

After a sigh, she opened her eyes.

A Mexican boy, his head down, rounded the short adobe fence. He trudged around a withered tree and into the center near a dry fountain. He pulled a horse behind him, the reins clasped in his hands.

She greeted the boy. "Hello there."

She recognized the weary animal.

Anna rushed to her horse and buried her face in the ratty mane. "Alita!" She breathed in the sharp smell of horse sweat, so welcoming and familiar.

Alita snorted and brushed her muzzle against Anna's side.

When Anna looked up, the Mexican boy had disappeared.

Although Alita wasn't saddled, Anna could easily leap onto her back and escape. Leave Jacob far behind. And leave Beth and her mother. Rachel and Becky.

Or Anna could find the city marshal.

The law wouldn't do anything. She held tightly to Alita's mane. No, the law surely knew girls were brought into his city with the hopes of selling them. And the law did nothing.

Sores spotted Alita's back, and her flanks were matted with sweat and blood. She'd been ridden hard with no care.

Oh, someone would get an earful from her. Perhaps a punch in the mouth, if she were lucky.

Anna felt a presence.

She spun. Jacob stood close to the chapel's back door, shrouded in a monk's robe. Even though his hood covered his head, the morning rays lit sparks in his eyes. His consuming lust for her engulfed the space between them.

He straightened, and the look was gone.

"No," he said, his mellow voice soft. "You can't leave. You're too honorable to leave behind your sister." His eyes begged her to respond.

She held her tongue, but keeping silent was the most difficult thing she'd ever done.

His robe brushed the red clay around his feet as he sauntered toward her. "There's a subject I've been loath to bring up with you, since it's . . ." His face contorted as if he'd eaten a lemon. "So beneath us."

Anna lifted her chin.

"There's a small token you possess that I need."

A horse's neigh echoed off the adobe walls, and Anna spun to see the boy returning. He used one arm to brush sweat from his temple with his linen sleeve. His other hand led a stallion.

Anna gasped. The animal's butternut coat gleamed in the orange light, its muscles the perfect mix of bulk and sinew.

Such a beautiful animal.

With head low, the boy handed the reins to Jacob, turned, and sprinted away in a cloud of dust.

Anna looked toward Jacob with raised brow.

Jacob caressed the stallion's muzzle. "Tell me what I want to know, and I put Beth on a train back to Mitchell."

Anna stiffened.

"Tell me."

She looked toward a flowering bush, then back at him.

He squared his shoulders, facing her directly. "The map."

Oh, Philip.

The map.

She'd forgotten.

"I see," he said, chuckling. "You know where it is."

Anna's mouth was too dry to respond.

Jacob stared at the ground. He ran a hand across his lips, looking thoughtful. "Magnificent animal, don't you think?" He took a step back to survey the horse. "When working, a man must furnish himself with the best tools, such as carriage. Clothing. Gun." He looked toward Anna. "Woman." He motioned to the stallion. "A horse is a tool that can save a man's life."

Anna felt heat burning her cheeks.

With a pale hand, Jacob touched the horse's white blaze.

"This tool will make me faster, stronger. So," he said reaching into a fold in his robe and pulling out a gun. "I don't need this one." He pointed the muzzle at Alita's head.

Anna gasped. Philip had described Jacob pointing a gun at Raven—the sheer terror and helplessness.

But not helpless.

With all her breath she pressed her lips together and blew. Oh, if her mouth wasn't so dry!

Anna sprinted toward Jacob as she whistled.

Did Alita's head rear back as Anna had trained her to do? Did she run as Jacob adjusted his aim?

The blast from the barrel sent her reeling to the cobblestones, covering her head. Ringing mixed with her scream.

Through the cacophony of noise came the most beautiful sound she'd ever heard—Alita's hoofbeats fading away.

His fingers grasped her hair, nails scraping her scalp. He yanked her to her knees. His vicious pull forced her to stagger forward. She tried to gain her footing, but he wrenched hard and she stumbled and slammed into the ground. He dragged her a few feet before the unbearable pain overwhelmed what little control she maintained. She swung her feet toward his leg, and another scream escaped her lips as his grip held.

Anna kicked again at his leg and connected with his knee. He let go of her hair and grasped the injury.

She leapt to her feet and charged for the stallion, hoping she could climb its back. The animal's strength would take her away, far away. Back to Mitchell, back to her father and mother and Beth and Philip.

Even remembering the truth, knowing Philip was far away, her mother in the chapel's dungeon, Beth tied beside her, and her father probably dead didn't stop her efforts to mount the horse.

Her tied arms draped over the high shoulders and she jumped.

Jacob's hand grasped at her back, and his fingers slipped and caught her pocket.

He tugged. The stitching gave way, and she fell back.

A single piece of yellow paper fell beside her, fluttering on the soft morning breeze.

"No!" She reached out to snatch the map.

Jacob was faster.

He straightened, holding the map in front of him, casting a long shadow beside her. She studied his face for a reaction, anything that might tell her what he was thinking. He remained in perfect control.

"Ah," was all he said.

He looked past the map and down into her eyes. She returned the gaze with as much defiance she could muster.

With a sigh, he tucked the map into the fold of his robes and lowered a hand. She felt the gentle pressure against her elbow as he directed her to stand.

Without thinking, she complied.

"I would be disappointed in you if I didn't respect you so much," he said almost piously. He led her toward the chapel. "You are headstrong. Filled with will and spirit. Misdirected, I must admit, and I've done my best to change that. But you're too simpleminded. Too dull for my tastes."

Between the ringing in her ear and her heart beating like a troop of galloping horses, she barely registered his meaning.

He kept talking. "Yes, dull. You move only a single direction. Philip is a distraction for a woman, not a destination. Poor farmers like he should be nothing to a beautiful woman like you. But you insist on resisting me because of him." He smiled and lifted the map. "But I think I'll give you one more chance to redeem yourself."

He led her through the back door and into the sanctuary. His voice echoed. "Perhaps you think you're a sparrow, and because you're so small the hawks will ignore you. Well, I'm giving you a chance to soar with the birds instead of flit with the insignificant."

She failed Philip, failed him miserably. But as Jacob threw her below the benches of the front row, her mind clamped down on her self-deprecation.

"You will marry me. Now."

She wanted to give in. End all this.

"The priest will arrive in a moment."

Long had she focused on truth. Since her atrocious relationship in Branson—the older man blaming her for deeds she'd never done—Anna put blame where blame was due. If her actions caused a problem, she wouldn't twist the circumstances to make others take the blame. The opposite was true as well. She wouldn't beat herself for others' actions.

Think, Anna. Work out what is happening. Because he's lying to you.

As she lay in a beam of sunlight before the altar, she came to herself again. Slowly crawling to her knees, she looked to the ceiling. The candle chandeliers hung by ropes from above, streaks of black where smoke escaped the flame, cold wicks as black and lonely as the fear that threatened to overtake her newfound courage.

She reached out her hand and touched linen on the crude altar. Her fingers brushed the silver communion chalice as she grasped the small, wooden cross. Jesus hung from tiny nails.

The words seemed to come from somewhere—bigger events were happening. She and Philip and Jacob, even the map and the past were part of a far bigger working.

Just past the cross, her gaze fell on Jacob as he reached up and grasped a rope. With a tug, the bell tolled.

She closed her eyes as the pealing chimes reached the end of time.

And she knew the pain she suffered wouldn't last a lifetime.

Lord, forgive my unbelief.

Help me.

The derringer. *Shoot Jacob now, take the girls and run.*

Jacob's bane is here.

Her heart pounded in her head. Fear was a dagger through her heart.

I can't.

Lord, my unbelief! I'm not bold enough.

The bell rang. For how long was she paralyzed? A dozen bottomless rings?

Too late, the voice seemed to tell her. Too late.

No, never too late! As if in a dream, she twisted her hand in the ropes so that her right arm reached for the tight band on her forearm. Her fingers clasped the gun. Once she pulled out the weapon, there was no choice. She had to finish the deed.

The barrel slipped from the tiny holster, past the filthy ruffle of her sleeve, and into the chapel's dusty air.

She would kill him at the altar. A shudder ran through her as she pointed the muzzle of the .22 caliber at his hooded head.

Her thumb reached for the hammer.

A shuffling sounded at her left, and a boot smacked her arms, sending the derringer spinning over the benches.

She scrambled for the gun as Jeb's voice tugged at her soul. "She had you dead to rights." His hands circled her waist.

"No!" she yelled.

Jacob stood over her as Jeb pinned her to the stone floor. A ridge dug into her back, but she dared not move.

Jacob's slap across her face barely stung.

"No time," Jeb said, putting a hand on Jacob's shoulder. "He's in town. We've got to move. Can't you hear the gunfire?"

Jacob's eyes narrowed. "How many?"

"We're not sure. They're close to the station, but it seems men are coming from all points of town."

"Plans have changed. Take the girls to Mexico. Meet the

buyer there." Jacob tugged Anna to her feet. "I'm taking her to—" With his other hand he pulled out the map. He studied the markings for several seconds. "Devil's Tower."

"D . . . Devil's . . . Devil's Tower?" Jeb chewed on something as he snatched the crucifix off the table. "Never heard of it."

"When you finish, meet me at Deadwood."

"Now that I did heard of." Jeb snapped the small figure of Jesus from off the cross with a crack that echoed through the chapel. With the sharp fracture near the feet, he picked at his teeth. "Bring you the horse?"

"I'm taking the horse." He tugged on Anna's arm. "And the girl."

Jacob led Anna with one hand, the stallion with the other. They left the courtyard and entered the street. The town was empty, and as they neared the train station she could hear why. Gunfire.

On the station's platform, barrels and bags of flour made for perfect cover. Jacob's men lifted their heads and fired, but Anna couldn't make out their targets. Her heart thumped louder than the blasts from the muzzles. Was Philip here? Were these marshals or rangers or U.S. soldiers?

Behind a short, pockmarked adobe fence rose a red head. His rifle fired, and he ducked behind again.

Scott Ladd had come. The dark hat rising beside him—and even from this distance the magnificent mustache—could only be Marshal Hill's face.

They'd come for her. Right here. Right now. She would be saved. Philip would stop this madness.

Jacob dragged her and the horse around the station's corner, up three long stairs, and onto the platform. Anna could barely catch a breath. She was in the heart of a gunfight! Shots rang out every few seconds, the sound of whines from ricochets, smacks from lead hitting wood and bags of flour, and crashing from shattered windows.

Anna kept her head down but stole glances from side to side. Where was Philip? Why wasn't he charging?

She bit back the thought. She'd never been asked to charge into bullets. But soon he would need to make his move.

Jacob shoved Anna toward the nearest passenger car. He called out, "We've got steam. We leave, now. I want to see the train moving forward in thirty seconds."

One of the men nodded, and a few scurried toward the engine.

Philip, hurry!

He yanked her into the coach and threw her onto a seat. The train lurched.

The desert outside her window seemed to roll under them. On the opposite side, the station began a slow retreat. Men pulled away from the fight and jumped onto the train.

She looked back toward the desert. In a small hollow protected by staggered rocks, Ryan stood with his shotgun pointed toward some of Jacob's men below her window. They exchanged blasts, and pellets slapped the wood at the end of the car. Between a crack in the rocks lay a body.

Her heart stopped. Philip.

She stared past the leafless brush, beyond the shallow rise of rocks, through the suffocating dust. She didn't take her eyes off him. Couldn't think but one thought—did his chest rise? *God, please, let me see he's alive.*

The train moved slowly away.

God, please!

Sandstone hid the body from view.

Philip! No!

She saw him again, stretched on the sand, unmoving. Too far away now to make out if he was alive. With both hands she reached for him, smacking the glass. The train moved beyond a small cliff, hiding the scene from view.

Jacob spoke to her, but all she heard was the pounding of blood in her ears.

The thought of never spending another moment with Philip again pierced her heart. She couldn't breathe.

Jacob had the map. The girls were probably in Mexico by now. Philip was most likely dead. Her father was dead. Leroy was dead.

Where did hope lie?

She collapsed into the seat.

Every moment of her life, she lived in defiance. She fought to wear what she wanted. Fought for pride when all the women around her settled for men while she waited for someone she honestly loved. Fought to work for her father when other women started families.

She had battled Jacob with every fiber of strength. But now, as they retraced the trail she'd taken to get to the hot southern territory, the fight in her was played out.

What had Philip said recently? Love was worth fighting for. What had she left to love?

Marry Jacob.

Yes.

Give in to his desire.

The answer was so simple. Why hadn't she thought of it before? Marry him, and all this goes away.

What had she learned from loving Philip, oh so deeply? He had lived a life looking for answers. Looking for truth.

The truth? Jacob was the most evil person in the world.

Should she marry him?

His thin, pink lips were curled in a sad grin as he looked at her, as if he understood her pain. A blond lock fell over one of his eyes, blue eyes that offered the sympathy she deeply craved. His arms rested on a seat, a set of arms she so desperately needed to curl around her, offering safety.

Truth. Honor. Trust. Courage.

Anna Johnston, she thought, wore riding pants.

"Jacob," she said, her voice cracking. She didn't know what to say next, but the words appeared, unbidden.

"Jacob. I'm going to kill you."

16

I fell into a bottomless void. Sensations of black mist whirled around my stretched fingers.

A marble floor rushed to meet me.

I woke before hitting bottom.

Voices echoed inside the building.

Touching my head, I opened my eyes. The blurry world sunk and spun, leaving my stomach far behind.

What happened? Had Jacob given me a beating again? I forced an eye open, hoping to see the furry face of my dog Trevor. Instead, I saw a silver cup.

I lifted my head. This wasn't my bedroom.

I forced both eyes open and looked at a makeshift table. Beside the cup rested a broken figure and a cross.

Where was . . .

I remembered.

The train. Gunshots. Ryan pulling me away. More gunshots.

Scott's voice cut through the fog. "I have Alita tied out back. She was just running down the street, riderless. But Anna. We tell him. As soon as he awakes."

"Tell me what?" I asked, slowly moving my legs to the side. With a hand over my eyes, I tried to sit up. "Oh, my." I rested on an elbow.

I heard wood scrape against stone, and a blurry image with a mane of red sat a few feet in front of me.

"We didn't get the girls." Scott's voice was firm.

Another voice cut in. "It's a mistake to tell him." Who was that? I remembered, the soldier Matt.

After a pause Scott said, "The girls were split up. I saw Jacob board the train with Anna. The rest of the girls went south."

"Into Mexico." My words sounded as if I'd just woken and was drowsy. I tried again sitting up, and this time my feet touched the floor.

A gruff voice to the left said, "Yes, Mexico. Running Deer is tracking the girls."

"And Anna?"

No one spoke.

"Anna?"

"Jacob forced her onto the train." Scott's tone was bitter. "We couldn't get to her in time."

My mind cleared and I looked around me. High windows allowed just enough light to make out an altar, a small podium to the right, and a door on each side. "This a church?"

"Yeah, you're in the chapel," the gruff voice said. I turned and saw Marshal Hill looking over me, concern in his eyes.

"Why not tell me about the girls?" I asked him.

Scott answered, his face close to mine, his elbows on his knees. "Some believe it's best to just tell you about Anna, since she's still close. And certain parties in our posse can go after her without repercussions." His lips curled in a snarl.

"I've no idea what you're talking about."

"Mexico isn't a place we can go," Jackson said. I turned to look at him, and the world spun again. "We won't be soldiers if we ride. Matt isn't ready to leave his career."

"No sir."

"I, however, am."

I nodded. "Thanks, Jackson."

"Hey, I worked hard to be a soldier. Ain't easy for a black man to get any respect in the world you white men control."

"You're following the rules," Marshal Hill said, holding out a hand to Matt and sitting next to Scott. "I would do the same."

"Got a lot of men looking to me." Matt crossed his arms. "And I can't let 'em down by running over a border you all think is okay to just skip across."

"He's got a point," Marshal Hill added. "We'll all jeopardize our careers. Worse, we might start a war."

"With Mexico." My mind was still moving slow. I rubbed my temples.

Scott kept his voice low. "Yeah, buddy. We've got to think this through. I can't get the girls by myself. You know that. But you can't get Anna by yourself. So we need to decide. Anna? Or the girls?"

I closed my eyes. *Think, Philip. C'mon.* I knew when making big decisions it was better to clear the mind than to keep the clutter.

A picture of Anna's face entered my mind. She would know. What would she do?

I knew what Scott wanted. I looked my best friend in the eye.

He returned the gaze.

I said, "What do you think?"

"You've got to ask yourself a very important question before we decide what to do. *Why* did Jacob split up, and *where* do you think his destination is?" His pronunciation was a poorly hidden conspiratorial tone, but I caught what he was saying.

Jacob had found the map. He was on his way to Devil's Tower. "You think?"

He gave a knowing nod.

So. Jacob was after the treasure. If he didn't have Anna, I would let him go.

"Marshal, how long before we get another train?"

"I can wire to get one sooner," he said. "But I'm guessing a week. Maybe two."

That sealed my decision. "We'll ride to get the girls. But Matt, I've got a mission for you to the north."

I stretched my legs and tried to stand. Wobbly as a newborn colt.

"Take it slow," Marshal Hill warned.

I sat down and bent forward so my forehead almost touched my knees. "What happened out there?"

"Not sure." Scott lowered his head close to mine, so I could feel his breath. "You okay? Feel like a good vomit? Make you feel better."

"No, Scott, I'm fine. I . . . I think Ryan saved my life."

"Yep."

"Where is he?"

Marshal Hill said, "Behind you. He's been wanting to show you something."

"Oh yeah? What's that?"

The big man's hand appeared over my shoulder. In his palm was a small derringer.

"That's Anna's." I turned to look at him. "Where did you find it?"

He pointed over his shoulder toward a bench.

I asked him, "How did you know it was Anna's?"

"She shot me."

"Right." I remembered.

I took the gun. Her initials, *A.J.J.* marked the butt. Still loaded.

How did it end up here? Holding such an intimate part of Anna's life was surreal and made the longing wrap around my heart like a snake choking a victim.

The oppressive heat didn't help either. I wiped a trickle of sweat that ran down the side of my face.

Think, Philip Anderson. Be smart.

I stood on weak legs. Scott sat directly in front of me, looking up. His eyes held a familiar expression. On the cliff top, he'd been innocent, eager. And after he marched into the wolf's mouth he stood his ground, gave as well as he got and accounted himself a man. Anyone can pretend to be a man. But his eyes always give him away.

Scott's lighthearted nature had returned. But now as he considered me, the wisdom and self-reliance stepped forward, not the whining or fear.

He measured me as an equal now.

I put a hand on his shoulder. "Good job today, buddy. Wish I could have fought at your side."

He pursed his lips. "Glad you're okay."

I walked away from the men, away from the altar, taking with me a longing to do the right thing. I would pray outside.

I tapped Ryan's arm in appreciation. Then I walked under a wooden archway and pushed open the double doors.

On the wide street I breathed in the cooling evening air. A few feet away, a stone wall stretched until it reached an adobe fence. I leaned an elbow against the dried mud and pulled back. The clay still baked, even though the sun hung orange and low against a bank of mountains.

Lord, I thought. Paths. Which do I take?

I wanted to go after Anna. But if I saved her without trying for Beth and her mother, she might never talk to me again. A pretty poor excuse for a decision, but in the end—thinking on Anna's strong will—potent.

The smells of sage and flowers mingled, and I dearly wished Anna stood by my side to experience the moment.

Shuffles sounded in the dust, and I turned to see Marshal Hill approaching.

His mustache glimmered in the dying light.

"Someday I'll grow a caterpillar like yours."

He grunted, looking back at the chapel. "Finding the girls sure changed the attitude of our posse." He raised both elbows out wide and leaned against the adobe and looked toward the sunset.

"Waiting for Running Deer's a trial."

"You're back to normal too," Marshal Hill said. He didn't catch I wanted a subject change. "Know what you want and how to get it. That's good."

I lifted a brow and faced him.

"Say what you've got to say, Marshal, please."

"You really want me to?"

"I sure would."

"There's a lot going on I don't know. You and Captain Smith seem to know each other far more than you let on." His dark face showed his emotions, usually buried deep, rushing toward the surface. "And what about you remembering Mrs. Custer? Scott said that's why you were in town when the girls were kidnapped. I remember you saying you knew Custer. How does all this fit in?"

I must be one of those rare people that didn't have to know things. Anna devoured information about people, places, and facts like I worked with horses—a fanatical devotion. While talking with me, she was listening to the conversation nearby as well but still somehow completely absorbed with me.

Marshal Hill was like Anna. Probably why he and I were close.

"And what about John Maxwell being your uncle? You've never fully explained that to me. What's going on, Philip? Does it have to do with why Jacob and Anna went North?"

There were some questions bothering me as well. "Tell me first, honestly, did you know my parents? Henry and Constance Anderson?"

He shook his head. "Never heard the names."

"Never spent the war in Virginia?"

"I was a Pinkerton." He stared me down. "Spent the war protecting the president."

I choked. "The president? Sorry." I covered my inappropriate smile.

"Don't like to tell people about that. But you're a good man. Won't spread it around."

"No," I said. "No, I'll keep that to myself."

He dug into his pocket and pulled out a cigar. "Need to think. Calm my nerves. You don't mind, do you?"

I shrugged a shoulder and looked back at the sunset.

"I was protecting a senator during the assassination." He scratched a match and I heard a burst of flame. "Did my job."

First the smell of sulfur, then rich, sweet tobacco filled the air.

"I never met Custer," he said.

"I did. As a child. I didn't like him."

"No." I heard him take a puff. "No, I expect not."

"I'm going to trust you. There's a map, split in two." Privileged information had gotten me nowhere. "Leading to something like treasure. Maybe another map. Maybe nothing, I don't know. It's why my parents left hearth and home for the Dakota Territory. Went right past their homestead and died at Devil's Tower."

He didn't look up, didn't move. He only stared at the ground with the cigar in his fingers, burning.

"John Maxwell had been looking for the treasure with only

half the map. I'm guessing he saw the other half that tells the exact location. I have the other half, the section that points to the part of the country. Mr. Wilkes knew about the map. Moved to the Dakota Territory just to be close to me." I shook my head. "Incredible the lengths people will go to for perceived wealth."

He grunted. I imaged he was thinking of train robberies and stage holdups.

"I've always thought my father was an amazing man. Turns out, my mother turned society's head." I ran a hand through my hair. The strands had never been so long. "My memory is cockeyed."

"Jacob know about that map?"

"I don't think so."

"Until now," he said, lifting the orange glow of his cigar at me.

"Anna had the map. Bet he just found it. Only reason he would split like this."

"Makes sense." He let his arms drape over the adobe's edge. He sighed, long and filled with emotion. "Love this country. Wife lives in El Paso." He lifted the cigar to his lips. "Wish you weren't so blamed angry at these people."

I took a deep breath as well and tasted the sweet smoke from his cigar. "All people sin. I forget that sometimes." This was hard to admit. "I guess pointing out other people's faults helps me forget mine."

"Hope you get to see the better side of them." Marshal Hill let out a long stream of smoke. "Thinking this'll be my last rodeo."

"Going home?"

"Going home. El Paso."

"Won't be the same, you not riding into my ranch dead of night."

"I'll still come by. For memory's sake."

I hesitated to say it but decided life was too short. "You think you might die?"

"Maybe." Another sigh that was filled with a sadness that drifted on the cooling air. "Worried you might too. You're getting a bit reckless."

"How do you mean?"

"I just see you getting into a situation where there's more bad guys than you have bullets."

"I do too." The thought was an instant nightmare. Raven had to carry more than her share of extra ammunition, because I never wanted to run dry. But I'd never formulated the words—making the fear spoken. Getting backed into a corner, without the hope of escape, out of ammunition. Yes, a nightmare. I better change the subject. "My special mission for Matt. He a good man?"

"Reminds me of John Scobell. Man we had on the Pinkertons. Former slave. Black man had something to prove. Worked to show himself as good as any man, and doubled the skills of everyone else. Let Matt try. He'll give it his best."

In the distance cactus rose like random soldiers waving, their long shadows cast across the desert. "You like the land?"

Marshal Hill started to say something then pointed over the wall we leaned on.

A form left the shadows and walked through the chapel courtyard. The dying sunlight splashed against a young Mexican woman, her black hair gleaming. Her white linen dress and brilliant red sash and shawl spoke of modest wealth. A cobalt blue belt wrapped around her slender waist. The closer she came, I could make out embroidered red flowers on her dress.

Her cloth shoes barely made a whisper on the cobblestones.

Despite her youth, lines of worry and despair crossed her forehead. She sat on a bench near the dry, central fountain. She lowered her head and brought a hand to her heart.

Perhaps I should announce our presence. Just as I opened my mouth, Marshal Hill tapped my arm. "Shhhh."

I held my tongue.

She sat, lost in thought, for nearly a minute. Her head jerked up at a sound, and over the wall a man dropped, landing lightly on both feet.

She gave a sharp cry, jumped up, and rushed to him. He opened his arms and she fell against his chest. He wrapped her as if her life were in danger. I dreamed of holding Anna, and I had to swallow the pain.

"Miguel," she said in a thick voice. Her next words were in Spanish.

So, the young man who helped us on the cliff top had a love.

Marshal Hill leaned close. "She's telling him not to go. To stay home."

"Go where?" I whispered.

"The chapel. He's wants to volunteer. Help us find the girls."

He wore an old pistol tucked into his belt.

"He has a mother, but his father is dead. Who will care for the farm? The goats? What will become of her? Her father is... is the mayor." Marshal Hill groaned. "Their love isn't approved by her father."

Miguel took the girl's hands. "Ana Maria, por favor." And I understood nothing more.

"He asks her if she always wants to be poor. If she wants to live in slavery or freedom. They were born free and no one—not even Valentino—could take that away from them." Marshal Hill groaned again. "Sounds like they all answer to this Valentino."

The marshal tilted his head to the side and started translating exactly as he heard.

"And now that these strangers come, these lawmen from

the North, they are willing to stand up to Valentino, to free us from these taxes. To give us a chance at happiness. And you would have me watch as you marry him? I will not have it, Ana Maria."

Why did her name have to be Ana?

"But Miguel, you cannot stand up to Valentino alone."

"Alone? Alone? I am not alone. Do you not understand who is in that chapel? Do you not understand what has happened here today? These men have come and chased away the man with white hair and his men. Don't you understand, Ana Maria? Please understand. These aren't ordinary men. These are gunmen. And it is not just a lawman who leads them. No, it is Philip Anderson himself. Ana Maria, he is the greatest of all men with a gun. Do you understand, Ana Maria?"

I was sure they could hear my heart pounding in my chest.

"Do you understand our poverty, Ana Maria? When the chapel bell rings, it reminds me I have nothing to bring our sweet Mother but the handfuls of grain that Valentino hasn't taken. Even our love he has stolen. Please, I love you, but I would rather die than see you in the embrace of him. I must try."

"No. I forbid it. I cannot live as his wife thinking of you dead."

The passion in her voice, even though I could not understand their words, forced my hand to move to my gun. These people needed protection.

When she spoke her voice was so timid I almost couldn't hear her.

Marshal Hill said, "She will kill herself if he joins us." In almost a growl, he added, "That way he will live."

The effect on Miguel was difficult to see in the growing darkness. He stood without moving. Finally he spoke and rushed back the way he came.

Ana Maria looked at the wall where his lingering presence

faded then rushed the opposite direction, through the gate and down the street.

Marshal Hill was silent as she passed us, her sobs so consuming I don't think she saw us. A pair of birds burst from a nearby scraggly mesquite with a flurry of chirps and darted across the street.

I watched her until she turned down another street.

One thought filled my head. "They are Anna and I, aren't they?"

Marshal Hill gave me his attention.

I closed my eyes and choked out the words. "What I wouldn't have done to have Philip Anderson march into Mitchell and take care of Jacob."

"So you understand these people better?"

I didn't say anything for a bit. Instead I let the heat from my body fade with the cooling night. "You think Miguel is out for revenge?" I was asking if I was hunting Jacob not only to save Anna, but to exact justice.

He shook his head. Looking at me, he said, "Hunting outlaws—my only regrets are when I went too far." He wiped his mouth with his opposite hand. "Revenge isn't wrong when you fight to stop evil. But when justice loses sight of the end, righteous anger becomes revenge and turns on itself. No, I guess he'd go as far as stopping Valentino."

Which meant I should go as far as stopping Jacob.

Running Deer stepped into view, pushing back a branch from the mesquite. Leather fringes hung limp from his sleeve, the buckskin stained and torn across his chest. His shoulders drooped.

I took a step toward him.

"*Miya Ca.*" Running Deer held up a hand. He took a leather pouch from his side and lifted it over his lips. Only a few drops fell.

"I'll get you some water." I started for the chapel.

"I have found them." His dark eyes were worn with fatigue. "But we must hurry. I believe they are in great danger."

17

I thought it ironic we moved from the chapel to the saloon. Conditions in the chapel basement were unforgettable. Ghosts from the girls' imprisonment haunted the very air we breathed. That was before we found the decaying body of a priest locked in a side room.

Running Deer scratched a rudimentary map on a wide table next to the bar. No one complained—the saloon was empty of all but the bartender. No one dared intrude on our planning. A sense of guilt seemed to saturate the very walls of the town. We were judge and jury and possibly executioner.

I expected Miguel to return. He did not.

The bartender, a short man in his forties with pale skin, was sweating profusely despite the cooling night.

Scott stood to my right, Ryan to my left. Jackson and Marshal Hill sat across from me.

Running Deer and I drank water. Scott held a cup of lemonade, sipping, making his lips pucker. Jackson and Marshal Hill took a shot of whiskey then drank nothing.

Matt had already left on the mission. "I'll do it," he had said, his broad smile infectious. He lit out into the darkness, and we heard him jump on his horse and race away.

Marshal Hill studied Running Deer's chalk drawing, the rough planks rising and falling, the lines curving with every building. An old town with an abandoned mission, the structures nearly made a fort.

Running Deer had seen the girls but couldn't find where they were housed.

I tried to hide my nerves. On the walk to the saloon, I'd nearly lost control. Two voices battled in my head. *Ordering, even encouraging men to battle is paramount to killing them yourself.* Then *Quiet your pride. They fight for a cause, not for you.* Leading wasn't coming naturally, and the idea someone might die because of my orders left me paralyzed. With all my strength, I forced down the rising fear. "Two dozen men?" I asked. "Maybe more?"

"Less one." Running Deer touched the knife at his side.

"And you're sure they're taking the girls farther south in the morning?"

With his hand still on the hilt Running Deer said, "He said so."

"Ah." I looked down at the map.

"Walls here, and here." Running Deer made a few scratches with the lump of chalk. "Broken. Come up to here." He tapped his chest. "Good cover all around. Buildings make a circle here, to this side."

I looked at Marshal Hill, who was reading a note. "We're not getting reinforcements, are we?"

"I received this telegram a while ago." Marshal Hill pressed his hands against the table. "No. Not in time." His smile was vague and unconvincing. "But they're coming. Texas Rangers are investigating what's happened here." He crumpled the telegram and stuffed it into a pocket.

"An outrage." Scott pounded the nearby bar and pointed to the barkeep. "Justice. I hope to prosecute each and every one of you."

The barkeep's droopy jowls seemed to sink lower. "Hungry children in this town. Sacrifice of a few for the betterment of all."

I stared at him. Scott started a reply, but the barkeep continued. "You think you know how to run our lives, coming here and telling us what to do." He mopped sweat from his forehead with a bar rag. "Spend time on this border, and you'll see how survival is. Walk in our shoes before you judge us."

Scott stepped over to the bar. "Trains follow the goods. Railroad wouldn't have laid tracks to this town without a diverse economy." He picked up his lemonade and set the mug on the bar. "You disgust me." He slid the pottery across the bar, and the barkeep fumbled to keep the cup from crashing to the floor. "And you make terrible lemonade."

The barkeep sniffed and disappeared into a backroom.

Marshal Hill's gaze went from the barkeep's trail to Scott, a modest look of respect in his eyes. "You have the makings of a good lawyer."

"You catch them, I'll prosecute." Scott made a chopping action with his hand. "Line 'em up."

I pointed back at the bar. "Probably in that Valentino fellow's employ. He's gonna tell we're coming. Doesn't matter," I said, pushing forward the strength I found from within. "Here is our main attack, at the short wall. Don't press. Just pin them down. Draw them to you. Everyone but Ryan and me." I kept my voice down. "I want Ryan to come this way, toward the buildings. Opposite of the attack. He'll search these buildings. While he moves in, I'll come this way and search these buildings."

Running Deer grunted.

"Marshal Hill, if you feel the cover is good and you've

drawn most of the defenders, send Running Deer to this point here so we can meet him. If Ryan or I find the girls or come into heavy resistance, we'll retreat then come back to find you," I said, looking at my Sioux friend. "And the three of us can get the girls. If Jackson and Scott can hold it alone, then Marshal Hill, you come with Running Deer."

They stared at the table.

"Look," I said. "I know it's desperate, but time isn't on our side. And numbers aren't with us either." I couldn't help the somber feeling that entered my voice. "What each of us needs to ask ourselves is are these girls worth dying for?"

"On the one hand," Scott said, "We may die and the girls will be trapped forever in unthinkable slavery. Or we can return to Mitchell and live, but the girls are still trapped in slavery and we may or may not be able to live with ourselves. Or we can send a message to these men that we won't let their actions go without legal trouble. Or we can free the girls and return home and be heroes, and girls love a hero."

He slipped off the barstool. "And if we all die, there's nothing to worry about. We're still heroes." He straightened. "I guess that's more than two hands."

"I've no pony in this race," Jackson said. "But I'm in."

"My job." Marshal Hill said, unpinning his star. "My job taught me to fight for what's right. Let's ride." He tucked the star into a vest pocket.

Running Deer simply said, "*Miya Ca* is brave. We will succeed."

I looked at Ryan.

He searched for words, his eyes moistened as he looked at the table. Finally he summed up his thoughts. "Rachel."

I nodded. "All right. Let's ride."

Our horses needed shoeing, fast. The local blacksmith, while competent, couldn't finish in time. The work was welcome, and I pounded the iron into the shapes we needed with ease.

Marshal Hill filed rough spots in the hooves as I worked, and Jackson hammered in the square nails.

Why did I always think about God most when working metal?

With every hammer blow, the memorized movements shaped my own spirit, my flighty will, into dependence on God. He was shaping me. Molding me. I wasn't quite right for Him, not quite what He needed. So God would pound.

Perhaps that's why I felt like I wouldn't die in the next few hours.

A thought struck me. The iron was smashed and molded until I shoved the finished product into cold water.

Lovely thought. God molded a man, all the way into the grave. Well, when I died I hoped to steam like hot iron.

And then we rode across a moonlit stretch of water, wider than my James River but shallow. And we were in Mexico.

Mexico. And I'd never been south of the Dakota Territory's border.

Running Deer led us through the moonlit desert. Did he have the eyes of a cat? The black world around us was a shadow, while the heavens shone with the brilliance of diamonds. Vast bands of distant light shot across the sky with a painter's brushstroke, losing individual stars to the band of spilled light.

Running Deer motioned and we stopped. "We're close."

"Time to split up," Marshal Hill said.

We tied up the horses then shook hands all around.

"I know," Scott said as we clasped hands. "Be careful."

"I would say don't do anything I wouldn't do . . ." I pulled my duster tighter over my shoulders against the night air. "But yes, take care. Becky will shoot me herself if something happens to you."

He buttoned his vest and slung his rifle over his shoulder. "Good point, there." Over his other shoulder, he hefted his saddlebag. He winced as I heard a loud jangle over the roar of chirping bugs. "I've got some extra ammunition."

"How much?"

"Mmm, maybe more than I need." He swiped at a strand and brushed the hair away from his eyes. Even in the dim light I could see he wouldn't meet my gaze. "Um. Two thousand rounds."

Jackson's voice cut in from behind. "Two thousand?" He choked. "We're issued one hundred rounds before a fight." He walked to the other side of his horse, mumbling to himself.

"Hey," I said to Scott quietly. "If it helps you to feel better, take that many with you. Preparation over devastation, I say. Even if that means toting eighty extra pounds. How did you find that many?"

"Been collecting for a few years."

He brought it with him all the way across the country. "All right, buddy. Take care."

He and Jackson wandered deep into the night until they were out of sight.

"Ready, Ryan?"

He nodded, and we walked past Marshal Hill and Running Deer.

"*Miya Ca*, prowl like a wolf." Running Deer held a bow and quiver in one hand, a hatchet in another. He would be quiet death tonight.

I clutched the claw at my neck.

Marshal Hill shook his head as he came close. "We've been far afield, you and I." He clenched his teeth. "I would never put you in harm's way if I could help it. But I have to admit, something inside wants to see you fight it out with the likes of the men here. Test your skills. See how really good you are."

I couldn't hold back a sigh.

"These men are battle-tested. They make their living by killing. Remember, these men are living by the gun, and any moment someone could get the drop on them. Everything might kill them. Weather, animals, people they consider friends, people they consider foes. All might mean death. And the law is on their tail. Yet somehow, they survive."

"And you're eager to watch me shoot them."

Even though darkness surrounded us, I could imagine the gleam in his eye. "Something like that."

I pulled a box of ammunition for the Smith and Wesson from my saddlebag. Scott's influence, no doubt. I let the shells slip through my fingers to fall into my duster pockets. "You're really saying you like me and I should be careful."

He chuckled. "Like you? Guess that's what I'm saying. But more like I respect you."

I pulled the Colt .45 from the bag and shoved it to the left side of my belt then pulled the Smith and Wesson from the holster and opened the chamber. "Sounds about like you're planning on not returning."

"It does, doesn't it?"

"I'd ask you to sit this one out if I thought you'd listen. Or if you wouldn't be given to some offense."

"I would be offended."

I slipped a cartridge into the sixth slot. "You know, I make sure the hammer rests on an empty chamber. A branch could bump the hammer and the gun accidentally fires."

Before I could continue he said, "Don't take chances?"

"That's right." I returned the gun to the holster. "Don't take chances when you don't have to."

He chuckled. "You're the gunman you never wanted to be."

"I suppose I am."

"Being a gunman's well and good." He studied the desert for a moment as if looking for an answer, some final bit of advice. He walked away, following Jackson and Scott. He called back, "But a pack of coyotes can take down a wolf."

I started off into the night, Ryan by my side.

18

The desert air was as motionless as a closed room. Brush around us stood so still the dark plants didn't seem real. I had to pinch my arm to feel alive.

Morning gray in the East was broken only by saguaro cactus that looked like men standing sentinel.

Ryan and I pressed south. My footsteps sounded unfamiliar, a crunch of gravel and sand different than the rich loam of the Dakota Territory. The grass and brush in the morning gray felt as if I had traveled to the moon.

Birds welcomed the morning, tired and vague, as if scratching out an existence was so exhausting that singing was a chore. Or perhaps that was my imagination. I would have to return when my attitude had changed, probably when the promise of gunplay was over. The desert could be beautiful.

The sky took on a shade of purple and pink, and instead of cactus, low buildings and three towers broke the eastern horizon. If I were to build a small village for a child with haphazard structures made of blocks strewn across the field of play, I would imagine the view something like what lay before us.

"I'll keep going." I held out my hand to him. "Be careful, Ryan."

He took my hand and shook it in his big grasp.

"And Ryan," I said, taking a step back. "You've proven yourself, time and again. I was wrong about you. Thank you for all you've done."

He gave a nervous laugh. "I'm a good guy."

"Remember, go in when you hear the sound of shooting. And meet back here if you run into much resistance."

Ryan reached across his belt and pulled a Bowie knife. "You might need this."

The thought of stabbing a man was intolerable. Odd. As if shooting him made him less dead.

"No thanks, Ryan. I'll use this." I tapped the revolvers. "And I've already a knife." I thought of the blade in my boot.

He slid the knife into its scabbard. Without another word, he walked toward the low silhouettes as if Sunday had arrived and he just stepped out of church.

Gunfire ripped through the morning calm.

I ducked, trying to calm my heart.

The sound was distant. Scott fought on the other side of these buildings. *God, keep him safe.*

I ran southeast, Smith and Wesson in hand. The first building loomed above me, a charcoal shadow.

Closer in, I could make out shapes of rain barrels under gutters and sagebrush piled in corners. Windows were high and glassless, blocked by bars.

The smell of filthy humans settled like a mist in the morning air.

I peered around the edge of the building toward the center of the compound. Buildings encircled a dry fountain, the front doors all facing toward the middle. This resembled something of Running Deer's map.

This end of the small village wasn't built quite like the side the others attacked, more circular here than the straight streets to the east.

Going in blind. *Reckless, Anderson.* Completely reckless. But the girls, and justice, waited. And in a few hours, with light, would come enemy reinforcements to take the girls further south and possibly out of our reach. Forever.

I kept my hands free of weapons but ready to draw if needed.

The gunfire was distant. The boys must be fighting maybe half a mile or even a mile away.

I watched for motion. Not a soul could be seen, but I could feel them. These buildings weren't empty. Did they hear the fighting? Would they run to support the growing volley of shots? Or were they drunk?

I stepped onto the first ramp and reached for the door. My courage waned.

Pull my gun? Or leave it?

I opened the door as if I had every right to be there.

The smell of dust and old wood assaulted my senses. My vision was already adjusted to the dark, and I saw a large room with nothing inside. I quickly closed the door and started for the next building.

Before opening the next door, movement across the circle caught my eye. I stood still.

Two men started in the direction of the gunfire, but they seemed unsteady on their feet.

The door near me opened and five men rushed out, all heavily armed and steady on their feet. I pressed my back against the wall as they sprinted down the lane that cut the circle's center. They followed the road between two low buildings and out of view.

Marshal Hill and the others were doing their job. Keep doing mine.

Before I could start again, another movement across the way caught my attention. This time I made out Ryan's size. I motioned and he lifted his shotgun, then lowered the barrel. He faced a nearby door and went in.

Keep going, Anderson.

My knees knocked as I kept moving.

I reached for the door to the building just vacated by the men, using my left hand.

Cans and broken bottles littered the floor. Bedrolls lined the walls—five, I noted after a quick count.

Three more buildings, and I counted nine more bedrolls. From the firing and the bedrolls, I was sure there were far more than two dozen men.

How long would I go undetected?

I neared the road when a flash and thunder sounded from inside a building across the way. I pulled my gun, and the door slowly opened. A man stepped out, his face pointed to the sky, eyes glassy. I held my fire.

He took another step forward out from under the porch covering.

Blood covered his chest.

He fell face-first in the dust.

Ryan stepped out of the shadowy interior and stepped over the body. "He almost got me."

I looked around. Nothing else moved.

"Good work. Can you clear that last building in this circle? I'll keep going. I saw a church to the right. You take the buildings on the left when you're done." I pointed down the lane.

He opened his shotgun, pulled out a smoking shell, and let it fall. Reaching to his bandoleer, he pulled out another and thrust it into the gun. With a snap, he closed the barrel. "I'm going to find Rachel."

"I know. Let's go."

I left the circle of buildings and hurried down the lane toward streets bordered with single-story adobe huts. In a large open space to the right, the church loomed like a lighthouse over the desert.

I stopped behind a barrel. The narrow church's bell tower, topped with a broken cross, was circled by a platform. Three men with rifles kept up a heavy fire toward the opposite direction.

From their vantage point, Scott and the others had to be easy targets.

I lifted my revolver but knew the tower was too high for accuracy.

I whispered a thankful prayer their backs were to me. Then I charged the closed church doors.

Many a foot had packed the hard ground I now ran. I doubted men such as these came to pray. The building with the broken cross was used for other reasons, and I was about to find out what.

I lowered my shoulder to crash into the paneled wood. The instant before hitting, I wondered if the door was barred from the other side.

The door smashed open with a loud crack. Sickening smells of alcohol and vomit hit me like a train. If it weren't for threat of death, I would cover my face. Instead I stepped inside, pointing the Smith and Wesson everywhere I looked.

Pink light flooded through stained-glass windows through the long room. Benches may have created rows at one time, but now they were strewn like logs after a storm. Cans, dirty rags, broken bottles, the carcass of a dog, books filled with bullet holes, and rotting trash I couldn't identify with a quick glance saturated the church. To my left was a closed door. To the right a spiral staircase, broken.

The far end of the church was too dark to see.

I pressed on, stepping over the charred remains of a Bible and smashed candles. My boot landed close to a crumpled bed-roll.

Shots rang out from above and ahead, the men on the tower still trying to kill my friends. The thought propelled me forward.

The front of the church came into view. An opening to one side revealed another spiral staircase that probably led to the tower. I pointed my gun at the other side. The lectern was broken in half.

Another step forward and I paused.

The altar came into view.

Amid the rubble was a human form.

Another gazing sweep around me, I started forward.

Her knotted hair was plastered to her face, and her dress was in tatters. Mouth open, eyes glazed.

Mrs. Johnston.

They had used and killed their least valuable woman.

I gulped air, despite the fetid smells. These men weren't human.

My gun rattled in my hands.

A vision of Anna passed through my mind. Was her fate similar? My heart brought first a choking cry, and then the same feelings at the death of my own mother.

And now Mrs. Johnston.

For every second that passed a new thought filled my mind, like a box opening. The first that opened was the love of Anna, the innocence of Beth, and how I wasn't able to protect either.

I questioned my own survival in that moment. I stood in the center of a church on the edge of a gun battle. A stray bullet could find me. But wild shots weren't my only worry. I was a marked man.

Another second went by. The fastest gun in the Dakota

Territory was south of the border, pitting himself against outlaws who used guns to kill, raid, and kidnap.

The last box opened, and I saw a man in the center of a discarded Catholic sanctuary, hat with a wide brim tilted down as he looked at the corpse of a good woman. His duster looked weighted down with extra shells in the pockets. He was lean, his cheeks gaunt from a long ride, skin dark from birth but darker from the sun. His eyes were as haunting as a wolf's eyes.

He had the look of a killer.

He'd lived a clean life, as honest as he could, attending Sunday meetings and helping others when he was able. He wanted nothing more than peace.

But an anger swelled inside him that flowed red-hot from his fingertips.

He was witness. He was judge. He was jury. They were guilty of crimes unspeakable.

My hands steadied. I held the Smith and Wesson as motionless as a stone.

I lifted my head and turned to a sound to my right. A man rose to his elbows from the debris, pushing an old hat from his face. He managed to stand. He weaved for a moment then looked at me. I stared back.

His gaze turned to the rifle on a bench, inches from his fingers.

I gave the slightest shake of my head.

He went for the gun.

My Smith and Wesson's blast, so familiar to my ears, sounded like thunder in the church.

He fell to his side.

I cocked the hammer back but didn't need a second shot.

Firing from overhead stopped.

Three long strides, and I stopped beside Mrs. Johnston. "I'm sorry." I eyed the opening to the tower staircase. "I'll save Anna and Beth."

Holding my gun ready, I marched to the opening and looked up. Each stair stretched from a vertical center beam to the tower wall, spiraling, so the only view was the bottom of the staircase as it wound its way up.

One step at a time I climbed, circling higher and higher.

I heard arguing coming from above now, sure they were preparing for someone to attack them from behind, but I didn't care. Some men would keep hurting people, no matter the discipline. Death was the only way to exact justice and end the horror.

Even now, I justified my actions to myself.

Silence from above didn't slow my ascent. Higher and higher, until the staircase narrowed to shoulder width. I couldn't duck to the right or left. There was no way to miss me here. I kept on.

Rounding the last turn, an archway let to the outside. A few steps higher and morning light shone in my eyes, but I forced them open.

I burst onto the tower's top.

And there the men waited, three shadows against the bright gleam, barely visible behind cover, their rifles pointed at me.

They should by rights have killed me.

But I had my gun drawn. And the world moved slowly around me, so slowly, my three shots sounded as one.

Two men fell, while the last grasped his neck and stumbled forward.

I fired again.

Shielding my eyes, I looked down. Toward the sunrise, rifle fire from enemies on rooftops kept Scott and the men trapped.

Shots to the left kept Ryan pinned as well.

I dropped all but one cartridge from the chamber and the spent shells fell to the stone floor with a clatter. Should I try to fight from here, using their rifles?

If I did, I'd be trapped.

As I descended, I reached into my pockets and pulled out a handful of bullets. I shoved them home then clamped the cylinder shut.

Every step I took down the staircase sent sparks through my body, adding heat to the inferno that raged through my very essence. My soul propelled my body on, setting fire to every footprint, splitting the air just before I passed through.

At the bottom of the steps four men stood in a semicircle, as if they'd just roused. Two rubbed their heads, and the others looked wobbly on their feet.

Did I let them draw? Did they all face me as I gunned them down, these men who slept after their night of reverie?

That I was the hands of justice or the grim reaper I gave just a fleeting thought.

The gun's metal burned my skin as I reloaded. Pain. A welcome feeling.

I crossed the church and stepped into the sunlight.

Beyond the lane, Ryan's shotgun blasted at three men behind barrels. They ducked as the wood splintered and exploded. He fired again, the blast lifting a man from the ground and throwing him back. Ryan leapt over a broken wheel, shotgun held high like a club, and he charged the remaining two men.

They rose as one and fired, both quick shots. One flew high, and the other made Ryan's left shoulder jerk back but didn't slow him.

The two turned and sprinted toward their fellows in the fight against Marshal Hill.

I fired at both, nearly thirty yards. The first crumpled in the dust. The second man's head whipped back and his feet flew high before slamming into the ground. They didn't move.

Ryan slowed and walked toward me.

I reached up and tugged at the hole in his sleeve, peering inside. A little blood.

He tried to turn his thick neck enough to see the wound but couldn't.

"You're okay." I reloaded. "They killed Mrs. Johnston."

Even now, his face was unreadable but for a deep frown and a narrowing of his eyes.

Ryan's chest heaved, and I heard his gasps over the sound of gunfire. After a moment, he snapped open his shotgun and flung the spent cartridges toward the church.

He reloaded.

His every breath came as a growl.

The Sioux called me *Miya Ca*, or Prairie Wolf. My eyes. But more than just a chance physical characteristic, I felt a bloodlust rush through my veins. I'd just killed, and my anger and hatred fueled a hunger for more.

Forgiveness and justice were washed away in the river of pulsing blood. I was an animal. A wolf.

Visions of the battle in the Badlands washed over me. I'd flanked outlaws and gunned them down. My first kills.

Not my last.

Pulling myself out of the Dakota canyons and into the Mexican village, I surveyed the buildings where my friends were locked in a struggle of life and death. Even though there was no wind, I felt fury blow around me like a gale.

I pointed to the left of the lane with my gun. I started toward the right, toward the heaviest gunfire.

Between two walls ran a narrow gangplank. Four men fired to the East, a small adobe barrier between them and Marshal Hill.

But no barrier between them and their deaths from behind.

As they toppled from their posts to the ground and seeped their blood into the desert, I started down the narrow passage.

The world around me moved slowly as I walked past

their bodies. Flies buzzed over the forms, as if they'd kept hidden in pockets, aware this moment would come.

I had given them as much a chance as Mrs. Johnston. I reloaded.

Pull your gun. Defend yourself. And let God decide who lives and who dies.

I squeezed between the two buildings and found myself on a wide boardwalk, and the street that passed in front of me bordered the desert.

To my immediate right along the boardwalk tipped wagons, bags of flour, crates and barrels lined the street. Rifles thrust through the cover and fired at invisible targets in the desert. I didn't take time to count the men in view before I glanced to the left and saw the mirror image stretched along the street.

Retreat would have been an option. Mercy as well. But their evil had to be stopped.

And one more bullet could kill any of my friends.

I was center and parallel to the line of men, like a keystone in a poorly built arch. The man to my immediate right must have seen I wasn't one of them. He brought his rifle to bear.

The black muzzle drew a straight line to my heart and threatened to split me in two.

I was a fraction faster.

The man beside him turned to see his fellow outlaw fall. He glanced at me. Before he had a chance to lift his rifle, he exploded into fire.

My Smith and Wesson did its work.

I heard a yell.

I spun.

To my left, they'd noticed me.

I fired, not chancing precise hits, but blasting each man in the chest—one shot, two, and a third man fell.

Two bullets left in the Smith and Wesson. But I needed to

fire in the opposite direction. I spun my whole body, and as I did I pulled the Colt with my left hand.

Both arms extended, I blasted away, standing like a star and using my peripheral vision. A man screamed and grasped his belly. The man behind him was aiming at me. I dropped him. Thankfully, the single action was in my left hand. My weak thumb wouldn't pull back the hammer without error. My right hand, however, was strong, the thumb powerful enough to pull the hammer and dispense death.

My Smith and Wesson dry-clicked, so I dropped to a knee and swept the Colt across my body and fired, finishing off the last rounds, killing the last man.

Vapors hung in the air around me like a death shroud. Bodies made a line from right to left. I'd killed them all.

Overhead, the thatched awning deadened the whistling guns.

I cracked the Smith and Wesson in half and let the cartridges drop, then slipped in another six fresh shells. Snapping the Colt's chamber to the side, I reloaded my second revolver.

One step back, and another. I lifted my arms and pointed both guns high, my duster loose and rustling in the hot wind. I kept walking backward until I broke from the roof's shadow. Every step back revealed more of the adobe front protecting the outlaws on the building's roof.

Did they expect death from where it came? I only saw their heads and rifles, but it was enough. I aimed to the right, fired. Then as I pulled back the hammer I sighted down the Colt and fired. Back and forth, dropping men just as they noticed me and tried to cheat death.

Sweat trickled in my face.

When the last man slumped forward and crashed through the awning, all fell silent but the ringing in my ears.

I kept my guns aimed high, arms spread wide.

Nothing moved.

Footsteps thumped behind me and I spun, guns ready.

Scott and Jackson slid to a halt, their hands held high.

Jackson's face was as red as Scott's hair. "Gah, have you ever—" He lifted his rifle over his left shoulder. "I must shake your hand. Never have I . . ." He opened his gloved hand and held it out to me.

I stared at it for a moment. "There's still another building!" I pointed at the far end.

"No." His grin was absurd. We were in the middle of a fight. "Running Deer."

Scott bumped my arm. I shook my head and felt as if I woke from a nightmare. "Running Deer cleared the men from the building?"

Jackson extended the hand farther, the smile still plastered across his face. I holstered the Smith and Wesson and grasped his hand.

"Incredible. Incredible." Jackson shook his head. "Honored to see it." He snorted and wiped his nose. "No one will believe me."

Scott tapped the Colt with his Winchester. "You never told me. Double action." He looked behind me, surveying the bodies. "I don't believe I'll speak to you again."

I rubbed my head to massage away the fog. "We've got to find Ryan. He was going to find the girls. There's still more buildings back that way."

Jackson's stupid smirk finally hardened. "Where?"

I pointed down the way I'd come. "But we go together."

Marshal Hill's slow gait reminded me of a mule as he closed the distance over the lane and onto the boardwalk. "They aren't all yours," he said, pointing on either side of us. "These boys accounted for some too."

"Marshal," Jackson said, cutting him off. "Ryan's going after the girls."

His face looked grim. "Lead on."

I started down the narrow alley.

"I'll find Running Deer," Marshal Hill said, and after taking a few breaths regained his strength as he marched off to the right.

Jackson on my left, Scott on my right, both gawked at the bodies that had fallen from the catwalk. They followed, their faces filled with a grim determination that mirrored my own focus.

At the building's edge, Scott lifted his rifle, pressed his back against the wall and peered around the corner. "I don't see a soul."

"Let's go." I led them back toward the center cluster of structures.

Guns at the ready, we kept walking.

A lean-to on the right stretched from the stone building. Three bodies lay under the ragged shade—bodies I hadn't put there.

These had arrows in their chests.

Jackson whistled. "Running Deer's been here."

Gunfire erupted ahead of us beyond a scattering of hovels, and I heard the blast of a shotgun.

Ryan had found the girls.

19

I sprinted down the dusty street, jumped over a broken water trough, and stumbled toward the fight. The others followed.

We ran through a wooden shack, passing two more bodies with arrows. Our footsteps thumped on the wood floor.

Out the back door, I grabbed the horse rail and launched over, the others following.

Beyond, a low villa curled like a sleeping dragon on the desert floor, an adobe wall trapping the beast inside. Ryan stood with his back to the wall, shotgun held to his chest as he peered past an open gate. A man lay crumpled at his feet.

We sprinted toward him, but before I could call out he charged past the gate and toward the main building. His shotgun blossomed smoke.

"Come on," I said, bursting into a full sprint.

My boots crunched over the gravel entrance, my gun sweeping from side to side. I focused on the wide double doors, their red paint shimmering in the sun. No movement came from my peripheral vision.

Ryan lowered his shoulder and burst through the front doors.

Well, the plan of attack was decided. Tragedy or victory, charging was how we'd do this.

Scott and Jackson followed me into the villa, the cool air energizing.

Ryan turned, saw us, and straightened. Chest heaving, he wiped his brow and swept the room with the muzzle of his shotgun. "Last place they could be. Looked in all the other buildings."

"Let's find them. Fast."

"Together?" Scott asked.

I paused. "Yeah. Together."

Hallways stretched from the open entry to the right, left, and straightaway. A staircase rose to the second story ahead.

Which way? I closed my eyes, and when Scott started to talk I lifted a finger to my lips. "Shh."

My heartbeat pounded in my ears, made worse by holding my breath. What made me think I would hear the girls?

Despite the throbbing in my head, I heard a scuffle. "Upstairs." I was on the third step before the others jumped.

At the landing, the stairs rose to a balcony in both directions. Which way now?

Scott and Ryan surged past me to the right, drawn by invisible cords of a compass. I followed them.

In an open room with high rafters they rounded chairs and tables, a billiard table toward the far end. I called out for them to stop, but the two ran around the corner.

I heard two blasts. Gun drawn, I crossed the room and peered around the corner. Two bodies bled on the gold Navaho rug.

At the end of the hallway Scott and Ryan stood side by side, staring at something in a room to the right.

Why did they lower their guns?

I stopped in the hallway.

Jackson bumped me as he ran by. He halted beside my two friends, his rifle raised. His pockmarked, sweaty face turned a deeper shade of crimson. He lowered his gun.

What could possibly make them stop?

From around the corner I heard, "Señiors, drop the guns."

The three slowly bent over and set their weapons on the rug.

The man's soft accent told me English wasn't his first language. He was also older and in complete control of himself and the situation. I holstered my gun and dropped my duster in a heap.

The voice came again. "Where is he?"

Scott's hands, lifted above his head, were shaking. But his voice was strong and confident. "President Lincoln, you mean? Well, sir, he was shot some years ago."

"Do not be a fool." The man's tenor didn't waver.

"But the president's killer was later shot dead. Justice served."

The creases at the edge of Scott's eyes showed deep concern despite his casual voice.

The man they faced had one of the girls as hostage.

I heard struggling, and the muffled voice of Beth. Something hit wood and crashed, maybe percaline.

"I will kill you." The voice came as a hiss. "There, much better. Now, produce Philip Anderson."

"Oh, no, no you wouldn't like to meet him," Scott said.

"His exploits, legendary. And now he's taken my fortress. Yes, señior, I would like to meet him."

This man was stalling. He knew his reinforcements were close.

Scott lowered his hands. "No, you really don't want to meet him. Because, well, simply put, he'll kill you." Scott leaned forward. "And dead's mighty permanent."

"I will put a bullet in this girl's head if he doesn't stand before me in five seconds, and as you said . . . dead's mighty permanent."

My mind swirled with visions. John Maxwell in Deadwood. My parents at Devil's Tower.

Scott took a step back. "Not sure why you want to meet him. I mean, I'm the handsome one, anyway."

"*Uno. Dos. Tres.*"

Scott's voice was low. "Philip."

"*Quatro.*"

I stepped into the man's view.

His smile was brilliant, eyes focused.

Short.

Beth was nearly his height. He ducked behind her, but the gun at her head didn't waver. His finger held steady on the trigger.

"I've read your exploits, *amigo.*"

The desk to his right swirled into a prairie and charged high into the night, erupting into Devil's Tower. Grass seemed to spring up from the wood floor, trees sprouting from the potted cactus, and from the open veranda to the side, the view of our battle turned into a moonlit river. Dozens of guns, swords, bows and arrows covering the walls turned into stars.

I was revisiting the night my parents died.

No. I had to think.

His finger calmly pressed against the trigger. I was fast. Was I this fast? He stood so close to Beth.

A gag tugged at Beth's chafed and oozing skin, and her lips quivered. Her swollen eyes looked up at me as if in a drugged daze.

What had she been through the past weeks?

"Valentino."

He chuckled. "I see my reputation is known to you as well. *Amigo*, I've waited for this moment for some time. When your

206

amigo, el fulano . . . Jacob Wilkes, *sí*, told me you would come to save these girls, I thought to myself, now would be a good time to test my skills on someone worthy. I've read all about you and know the talents you possess." He chuckled and motioned his head toward the open veranda. "And you live up to your reputation, eh?" He laughed.

His right arm wrapped tighter across her body, while his left hand pressed the gun against her temple.

I couldn't get a shot. Not one that wouldn't injure Beth.

"Your eyes. They really are the eyes of a lobo. Perhaps you're *Ahuizotl.*"

I had no idea what he was talking about, but every time he laughed, I watched carefully for an opening. "Where are the other girls?"

"Eh? Behind me in the closet. They smell worse than this one. Perhaps you care so little about the others that you need to be enticed. Little girls do just that . . . entice." The end of his word whistled.

A bullet through his gun hand was possible. Would the shock of the .44 cause him to pull the trigger?

I couldn't risk the shot.

"So *amigo*, *el juego* is simple. I stand behind her and shoot you." He stared into my eyes.

Valentino was going to shoot me while I was supposed to let him?

What he meant struck my soul. He was asking me to send a bullet through Beth so I could kill him and save myself.

I was a child again, beside the fire on a cool, Dakota evening. Thieves stepped from the brush and into camp.

I had to stay in the moment. Beth's life depended on my clear head.

Impossible.

In the few seconds since Valentino's declaration, silence filled the room.

I needed help. *God, please.*

"So, shall we begin?"

Beth's captor slowly lowered his body completely behind Beth's and brought his revolver to bear, right at my face.

My breath caught. I couldn't shoot Beth.

Please let Anna know why I'm not coming to save her. I closed my eyes.

A soft whistle crossed the room, followed by a thud.

I opened my eyes.

His gun's barrel slowly lowered until pointed at my feet.

The revolver slipped from his fingers. He staggered to the side, and my Smith and Wesson was trained on his head. But there was no need to pull the trigger. The man grasped at Running Deer's fletching embedded in his neck.

I looked through the open veranda. At the gate, Running Deer held his bow high, another arrow notched.

Beth gasped and took three leaps into my arms.

She smelled of unwashed body, and her tears trickled down my neck as she clawed at my skin. I held her close, unsure how to help her control the sobs.

Scott and Ryan charged past me, around the wide desk. Jackson held his position at the stairs in case there were more guards.

I held Beth tight and watched my friends fling open a door at the far corner and disappear inside the room. Their footsteps dimmed, as if they marched down stairs.

A new set of footsteps shuffled behind me. I spun, standing tall but still holding Beth.

Running Deer had climbed up the veranda and stood by my side.

I motioned with my head toward Valentino's body. "Thanks."

Running Deer's buckskin and dark war paint didn't scare Beth. Instead she seemed to calm down, working into hiccups.

"Beth," I said quietly. "I've got you."

Jackson still kept a lookout on the stairs, but I knew there was no one else here. "Marshal Hill?" I asked Running Deer.

"He took the long way."

He meant the marshal didn't climb up the lattice to the second story.

In the silence that followed, Running Deer's presence seemed to calm Beth. Then she spoke in a quiet voice. "I remember you."

He looked at her.

"At the trial. This summer. I saw you in town."

Running Deer didn't blink. Instead in a noble tone said, "You were brave today, young warrior."

Beth's body relaxed in my arms, and her grip on my skin loosened. Blood swelled from several scratches she'd inflicted. I didn't care.

Scott stepped from the closet, Becky close, her arms wrapped around him. Her hair was a nest of dirt, her face pale and eyes filled with little life.

Rachel came behind them, pulling Ryan by the hand. Her dark skin was filthy, but her gaze still held a defiance that made my heart surge.

Scott reached to a pitcher on the desk and poured water into a basin. Becky dipped her hands in and soaked her face.

Rachel came close to me. "Did she survive the night?" she whispered.

My chest tightened as I shook my head.

Rachel sighed as if the world's last vestige of hope and goodness had died with Mrs. Johnston. "Tell her."

I glanced at Running Deer, and he gave a single nod.

The lump in my throat wouldn't allow me to talk, and I struggled with the heavy onslaught of emotions. I forced myself to say, "Beth, your mother died last night."

"Mama!" She clung to me again. Her sobs were no longer

screams of terror, but instead her body heaved with sorrow. "Mama," she kept saying over and over. She reached out to Rachel who took her.

"We're going to take you home. Your father sent me to get you."

"No, he's dead too." Wet oozed from her nose.

I pulled a handkerchief from my neck and cleaned her face. "He's alive. Home in Mitchell. Missing you. He's going to need you, Beth."

"Jacob took Anna."

"I came for you first. But now I'm going to find her."

"Philip." Marshal Hill's gravelly voice filled the room, and I spun to see him turn the corner. "We've a problem."

I grabbed the handle of my gun.

"Follow me," he said and started for the balcony.

With a hand that killed over a dozen men, I touched Beth's face. "We'll be right back." And I left.

I shielded my eyes from the sun as we crossed the veranda, and he led me to a ladder made with thick poles. I followed him to the roof, and as he climbed over he groaned.

He was getting too old for this. Was any age right?

At the top, I looked where he pointed.

From our vantage, I could see for miles. To the East, the sun was already baking the land. To the West, away from the brilliant light, the village spread out before us to the church that acted like a bookmark.

To the south, past the buildings where our shootout had raged, the desert looked in turmoil. Dust roiled in a long line as if charging for us to engulf the city.

"And there," Marshal Hill said, tapping my shoulder and pointing.

I looked to the North. If the dust from the south was an oncoming storm, the North itself was collapsing on us, as if the whole world folded in on itself with us in the center.

"We're trapped," he said.

"Ideas?"

He blew through his thick mustache. "You come across a defensible location when you came through?"

"The church."

"Last stand defensible?"

Why didn't I have emotions? I should be terrified right now. "Put men in the bell tower. I'll hold the stairs."

He held his hand against the sun and studied the oncoming reinforcements. His voice was a growl. "Was good fighting with you," he said.

"We'll make them pay."

He sniffed, swallowed, and nodded as he looked down. "Yep. We made a lot of bad men pay today."

"We've got just a few minutes. Let's try to get the girls out of town. Maybe they'll find the horses."

Marshal Hill smiled as he looked at me. "I like you, Philip."

"Just because you read a dime novel about me." I decided as we started for the ladder, I should have taken him seriously. Marshal Hill did like me. Enough to die beside me.

I felt movement to my right. Running Deer stood by my side. His gaze was focused to the south.

How did he move without being seen?

I didn't believe I would die. I might feel differently when the last bullet struck, but until then I would hold on to hope. We would make it. We didn't come this far to be stopped here. We would survive.

God, help us.

Finally, Running Deer shook his head. "They could not surround the town. I scouted." He motioned south. "They ride as one. A straight line. Still far off but moving fast." He turned. "Look. Staggered. Spread a long distance apart, not waiting for full strength."

"What are you saying?" I asked.

His eyes looked back. "Warriors." Then north. "Farmers." He turned to me. "The farmers will get here first."

"What do you think?" I asked Marshal Hill.

He studied the oncoming storm and grimaced. "Too late. Here they come."

I could make out individual men in the swirling clouds. Their charge was like a tornado swirling over the sands. I watched in morbid fascination, although I needed to prepare some defense. But I stood as farmers swarmed through the village, pressing past us in a cloud of dust—more numerous than I could count—some on horseback, a few on burros, and finally dozens on foot. They carried rifles, pitchforks, old swords.

I could just make out the leader.

Miguel.

We did nothing. We waited on the rooftop watching the two dust clouds come together, and after nearly half an hour the dust died down.

Farmers walked back. Cheers of victory on their lips.

"How do you say *come here?*"

"*Ven conmigo.*"

I passed Scott, Becky, Rachel, and Ryan. I noted that Beth was calm and patted Jackson on the back. "You've been here a while. Check up top. I think we're going to be okay."

I entered the front courtyard as the first few men trickled by. They paused to look at me, taking in my tall frame, hat, and duster. They waited at the gate and watched me, pitchforks in hand. A rifle was trained on me.

Miguel stepped into view. He took one look at me and barked at the men nearby. They took a step back.

Miguel approached, a pistol in his belt, his eyes wide. "Philip Anderson." His accent was heavy.

"You speak English?"

"Ah. Ah no."

"*Ven Conmigo.*"

Miguel looked eagerly at the tiled floor inside, the arches and velvet curtains. Pots and swords hung on the walls, and he paused at a brace of pistols and compared them with his. He shook his head and followed me.

Upstairs, he paused at the bodies. He looked at me and said something, but his meaning was clear. He liked what he saw.

We entered the main room, and he paused and nodded toward the ladies and swept off his hat.

I motioned him to follow. I led him around the desk, but Scott said, "We moved him into the closet. He's on the stairs."

Miguel's face when viewing the body turned from disbelief to wonder to utter joy.

"Philip Anderson," he said, grasping both of my shoulders. I was worried he would kiss me. "Philip Anderson."

"Running Deer actually—"

"Philip Anderson." He shook me.

I looked past him at the marshal.

"Don't look at me," Marshal Hill said, tipping back his hat. He had a modest look on his face. "You led us here."

"Ask him what happened."

Marshal Hill and Miguel talked so quickly in what seemed to me gibberish, I lost interest until Marshal Hill began the interpretation.

Miguel described gaining support in the town square, telling the people how Philip Anderson was here to liberate their city, how Philip Anderson was there to clean the evil from the streets. The people had taken up arms.

Rachel had washed, found a dress in the house for herself, Becky, and Beth. All three girls sat on a couch downstairs with cool glasses of water. They huddled together. The fear in their eyes was heartbreaking. Time. They needed time.

Running Deer was gone. Marshal Hill sat with a mug of water. Scott paced, while Ryan stood over the girls with his shotgun tight in his grasp.

Jackson was watching the looting from atop the roof.

The city folk had known of this massive outpost just across the border, and Miguel had finally gathered support to take it.

"They are going to make Miguel town marshal." Marshal Hill took a long drink. "Ah, I needed that. Anyway, he'll earn enough to expand his farm. Marry Ana Maria. Happy story."

"I was wrong. These people are incredible. They just needed hope."

"Just like anyone else."

I should have been elated. Playing a part was an honor. But Anna was still in the clutches of Jacob Wilkes.

And he had the map.

20

Rope and chain imprisoned Anna to the bed.

She lay on a white quilt. Well, it was white when Jacob first shackled her wrists and ankles. Now with her disgusting clothes, pockets of dirt lined the seams.

She tugged on her left arm, the rope tied to the bedpost stretching taught, while the other wrist was chained to a thick pipe several inches beyond the frame. Her legs were fastened with iron links to the posts at the foot of the bed stretching her limbs wide like a star.

Jacob turned at the sound of her struggle and stood at the foot of the bed, his cream suit nearly the same color of the hair that swept over an eye. He laughed to himself then returned to the window. With one hand he brushed the lock away and with the other pulled back the curtain. She studied his profile as he peered down at the street, the straight nose and firm, pointed chin, handsome and dangerous.

Despair wasn't half her stormy emotions. She wanted to kill this man.

He killed Philip.

Philip's death was the only reason he wasn't here in Deadwood exacting justice.

First she would end Jacob's life, either with the law's help or without them. Next Jeb would die. No second chances for him. And then she would find her sister, somewhere in South America or Africa or some other country. Then her mother. Then the other girls.

She would continue Anderson's War. Anna's War.

Jacob's thin lips pressed together, and his eyes narrowed. When he spoke his voice was quiet. "This very room." He looked at her. "Philip spent his nights in Deadwood in that bed."

She didn't question how he knew. He just knew things. Spies, no doubt.

"Below, Philip met the prostitute Rachel." He looked at her, the wicked gleam on his face tore through her heart. "The bed you lie on—"

"Stop. He didn't."

He grabbed his sides and laughed.

After calming himself he said, "Ah, Anna. What fun we'll have together." After another glance out the window, he pulled out the map and looked at it again. "The thrill, the tickle at the back of your neck—not knowing. Could it be jewels? Cash? Gold? I believe gold."

Anna kept quiet.

He settled on the bed beside her, and as he sunk into the mattress she struggled to get away.

"What, Anna? Can't you see destiny?"

She looked away, and when he touched her cheek she tried not to scream. An aching and bruised stomach had been her penalty for screaming.

He stood and returned to the window. His mind was churning like a swollen stream, devising plots and scenarios, riches and renown. She could only guess at what his next moves might entail. Sanctuary, family, and peace meant nothing to him, like they sustained Philip. Jacob loved hurting people.

"Mmm, yes." He tugged at his suit's sleeves, straightened his collar, and gave the tie a quick check in the mirror.

A knock came from the door.

Jacob took three short steps. He reached out and grasped the small, ivory knob. He turned the knob with a quick flick of his wrist. The door swung open several inches.

Jacob looked up at a man several inches taller. Instead of opening the door wider, he turned his back and walked toward the window, leaving the man to push the door open and step in.

The man's height shrunk the room. His clothes, worn from the elements, were two decades old and frayed. She guessed he was a meticulous man, however, since many of the frayed edges and tears were carefully patched.

Another man, shorter, rounder, and heavily bearded, stepped in behind him.

"Close the door," Jacob said.

The short man complied.

"Have you spoken with the others?"

"Aye," the tall man said. "They're yours. At your price."

"Forty a man." The short fellow's gaze fell on Anna. He licked his lips, reached over and ran a hand down her face. His rough fingers pressed hard and scratched her cheek and neck.

His fingers hovered over her top button. She shrunk in horror.

"Excellent." Jacob reached into his suit coat and pulled out a leather wallet nearly as long as his forearm. The short man turned to watch.

Jacob opened the flap and pulled out a stack of unwrinkled notes. He returned his wallet to his pocket and stripped off two bills and set them by the water pitcher. "Get this man out of my sight. He is to be banished. On threat of death."

"Hey." When the short man jabbed his elbow into his friend, it stabbed at the tall man's thigh. "What'd I do? He can't do that."

The tall man looked away, and his indecision—Anna knew—wouldn't win Jacob's favor. After several seconds of silence the tall man finally said, "I need every man."

"Do you?" Jacob removed the wallet again. "It seems I've erred. I believed you when you said the Maxwell Gang was reborn."

The tall man closed his eyes tight for a moment then shook his head. "Leave, Tony."

"But—"

"Now!"

The short man jumped back, fumbled at the door, and nearly fell on his way out. The tall man focused on the rug. Then he slowly lifted his arm and without looking closed the door.

"Excellent. I pray that won't be a problem."

He looked up. "No, sir."

"Because I would hate to think you cannot keep your house in order."

The tall man's voice was sharp when he said, "I said no problem, sir."

"Excellent." Jacob crossed the room and reached for the cane that was resting in the corner. He took the white wood in both hands and held the slender rod at chest level.

Anna shivered.

"Your men must follow my orders explicitly. Even if they seem . . . somewhat contrary."

"No problem there, sir."

Strange, seeing such a large man so submissive to Jacob. He reminded her of Ryan.

"Good. Camp on the north side of Devil's Tower. I'll meet you there tomorrow afternoon, as soon as I get an exact location."

"Yes." He turned to go then paused. He added, "Sir."

"You may be asked to fight rival gangs." Jacob glanced out the window.

"Even better. Plunder."

"You're not pirates." Jacob shook his head. "Go quickly, before darkness keeps you."

"I like dark." He slipped from the room.

Jacob fidgeted with the cane's golden handle and the staff slipped, exposing a few inches of wicked steel.

He set the cane's tip down and leaned on the support. A few deep breaths as if gathering courage, and then the door opened without a knock. Mr. Wilkes stepped inside.

Anna's eyes widened and she sat up. "Mr. Wilkes," she stuttered. "Please, help me."

His thick chest was covered in riding flannel, stained with sweat. He took off his hat, dirty from a long ride, and he held the brim in his hands as he looked down at Anna. "Oh, Jacob." He pointed at her with the hat and looked at Jacob. "Why?"

"Allow me this, Father. This one concession."

His voice. She'd never heard him use this tone on his father before. Usually respectful, he now spoke in a monotone voice, condescending, as if he spoke with those businesses in Mitchell who owed him money.

Something had changed between them. What had once been father and son interaction—similar to her father and older brother John—was now a game between two men both after the same thing.

The map?

Mr. Wilkes stiffened. A bemused look crossed his face. He took a few steps toward Jacob. His hand darted like a snake and grasped Jacob's neck in an iron vice. As if picking up something as light as a cat, he lifted Jacob from the floor and drove him to the hard planks with a thud, not letting loose his grip.

Anna jumped.

"We've waited this long for the map," Mr. Wilkes growled. "Don't ruin everything now."

Jacob struggled for breath, a strange picture of a finely dressed man writhing on the floor.

"Did you get the other half of the map?"

"De . . . destroyed." Jacob coughed. "Philip."

Should she call out Jacob's lie? She decided evil implodes itself. Wait.

Mr. Wilkes considered Jacob—five seconds, ten—and finally he let go. Jacob heaved and gagged.

Mr. Wilkes stood, eyed Anna, and turned back to his son. "I found the monk."

Jacob stopped rubbing his neck, his mouth open, eyes wide. "Still alive?"

He looked away and dipped his hands in the basin of water, letting the droplets fall on the floor. "You had your chance to be honest with me. You know where the treasure is." He shook his fingers. "You found the map."

"Is he still alive?"

"What difference would it make to you? He was an old fool."

"He cared for me." Jacob scrambled to his feet. "He loved me more than you ever would."

Anna watched, unmoving.

Mr. Wilkes splashed water on his face. "You only say that because you're angry." He reached for a towel and rubbed his eyes. "He talked."

Jacob held his cane in both hands, facing his father. "You don't need the map. You don't trust me."

Mr. Wilkes pulled the cloth away and turned to Jacob. He

dropped the towel and looked at his son directly. The two stared at each other, and Anna could feel fire burning between them, an inferno swirling into a lake of fire.

Mr. Wilkes laughed. "He drew what he remembered."

"You know." Jacob said. "You know where the treasure is."

Mr. Wilkes smiled.

"You could have questioned him before." Jacob took a step toward Anna. She drew away from him.

"You weren't ready." He flexed his thick shoulders and rubbed his ample belly. "And I believed he'd only seen the map I had."

Anna tried to wrap her mind around the intrigues of these two men. Jacob knew exactly where the treasure was and was trying to decipher exactly what his father knew.

Why?

And what was the game Mr. Wilkes played?

Jacob took another sideways step toward her.

Now she knew exactly what the conversation with the men had meant. Jacob had his own army. Chances were Mr. Wilkes had mercenaries as well.

These men were feeling each other out.

"Jacob. She's heard too much. She'll have to be dealt with."

"She's under my care." His brow rose. "If she talks, the alternative is silence."

"You would? Are you capable?"

"Your bank guard fell easily enough."

Anna's head was spinning.

Mr. Wilkes pursed his lips and considered her for a few moments. Anna looked past him and out the window at the distant mountains. "She's like your mother."

"How would you know?"

"Your mother and Constance." His eyes glazed over, as if looking through time. "Philip's mother and your mother were friends."

Jacob tucked his cane under his arm and straightened his jacket. "There is nothing Philip and I have in common. You're mistaken."

"The past cannot be altered by—"

Jacob's face had turned purple. "The past can be rewritten. By the future." He pointed his cane at his father with a sharp whoosh. "And I am the future."

"Your mother—"

"Was not my mother!" He took a step closer. "And you are not my father. Look at us. You and I are nothing alike. I am the prodigy of God, cared for by a monk, so that I may do great things on this earth."

Philip and Jacob attended the same church. Raised by a monk but attending a Protestant gathering?

Mr. Wilkes eyed Jacob with a shrewd look. "You're not God. Nor are you chosen by God. You're simply a boy the monk forced upon me if I wanted my portion of the map. A boy who would show me the path to God. It's what he believed."

Jacob's bottom lip trembled. He spun and gripped the window sill. "Leave me."

"I raised you as my own son. Taught you business. Aggression. Passion." Mr. Wilkes pointed out the window. "I gave you the world! And you frittered it all away on this girl. These hopeless dreams."

"Leave me."

"I don't need you, Jacob. I do you a favor."

Jacob spun. "I said leave me!"

Mr. Wilkes snarled, his teeth gritted tight, and he turned and slammed the door behind him.

Jacob leapt across the room, a movement so sudden she caught her breath. He reached into a wardrobe and yanked out a stunning blue dress, snowy white lace scooped low, sleeves ending in the icy stitches, and wide skirt with looping garlands of similar lace. He threw the dress over a chair. "Tonight, you will dress for dinner. I will have a bath brought up."

"I think not."

His eyes remained focused on her, unblinking. He gripped her neck, much like his father had done to him. "Where is the treasure, Anna? Tell me."

He didn't know? He hadn't seen his father's map. Did he think Philip knew and told her? She leaned toward him as far as the bindings would allow and spoke through her closing throat. "Who do you have left to kill, Jacob? Who left can you dangle before me to force me to do your bidding?" Emotions burst from her chest, and she allowed the words to spill through her tightening throat like lightning from a Dakota thunderstorm. "You can destroy the world, one person at a time. You've proven yourself a big man. Oh, so important. What has it gotten you? Yes, fine, you're in a fancy hotel room with a map to a treasure. Philip's room. Philip's map. Philip's girl. Philip's treasure. You can't even create your own life. You're just a child!"

The wild look in his eyes broke through her anger, and she stopped. He reeled back.

"I am not a child!" He fell to the ground, his eyes swollen and wet. He lifted an arm over his face, as if protecting himself from a blow. "Papa, no, please, no! I won't do it again."

His breath came in gasps, and his body shook. Why did his voice sound like a child's?

"Papa, stop! Papa, stop! I promise I'll not do it again."

He lifted an arm over his face and jerked as if someone beat him. He reached out a hand, fingers open and empty. She blinked, only a fraction of a second, but when she opened her eyes again he held the cane in his hand.

Jacob yanked the cane from the invisible attacker and slowly rose to his feet.

Anna had seen this before with Philip. His mind was

locked in the past, and what he saw, heard, and felt really happened. It was happening now, in his mind.

Jacob had lost what little reasoning he had.

"Wake up!" She screamed. "Wake up!"

"Now it's my turn." He drew up to his full height and swung the cane, so that the sheath slipped from the blade and spun through the air. It crashed into the pitcher, sending shards across the room.

Jacob bore down on the bed, sword raised high, only the chair with the dress between him and her.

His sword whistled through the air and slashed through the arm of the dress. Another swing tore through the rich fabric, sending ivory buttons bouncing across the floor. He raised his arm and brought the heavy blow down again, splitting the chair in two.

Anna reeled back, as far as the rope and chain let her. "Jacob! Wake up!"

"You can't run from me!" He lifted the sword over his head and swung, slicing through the batting in the quilt. In a blur, he raised his arm again and the blow sunk into the wool mattress, inches from her leg. He swung so fast she couldn't see the blade as it chewed inches from her feet.

"Wake up!"

Horsehair flew across the room as he chewed through the bottom mattress. "How does it feel? How does it feel? How does it feel?"

She watched him in horror. Blow after blow. "Jacob!"

The sound of the sword falling to the floor gave her a surge of hope. Jacob was reaching out to the tattered bed. "I killed him," Jacob whimpered. "I killed him." He curled into a ball.

Anna brought a hand to her neck as a tsunami of terror washed over her like a drowning wave. Now she knew how Jacob had become an orphan and found himself in the care of a monk.

Yes, maybe the deed was self-defense. But she knew how Jacob Wilkes—or whatever his last name had been—became an orphan.

Jacob had killed his own father.

21

The railcar swayed gently as we crossed the prairie. Buffalo grass swept in waves as the train raced through Nebraska toward Rapid City, then Deadwood.

My compass was pointed straight toward Anna. Nothing would slow me down. Nothing would stop me from taking her home.

Deadwood, where the stationmaster said Jacob was heading. Deadwood, where I gunned down John Maxwell, my uncle. Deadwood, where I tried to hide the fact that I played a role in taking down the Maxwell Gang. It didn't work. I was famous in Deadwood.

We'd hired out the entire car and sat in peace. We could hear the churning iron against iron and the faint grinding of the engine just past the tender. Every so often the whistle shrieked.

I looked away from the window toward Jackson. His Mexico farm clothing looked out of place against the grassland, but he didn't seem to care. He was embroiled in an argument with Scott. They were trying to decide if I was the fastest gun of all time.

How had Scott's clothing stayed perfectly clean? His suspenders stretched over crimson fabric that seemed to light his hair afire.

Becky sat across from the two men, and all I could see was the back of her freshly washed blond hair in a bun.

On the other side of the aisle, Marshal Hill rested across from Running Deer. The two conversed every so often, but they spoke Sioux so their words were hidden from Beth, who was tucked under Running Deer's arm. Somehow the stories I'd told of him to the family had caused her to fall completely in love with him. For the moment, she was at peace.

I remembered Running Deer with several children in his tent when I gave him the mare Princess. He had a gentle way with children.

Down the aisle, Ryan held Rachel as she slept. He stared at her face, his small mouth open, a look of love in his eyes.

I turned to look out the window again, the thick buffalo grass a carpet as far as I could see. Tufts of bluestem survived along the tracks, and blue grama's light, feathery wisps eked out a weak survival among the other grasses. Raven would bask in glory at the buffet. But first we had to save Anna.

If she was still alive.

I pushed away the thought and glanced at Scott again.

What made these men follow me? Jacob had to buy loyalty, force people to do his bidding through fear. A friend who will fight beside you, defend you, is the most valuable treasure on Earth. No *X* on a map could ever equal their value. But yet here we were, racing toward that *X*.

The trail of engine smoke left a shadow of dark green.

All the men had done to Beth was kiss her, Rachel said. But days after saving her, her lips were still cracked and swollen from the gag. Red circles surrounded her eyes.

I pictured Anna and me on my land, taking in Beth and allowing her peace again. The thought came so suddenly tears burned my eyes. Her ordeal cut through my heart, and I closed my eyes to chase away the horror.

I took a long whiff of coal smoke drifting in from my open window.

Alive was alive. Even filled with pain, alive was alive. There was always hope for healing. A person never knew what might happen next.

But I would do everything in my power to help Beth heal. And save Anna.

I closed my eyes and dreamed of the farm, the horses, the pasture that was probably filled with weeds. Planning the new cabin with Anna, building a home together, and starting a family. My nerves calmed.

I was lying in bed, a child, and my mother stepped into the room. "Good morning, sleepyhead." She tried to speak in an American accent for the word *sleepyhead* but sounded more like a man with a sore throat. "Your grandfather is joining us for breakfast."

In less than a second the soft quilt was shoved to the floor and I was tugging on my trousers. I ran out of my room, down the hall, and saw Grandfather sitting at the table, a newspaper open in both hands.

"Philip." Grandfather's voice, no longer British, resembled Marshal Hill's.

"Hey, Philip."

I opened my eyes and looked up to see Marshal Hill settling in the seat across from me. He straightened his mustache with two fingers. "Still a lot to do."

I grunted, rubbed my head to chase away the memory, and crossed my arms. With a dry mouth I said, "Wish we could get more marshals involved."

"If we did, they would take you to the Senate hearing."

"Funny how things work," I said, not really amused at all. I rubbed my face again. "You'd think they'd invest more time finding Jacob."

"The job that's standing in front of them usually comes first." He leaned back against the smooth, cloth seat. "We don't want you standing in front of them."

"Law isn't going to help me with Jacob, is it? I'm going to have to kill him."

"In self-defense, maybe. Yes."

I leaned forward, elbows on my knees. "I've got an amazing colt. I can't wait to get back to him. Such spirit, such fire. He's incredible."

"Will he replace Raven?"

"Someday."

"What's his name?"

I couldn't hold back my smile. "Mustard."

He laughed, his chest rumbling. "The fastest Mustard on the plains."

"I don't need to impress anyone."

"Those who don't try do the real impressing." His sigh was as loud as the train whistle. "Deadwood is much safer with Seth Bullock around. But do you want Beth there?"

"Turn the girls toward Mitchell at Rapid?" I asked.

"That's what I was thinking."

"Beth has clung to Running Deer."

He pulled his badge from his pocket and repinned the star to his chest. "It may be hard to separate the two."

"I visited the tribe last year. He's close to his family. The children love him."

He made a temple with his fingers and considered me for a moment. "This treasure. Have you considered what you'll do?"

"Anna is first on my list." I looked out the window. "Haven't thought past that."

He lowered his voice. "When it's time, Philip—after you've saved her and if you find the other half of the map—go find it. I'll take the men far away if you'd like to do this alone, but this secret seems to have destroyed many lives. I think you should end it."

"Why would you say that?"

"Because you want to be left alone, and that won't happen until the treasure's found and the maps are destroyed."

I sat up. "How many people do you believe are involved?"

"Mr. Wilkes? Who would have guessed? How many more are out there?"

I admitted he had a point.

"And Captain Smith? He knew who you were for how long before he told you about your past?"

I studied his bright eyes, the wrinkles of age a trophy of wisdom. "And you believe there's more."

"Custer! Custer! The loudmouth would have told the whole world!"

"Libbie Custer admitted as much."

He set a hand on his knee and looked back at the men. "We need to hold a council of war with them."

He was probably right. Just charging in to find Anna wasn't the wisest decision. I stood, and as I walked by the marshal, I set a hand on his shoulder. "Thanks."

"You're worth it, Philip." He swallowed, considered for a moment, then nodded. "You're worth it."

"I'll take your word for it." I looked toward Ryan, and Rachel shifted and opened her eyes wide, gasping and leaping forward. Ryan's arms circled her and drew her close.

She melted like butter in a warm skillet, but her knuckles were white.

"Bad dream," she said, her voice deep and husky.

Ryan kissed her wide forehead.

She put a hand on his chest.

The train rocked, and I grasped the back of the seat. "Sorry Ryan, but at your convenience, we need to hold a war council." I hated taking away Rachel's source of comfort.

She shifted to one side. "Go." Her smile was sad but still held determination. "Philip helped save me. Now go save Anna."

I stepped back to let Ryan pass, and I pointed to the back of the car. He started that way, and Marshal Hill followed.

I turned to tell Scott and Jackson but felt a hand encircle mine.

"Philip," Rachel said. "You'll protect him?" Her chin was high enough to show her pride, but her eyes pled with me. Old memories lingered. The last she had seen, I'd been angry at how easily everyone accepted him.

But Ryan had proven himself.

I squeezed her hand. "I like him too."

Tears formed in her eyes as I started for Scott and Jackson.

"Hey, what's it like to be you?" Scott asked as I approached. "We were just talking about if you were two people, who would be faster."

"I'm about out of my mind," Becky said, holding her head. "They've analyzed the entire fight forty ways to Sunday."

"I'll give you a reprieve. We're meeting back there. War council."

Jackson jumped to his feet and walked down the aisle, pausing seat-by-seat as the car rocked.

Scott moved to stand.

Becky grasped his arm. "Scott, no." Her voice was in earnest.

His face blushed. "Becky . . ."

"Please."

"I have to."

"I can't lose you again, Scott."

He looked at me, then back at her. Then back to me.

I shrugged.

"Scott," she said. "If you go with him . . ."

His gaze lowered to her hand, fingers white as they gripped his arm. "Philip saved you." This time, he sounded like a man scolding a child. Where had that voice come from? Since his gun battles?

She tilted her head. Her closed lips were as pale as her skin. They parted and she said, "I can't lose you."

"I am a man who repays his debts." He pulled from her grip, and the air was sucked from the cabin. He passed me and followed Jackson.

Becky's breath came in heaves and her lips trembled. She brought a trembling hand up to wipe the falling tears.

"He'll be okay," I said but was unconvincing, even to myself.

"If something happens to him, Philip Anderson," she said, her jaw tight. "I will kill you. With my own hands."

I opened my mouth to respond, but no sound came. My blood ran cold.

She meant what she said. And what was more, she looked eager to follow through. I needed her to support us, to agree with what we did. For Scott's sake, at least. But in the end, her obstinate hatred put us at such odds I was forced to ignore her. Scott had proven his skill in battle, and I needed him to save Anna.

Turning my back to her was one of the most difficult things I'd ever done.

Some men are chosen to exact justice.

God, why us?

Because no one else was going to get Anna.

I approached the men, their grim faces attesting to a firm knowledge of what the future held.

Running Deer set Beth on Rachel's lap and joined the council.

Marshal Hill, Scott, and Jackson faced forward. Running Deer settled in beside Ryan and I next to the Sioux. We faced the back of the train.

Marshal Hill was saying to Scott, "Back in my day, we did

our job with no feelings involved. Families were happy for the work, the coin."

Scott rubbed his jaw. "That what they taught you in George Washington's army?"

"You know what we do with tadpoles?" Marshal Hill asked, and a smile slowly crossed his face. "Nothin'."

I cleared my throat. They all turned to me and quieted when they saw the serious look on my face.

Time to be clear. And to fill them in. "My father had three close friends—John Maxwell who was my mother's brother. Mr. Wilkes, a business partner. And my grandfather. My father split a map in two, kept one half, and gave the second to my grandfather. My grandfather died and left the map with a monk.

"To get the map back, the monk forced Mr. Wilkes to adopt a boy he named after himself, Jacob Wilkes."

"Interesting," Scott said.

He opened his mouth to say more, but I interrupted. "My father, who had seen the entire map, decided to go after the treasure himself. He packed my mother and me into a wagon and passed our land near Yankton. He stopped at Devil's Tower where they were killed." I nodded at Running Deer. "That's where your story comes in."

He touched his heart but kept silent.

"I lived in an orphanage. While there, I learned to use this." I tapped the gun at my side. "General George Custer knew my parents, knew I was alive, and that I was in Sioux City. He checked on me. Stopped in just to see if I had a map. Then rode off." I grunted. "Wonder what would have happened if he lived.

"Then Mitchell, where Mr. Wilkes had opened his bank shortly after I arrived. Somehow, he learned I survived too— I'm guessing he came across my name when I filed for a land grant. Maybe he and Custer were working together. Anyway, he bided his time. I remember now that for the five years I lived in my cabin. I would come home and find items rear-ranged, as if someone had gone through the house while I was in town. He was looking for the map."

I looked out the window. The grass rushing past made me feel as if we moved at terrific speed, while the distant trees made the world stand still. I continued. "Devil's Tower. The map leads there. But Mr. Wilkes's half of the map has the exact location." I looked each of them in the eye, and said slowly, "and I don't know where that is."

"But Mr. Wilkes and Jacob have both halves of the map now, right?" Scott asked. "Somehow Jacob found it on Anna?"

I tried not to think of it. "And they have Anna."

"I wonder," Marshal Hill said. "I wonder how the two Wilkes men will work together. I can't see Jacob taking orders from his father."

"A duel between the two would be nice," Scott muttered.

I sat back, thinking.

Marshal Hill's voice cut into my thoughts. "What? You know something. Wait." He swore, jarring me. "You know... Philip, you are the most . . . You don't need the map."

"What?" Scott looked at me then back at Marshal Hill. "What? What did I miss?"

"He knows."

"Knows what?"

Marshal Hill studied me with his keen eyes. "You had a vision. You remember where the treasure is."

I crossed my arms and moved my gaze out the window.

He clapped his hands once. "Oh, this is gonna be good. I can't wait to see what happens."

"The truth is, I didn't remember. I just remember . . . something else." They looked at me quizzically. "I don't think they'll find anything where the map points."

Marshal Hill laughed. "You know where the treasure is, don't you?"

"Philip?" Scott asked.

Finally, I looked at him. I gave a single nod. "Jacob is in for a disappointment."

22

Anna's gaze went from her horse's saddle horn to the rope tied to Jacob's stallion. She studied the knot fixed to her saddle. Could she untie it and run?

No, not on the sorry roan she rode.

They wound around pines in a long row, probably twenty men in all. Mr. Wilkes led the way with Anna and Jacob in the center. The scent of fresh grass and warm sunshine overhead would have made for a lovely ride if the most detestable man in the world wasn't within earshot.

"Have you seen Devil's Tower before?" Jacob asked in a voice far too conversational.

What more could he do to her? Bruises covered her thinning body, her spirit was just as battered and starved, and to her utter shame she had cowered at times. She wasn't proud of anything now. But something about the warmth, the wildflowers, the sense of home renewed her fighting spirit.

Jacob repeated the question, this time in a stern tone.

"Yes, many times," she snapped. "I have a home here."

He raised his hand to backhand her.

"Beware," she said in a low voice, "Or I will tell your father your plans to take the treasure from him." She curled her lips into a wicked smile. "Where are those men you paid? Around the next bend?"

His hand slowly lowered to his side.

Did Mr. Wilkes suspect? Whether Jacob had truly wanted the treasure was beyond her to know, but he was a man who planned for every eventuality. His father surely guessed.

"I'll kill you, of course," he said, "before you tell him." He chuckled. "You'll be dead, and I'll be a son who respects his father's advice."

Her shoulders slumped. "I'll talk fast."

"You do enjoy talking, don't you?"

If only Philip rode beside her instead of Jacob and these men were paid workers to help find the treasure, she would talk until she had no breath. The thought sent unwarranted hope through her heart then drove her to the depths of depression. He couldn't be dead. Had she seen his chest rise?

No one was coming after her.

She looked away, toward the patches of trees. Her best chance of escape was when they found the treasure and were distracted. Somehow, someway she would ride Jacob's stallion away and never look back. Then she could gather herself and prepare to find her sister.

Against the vast blue sky, a tower rose from the green hills, a giant, gray thimble on the fabric of earth. The imagery she chose to describe Devil's Tower, coupled with the hope of escape, lightened her spirits. She would run when their attention was on things they felt more precious than her.

The best laid schemes o' mice an' men. If there was one thing she'd learned over the past month, nothing happened as she would have it. Plan, then act and hope for the best.

Ahead, Mr. Wilkes held his map in front of him. He tucked the aging page away as they approached a river. He started down the small embankment, his horse picking out a path.

Behind, the long trail followed.

Anna's borrowed horse stumbled down the bank. Her mare had seen happier days. Oh, if only she knew Alita had fallen into friendly hands!

They crossed a vast deserted plain. The ground was covered in dry gravel, broken poles, ripped strips of leather, smashed cans, and other debris. This must be where the Sioux had camped for their dances. Philip had been here.

An imaginary lance pierced her very real heart.

Jacob rode beside her, his cream hat set tight atop his wispy, white hair and pale fingers holding the reins high above his saddle horn. His face was turned toward the tower, a thoughtful, contemplative look in his eyes.

This man had orchestrated this unthinkable moment, stealing Philip's past and present to destroy his future.

Hot blood coursed through her veins. Every heartbeat thumped in her ears. She would never see Philip again.

Jacob had stolen her life.

She closed her eyes and tried to gain control over her surging emotions. Her hands, tied to her own saddle horn, twisted against the ropes. Weeks of chafing had toughened her wrists, and they barely felt the bite on her skin.

This was near where Philip's parents had died. She wanted to stop and think about him. They kept on.

Jacob. A namesake who had stolen a birthright.

With every step rage filled her mind, whispering *death, death, death, death.*

With death she could be with Philip again. With death she would see her father. With death she would have peace.

Beth and her mother would not be far behind.

Anna barely felt the hot wind on her face. The breeze was cool compared to the fire inside her.

Her horse jerked to one side, but she kept her eyes closed.

Jacob had destroyed her family. Happiness wasn't even a question anymore, nor was peace. Because of Jacob.

She growled, straining at the bindings. The ropes around her wrists snapped.

Her eyelids flew open, and her gaze pierced Jacob. Without knowing what happened, she was soaring through the air. Her shoulder slammed into his midsection as her arms wrapped around him. They tumbled over the stallion and slammed into a scraggly bush.

Air whooshed from her lungs.

Even though she couldn't breathe, her fists pummeled him, connecting with bone, then softer parts of his body. The smell of sage couldn't drown out his perfume, bringing memories of the murder of Beth's horse to mind, the day he tried to kiss her.

Beth's horse, Spink.

Jacob had ripped the heart from all of them.

She reached through his flailing arms and gripped his hair. With a knee in his gut, she smashed his head back against a mound of cropped grass. Voices screamed in her head but she ignored them all, instead letting the rage control her hands. "I hate you!" she screamed, words she never would have dared before. But what more could they take?

From behind, a voice. "Stop."

She lifted a hand and slapped Jacob's cheek.

"Stop."

Again, she reared back and inflicted pain, praying beyond hope her agony would pass from her into him.

"We're here."

Fingers entwined in her hair and jerked her body back. She slammed into the ground, panting.

Mr. Wilkes stood over them, his shadow crossing his son's haggard body. He held the page in his hand and pointed to the monolith within a stone's throw. "We're here."

Rising from the earth like a massive spear rose Devil's Tower, splitting the sky in two. Grooves the size of a house rose as far as she could see.

Her gaze stayed fixed on the stone pillar. She scrambled to her feet and backed away.

Had she ever seen anything so enormous, so imposing?

This stone rock was truth. Nothing could be done to move it, to destroy it. Jacob was powerless to control the giant. Its strength gave her strength.

At her feet, Jacob dabbed at his bleeding lip with a handkerchief. His eyes shimmered with two mixed emotions. The first was anger, a feeling she'd grown used to seeing. The second, however, scared her to the core. She'd hurt him. Not physically. There was no look of pain on his face. No, she'd hurt his feelings.

Had he honestly felt she would fall for him?

Her denial had finally touched his heart.

No hope she loved him, no chance she ever would. Now he was capable of killing her.

The emotion was quickly devoured by the cool pretense he usually wore. Pressing a hand against the earth, he rose over her, slowly testing his limbs. He stood between her and the tower, looking down on her.

He reached into his pocket where he kept his gun.

Mr. Wilkes put a hand on Jacob's shoulder. "Let's find it."

Jacob stared at her then let his hands drop. To a man nearby, he said, "Tie her tight. Bring her along."

Rough hands spun her around on her belly and thick knees pressed into her back. An elbow drove the side of her head into the red dirt. Every breath blew small puffs of crimson dust into the still air.

Her heart and mind were numb. The next moments were surely her last.

She closed her mouth and tried to swallow. They yanked

back her arms and tied her wrists together, but she barely felt the wrenching on her shoulders.

A purple flower inches away bowed its trumpeted head toward her. A harebell. The name was important. Why? She didn't know. But the name was vital.

The strength of the tower behind her. The beauty of the flower beside her. Somehow she knew God had put them there for her. For courage. For hope. All was lost, but yet the flower had not been crushed as she fell. And the tower's strength would stand the test of time.

Ironic, she thought as they jerked her to her knees. Devil's Tower. That name would fit the men who bound her. She'd remember the monolith by the Lakota name, Bear Lodge. More befitting her spirit.

A rope was wrapped several times around her, trapping her arms to her sides and her hands behind her. Her legs were left free, and as they walked along the tower she almost laughed at the thought of escaping and running across the prairie like a bizarre creature without arms.

Surely her torpid heart explained her laughter. But there was more. There was hope. A known future? Did she have a single possession? Was there any person left alive who loved her? Whom she loved? Now that everything was gone, what was left?

What was left was God, and He was still just. Philip loved—had loved—talking about justice. And no matter what happened to her, justice would be done. Even more compelling, after all that Jacob had done, all the evil he'd committed, he wasn't one iota happier. Just the opposite.

The band of men explored closer to the tower. They followed.

The rope around her neck pulled her along like a lasso.

Jacob walked close, keeping an eye on his father.

They split around boulders like water in a stream. Scraggly

pines were sparse around the tower's base, and as they paused she shifted into the meager shade.

Mr. Wilkes held up the page and slowly spun in a circle, looking past the map at the landmarks, then back at the faded ink.

Despite the dangers, Anna felt interest growing inside her, and her wonder at where the map would lead overshadowed some of her fear.

Mr. Wilkes walked several paces away from the tower, holding up a hand to shield his eyes from the sun. He lifted his arms. "I can't figure this map."

Jacob took the map from him. "Shall I?" He studied the faint writing, a brow raised, then surveyed the rocks. "Ah." He handed the map back to Mr. Wilkes and crossed in front of the men to a boulder.

Anna was yanked to the front, where everyone shifted to watch. What was it about Jacob that inspired such interest? His smooth movements, as well as his calm features inspired confidence. Dangerous.

Jacob ran a hand around the curved angle at the bottom of the rock. He paused, his fingers spread. A grin, close-lipped, crossed his face.

He'd found the treasure.

Jacob pressed his back against the rock.

If Jacob kept her alive because he thought she knew, his reason just ran out.

She tugged on the rope, eager to escape. Even with all her strength, her efforts barely caught the attention of the big man. He snarled at her then shook his head and tugged. She fell and decided just to remain there, looking at the sky.

When she was dead, before being reunited with Philip, she would float up to see what the top of the tower looked like. She imagined a colony of animals, escaped from the clutches of hawks. The animals had fallen in love, married, and had families.

With a groan, Jacob pushed. The rock, just larger than Jacob, leaned to one side, rolling on the rounded edge.

Anna scrambled to her feet.

A crack as tall and narrow as Jacob whistled as air rushed from the dark confines.

"A lamp," Jacob called. No one moved. "Now!"

Several men rushed to the horses.

Jacob's gaze fell on Anna, cold and hard. He considered her for a moment, but she knew the look. His mind was calculating. He lifted a hand, both pointer and middle finger extended, and he waved.

A signal?

Nothing moved that direction, only the extending shadow of the tower and beyond that miles of hills and trees. In the distance storm clouds gathered, their visual strength muted by the curve of the earth. Tonight the fury of God would be unleashed.

The lamps arrived.

"Father?" Jacob lifted the light. "Shall we?"

Doubt crept into Mr. Wilkes's eyes. Jacob was in control of this situation now. The older man worked his jaw for a moment, looking at the men, then considering Jacob. "Fine. But just us. You and me."

Jacob brushed dust and cobwebs from his suit with his free hand, slowly, deliberately. "Yes." He gave the lamp to his father, freeing up his hands.

The move wasn't lost on Mr. Wilkes.

Before Jacob started into the cave he looked at her, a gaze so soft that if she wanted to she could believe him compassionate.

In a soft voice he said, "You deserve to know." He took her rope.

Men who show the extremes of kindness and cruelty are not to be trusted. But what could she do? A shiver ran down her spine as he took the rope and led her to the cave.

Mr. Wilkes stepped inside first.

Jacob pushed her toward the entrance. A cool wind brushed her hair away from her neck. In one moment she walked in blinding sunlight, and in the next she was plunged in darkness. The wind stopped.

Jacob's footsteps against the gravel were close behind, echoing in the passage.

Anna kept her eyes focused on the lamp, the black around her whispering terrors of unknown creatures, monsters from the depths. What roamed in this darkness? What lurked in the deep? They continued into the abyss.

Her eyes finally made out the orange glow splashing against the rough cave wall. Craggy shadows sprang at her as the flame flickered despite the still air. A faint whiff of bat guano, an aroma she smelled near Branson in the Lost Caves, spiked fear through her. She hated bats.

The weight of the earth above pressed down on her.

Breathe, Anna. Breathe.

The passage continued straight and down for some time, as if this were a chute for lava in the past. But the cave took a sharp left turn then rose and widened.

Mr. Wilkes stopped and lifted the lantern.

A crevasse, longer than Anna was tall, blocked their way. Too far to jump.

Mr. Wilkes dropped to a knee and swung the lantern to one side. "Look."

Jacob led Anna forward. It would be so easy to push Mr. Wilkes over the edge, and Jacob must have realized the danger. Jacob's hand held her in front of him, so that she teetered over the rim of a bottomless pit.

She cried aloud but didn't dare move.

Jacob chuckled and leaned down to see what his father found.

A log stretched over the emptiness.

"Tracks," Mr. Wilkes said. "Several. They could be old."

"Could be ancient," Jacob said, surveying the passage beyond. "She'll go first."

Anna shook her head.

He lifted a hand to his pocket.

A bullet was sure death. Balancing on the log, she might live.

How old was the narrow bridge?

She pressed a foot on the wood. Solid. More weight. Still held.

Her mouth was dry and her heart hammered against her chest. Jacob would kill her. Her hands were bound and arms tied close to her side. Useless for balance.

Be fleet of foot. Move fast. Don't look down. Focus on the log. Will yourself across. God, please.

Three quick breaths and she jumped.

Her toes grazed against the wood's edge, and her other foot landed in the center. Like a dancer she pressed as lightly as she could. What if Jacob tugged on the tether? Before she could formulate the full thought, she landed safely on the other side.

Jacob and Mr. Wilkes crossed.

"Follow the tracks," Mr. Wilkes said.

They walked for about two minutes, and the walls on either side retreated so the lamp's light fell short of extinguishing the blackness surrounding them. The air was thicker, and she could smell water.

Mr. Wilkes stopped. "Best go around." His face was ethereal. "Must have fallen recently." He looked up.

The tracks led under a massive boulder.

Anna kept her mind off the implications of falling rocks, but being buried under the tower for all eternity ripped her sanity away. She jerked back. Jacob shortened his hold and jerked her to the ground.

She lay in the dirt, panting.

Jacob knelt by her side. "Keep yourself together."

She closed her eyes and swallowed. *You're okay, Anna.* She struggled to her feet.

Mr. Wilkes led them around the boulder, and this time when he stopped Anna ran into him.

He didn't notice. Instead, he took several deliberate steps forward.

Anna couldn't help but gasp.

With every stride, the world around them grew brighter.

They stood in a vast cavern. Ahead, a lake was so clear, so perfectly calm and smooth stretched beyond the light's extent, she barely knew the reflection was water. Lamplight reflected off the depths and scattered through the cavern and danced on the ceiling. To the left the lake stretched forever into darkness. On their right a sharp wall, identical to the tower above, gave the cave and lake an abrupt end.

There was no gold. No jewels. Just dark rocks wherever they looked. Under her feet, dark rocks—perhaps crushed lava—made up the shore. Under the water, however, ragged quartz reflected light.

A soft drip was the only noise.

Jacob's sigh caught her attention. He bent down and traced a round indentation in the rocks, perhaps the size of a barrel.

There were no other tracks.

Jacob looked up at his father. "It's gone."

Mr. Wilkes set the lamp on a flat rock and pulled the map from his pocket. "It has to be here. We're right here."

Jacob stood and brushed off his hands. "What's lost can be found."

Mr. Wilkes crushed the map in his fist. "But the money. Where's the money?" He threw the paper to the ground. "Henry. Henry Anderson took it. I knew it. I knew it." He swore, and the sound echoed through the cavern.

Anna crept a foot away, hoping God would drop a rock on him for his foul language.

"Father," Jacob said softly. "You said he was dead."

"It's true." He grasped both sides of his head.

"Then Philip must know where the treasure is."

"Yes," Mr. Wilkes said. "Yes, you're right. But he's dead."

Jacob craned his neck to watch her as he said, "He's alive."

She tried to control her face, tried not to give him the pleasure of seeing her emotions, but her heart burst. A sob escaped her lips. Renewed hope and anger and dreams and fears took the place of her grief, creating a whirlwind in her stomach.

But there was a reason for Jacob's admission. "Father," he said, still looking at Anna. "It's time you step aside and let someone else take care of matters now."

"Don't be preposterous."

"You know Philip's skills. You are no match for him. It's time you let my generation take over what you have started." Jacob finally turned away from her. "It's time to return to your bank."

"But—"

"Father, it's finished."

Mr. Wilkes's fingers drifted to the gun at his side but thought better of it. "You've bought them, haven't you?" When Jacob was silent, he said, "Are any of my men still loyal to me?"

Jacob held up two fingers. "And they'll follow you back to Mitchell."

The war that played on the large man's face attested to the battles within. Would he fight? What chance did he have? Both Anna and Mr. Wilkes knew Jacob would kill him.

"I have to know," Mr. Wilkes said. "I have to know what's inside. It's money. I know it is."

"I will tell you." Jacob lifted his head as if searching for something. "When I find it."

Mr. Wilkes squeezed his eyes closed tightly, and when he

opened them they held compassion. "Here," he said, holding out a hand. "Give me the girl. I'll take her with me."

"I've other plans for Miss Johnston," he said and he tugged on the rope, pulling her along the shore. He stopped at a thin boulder, half buried, and pressed her against rough stone. He wrapped the rope around the rock and knotted it to one side.

She pulled on the rope. Nothing. The fibers didn't give.

Jacob took the lamp and started back down the passage.

"No!" Anna called. "No, you can't leave me!"

"Jacob," Mr. Wilkes barked from the narrow cave. "You can't."

But the light dimmed, slowly fading until darkness surrounded her, prickling her skin.

Anna screamed. "No!"

23

We stormed through Deadwood like a hurricane.

The town was used to wild miners looking for a good time, men who have been away from any settlement far too long.

I wasn't looking for saloons or parties.

Without the influence of the Maxwell Gang Deadwood had quieted, which suited me just fine. But that didn't stop us from bursting through saloon doors and asking questions.

The townsfolk seemed to know we weren't there to cause a ruckus. Most were helpful.

Marshal Hill checked in with City Marshal Seth Bullock.

If Jacob was in town he'd kept a low profile and didn't show his face. I thought Jacob would have wanted to live a finer lifestyle and would have been noticed. But Seth Bullock was an honest man, Marshal Hill said.

A goods store at the edge of town said a few men just came through the day before and fitted up for either a long duration or their haul was for quite a few riders. They'd overheard them say Devil's Tower but guessed the men were just chatting, since the Indians had all left and there was no longer trade there.

"Philip," Marshal Hill said. "We going to Devil's Tower?"

My compass was pointed toward Anna, and if Anna was there that was where I'd be.

On the Deadwood streets Scott pulled on his reins and led his horse closer. "It as tall as they say it is?"

"Yeah," I said quietly. "It is."

Marshal Hill matched the softness in my voice. "I hope you have a plan, because Jacob's got a lot of men."

"Matt will come through," I said.

Matt had to come through.

Our horses thundered toward Devil's Tower, and even though they were rested, the journey took three days. Raven could have covered the trail before the sun set, and we could be under the shadow of the tower. But I wouldn't abandon my friends.

I needed them.

Running Deer had ridden ahead to scout.

Scott rode to my left, Ryan on my right. Jackson kept an eye out from behind, and Marshal Hill led the way.

The sun had passed its zenith, falling toward the thunderclouds building in the West. The sharp orange glow bathed the blades of grass in sharp contrast to the rusty dirt. Pines offered shade in stoic silence, growing tall around rocks and clinging to ravines.

Devil's Tower came into view and my body tingled, memories rushing back with the force of the promised evening storms.

Marshal Hill pointed with a gloved hand. "Dust up ahead."

To every man's credit, no one had to be told what that meant.

"What's wrong?" Scott asked in a quiet voice.

"A little worried. Hopefully that's Matt ahead."

"You've got the look again. The one that says the past and the present are merging."

I breathed through clenched teeth. "Strong this time."

"Hold on there, buddy."

"Up ahead, where the dust is?" I let the reins fall loose as Raven lowered her head. "My parents' grave."

Scott was quiet for a bit. He said, "Strange coming here, after hearing all the stories."

"Good to bring you here." Like two planets colliding, my best friend and the past rolling up into one. "Can't say what will happen, but getting Anna back . . . I need her."

Was my mother watching? Had my father, in death, regretted his actions? Did the heartache of the present touch the past? No, I didn't think so. They slept in their cold graves, their souls in another place. The past lived in the past, but the ripples influenced who we are, what we do, who we know. My choices had already changed the men I rode with.

My hands felt weak at the implications of what was coming. I held tight to the saddle horn, the reins weaved in my fingers.

Marshal Hill turned and said, "I wish I knew your mother, Philip. I think Captain Smith was in love with her. Tell us about her."

I took his attempt to calm my nerves. I told of her love for everyone, the parties she threw, the joy she found in her son. The longing in my voice surprised me. "Someday I will learn why she married a man like my father."

We topped a small rise, passed through a thicket of trees, and paused at the edge of the familiar clearing. The far end was bordered by the Belle Fourche River, the water edged in brush and trees. In the center a lone pine stood surrounded by riders.

My heart leapt at the sight of Matt's beautiful black skin. He'd finished his mission. I wanted to hug him.

As we rode up my gaze turned unwillingly away from his brilliant smile to the riders who tended their horses. Lean, skin weathered, clothes thick but worn. Their keen eyes regarded us. Then they turned back to their work with brushes against the shining flanks of their horses. From downwind, I could smell the welcome stench of the men, hide, and horse.

In the quick second it took to see us they'd counted us as friendly.

All twelve were heavily armed, but none wore the look of killers, like Marshal Hill's men might. To a man, each had rope hanging from their saddles.

These were cattlemen.

Matt lifted a hand and called out, "Jackson!"

Beyond was another man. With medium height and sandy hair, thick chest and trimmed mustache, he barked orders. "We'll send patrols in fifteen minutes. Camp setup for the rest. Look lively!" Was he bouncing?

He spotted us, and as we approached he stepped away from his men.

"Mr. Anderson," he said, snapping his words short. "Well met. This is bully."

I dismounted and took his hand in a warm shake. "You asked to be in my next adventure, Theodore."

"Wouldn't miss this. No, wouldn't miss it for the world. Honored you thought of me."

Marshal Hill descended from the saddle and was next to get a hardy handshake. "Marshal, a pleasure again. A pleasure."

"Mr. Roosevelt. Glad you could join us."

Roosevelt's smile faded. "Winter was hell, my friends. I've no cattle left. All frozen at the hoof, snapped their legs clean off. Terrible loss. But this," he said, lifting a hand as if to encompass the men. "This is simply bully."

Did he think of this as a glorified camping adventure?

"Sir," I said in a low voice, "I'm afraid Matt may have misrepresented our predicament. There's a fight ahead."

"Why I'm here," he said, "is for the fight. Wouldn't miss it."

"You want to be in a battle?"

"Glory? Honor? Bravery? They're not just words, lad. I search for them daily." He stood directly in front of me and thumped his chest with a fist. "I want this fight. I seek it. I crave to test myself."

Past his shoulder, the men continued rubbing down their horses. How many of them felt the same?

I couldn't hide my frown. Several of the men worked atop the ground my parents were buried.

"Mr. Anderson?" Roosevelt asked.

Perhaps I shouldn't say anything. But this mattered. I pointed "Those men. They couldn't have known, but that's where my parents are buried."

Roosevelt spun. "You! Men! Move!"

All the men looked up, and the offenders saw Roosevelt pointing to them. They grasped their reins and quickly moved from under the pine tree. They quickly backed away from the shrine I held so dear to my heart.

The small rock with a cross etched in the center came into view, and the men parted as I walked forward.

How many of these men knew of my past?

Conversation died. A few men removed their hats. Then more, and finally all held hat in hand. They bowed their heads as I stood over my parents' grave.

Their naked scrutiny sucked the emotion from me, leaving me hollow. There were no visions, no thoughts of the past. Only the observations of men who knew me through a dime novel and the newspapers.

Privileged information was no longer held sacred. My life was irrevocably public.

A hum from the men rose, growing louder, swirling around us like leaves on the wind. As a tenor pierced the air with a clear voice—the words sharp and beautiful—a bird's call for the world to listen.

Amazing grace, how sweet the sound.

A spellbound blanket fell over us, the emotion of my past singing from the rocks around us. The tree in front of me. The sky that held witness to the deeds on this very spot.

Tears trickled from my eyes.

And grace my fears relieved.

Do men really cry?

Running Deer had said the men who killed my parents were gone. I had built my life without revenge. But now here—I wanted Anna so powerfully, I couldn't hold back the storm of emotions now. Clenched fists, tears, gritted teeth, straight shoulders, heaving breath.

The song was nearly ended when I remembered I wasn't alone. I peeked to see I wasn't the only one who cried. Roosevelt's face was blotchy and wet.

Yes, my life was privileged information. But at that moment, I wouldn't trade the shared emotions for any amount of money. These men, willing to fight for me before, were now as my brothers—willing to die for each other. All had mothers. All had loved a girl sometime.

Those feelings were worth fighting for.

I lifted my voice. "Jacob Wilkes has committed crimes so heinous, I will not utter them here."

"Matt's told us," Roosevelt said, and many agreed as they quieted.

I gave Matt a nod, and he closed his eyes and continued to hum.

"The wrongs can't be undone. But they can be made right."

"He's right," a few said.

Roosevelt's men were circled around me and as I spoke I made eye contact with each of them. "You, standing here with me on the edge of battle, is an honor. Sometimes. . ." I rested my hand on my gun's pearl handle. "Sometimes we must allow justice to take her course. But in this case, we must stop evil dead on the trail." I faltered, aware of their presence, unsure of what to say next.

Roosevelt's high-pitched tenor rang across the prairie. "Forces that tend for evil are great and terrible, but the forces of truth," he said putting an arm around me and lifting his head, "truth and love and courage and honesty and generosity and sympathy are also stronger than ever before. Today we ride for honor!" He lifted a fist and roared. The men howled.

Roosevelt was a natural speaker.

A few of the men asked questions about the Maxwell Gang, and I downplayed my role as best I could. Scott, though, wouldn't let me. After he set the story straight, he wouldn't stop.

"This gun," he said as the others looked on, "in Mexico, took down dozens of bandits." And he told the story that mesmerized even Roosevelt.

Blessedly, as I felt the pink creep across my face, Running Deer stepped into the clearing.

"We need patrols," I muttered to Roosevelt.

"Right," he snapped and took to his work with the energy of Trevor.

I waved to Running Deer as he approached, his gait as fresh and confident as if he'd woken a moment ago.

"What news?" I asked as I stepped close, Marshal Hill close behind me. Scott and Jackson seemed to prefer storytelling.

"*Miya Ca*, there are many." He reached to his side and brought a long, leather water pouch to his lips. "I have seen the bank owner. And his son." He wiped a frayed sleeve across his mouth. "They fight with each other, I think."

"There's an advantage there," Marshal Hill said.

"Older Wilkes left and rode away with two. The son stays, but there are many men."

"How many?" I asked.

"Twenty-five."

We were outmanned almost two to one. I glanced at Marshal Hill, and I raised a brow.

"Do they have Anna?" I grasped his shoulder. "Have you seen her?"

Running Deer dropped to a knee and ran his hand over a dirt patch. Did he remember it was here the wagon burned?

"Bear Lodge," he said, making half a circle. "Sun setting here. Jacob's men, some miners, some ranch men, some paid fighters." He looked up. "All paid fighters." He reached across. "Horses here." He drew a short half circle. "Men in rocks here."

"But where's Anna?"

Between the men and the tower, Running Deer thrust his finger in the dirt. "In a cave."

Marshal Hill groaned. "They've found it."

I studied the crude map, concerned that Running Deer had drawn as poorly here as in Mexico. "You saw her?"

"Jacob, his father, and Anna walked into the cave. Jacob and his father left."

Marshal Hill and I exchanged glances. "She's still in there," he said. "I'm sure she's alive. She's his insurance. Same maneuver as Mexico?" Marshal Hill asked. "We feign into the sunset so the enemy can't see as well. We'll keep them occupied and you go into the cave, save Anna, and let's get out of here? We're not capturing him under these conditions."

"No, we're not." The cover was atrocious, unlike the buildings in Mexico. "Let's go. Now."

I turned to go, but Running Deer hunkered down. "There's more?" I asked him.

"Here." He stretched his other hand as far as he could reach. "Another outfit. Rich. Powerful. Strength there. Eight men." He looked into my eyes. "Killers."

Killers. "Who are they?"

His mellow Sioux accent was strong when he said, "I do not know."

"Let's make this fast. Get Anna and come right back here." Roosevelt's men continued to mingle in the distance, but I could feel their energy. "Jacob doesn't know this place. We're safe here."

Marshal Hill swept off his hat and rubbed his face with a sleeve. "Want me and Roosevelt to take the men then?"

"I'll leave now and scout the cave. When I hear gunfire, I'll make my move."

"Scott and Ryan are going to want to go with you."

Should I leave now?

What kind of friend would that make me?

Telling Ryan was easy. He put a giant hand on my shoulder and squeezed. My left arm almost fell off under his strong grip.

Roosevelt was so eager to get his men moving, all he said was "Bully!"

Scott's freckles were sharp in the evening light, a testament to the sun he'd lived under the past weeks. "Stay safe," I said.

"Philip, you and I can work together. There's no reason—"

"Two men are easier to spot than one."

He reached out and snatched a seeded grass top and twisted the stem in a circle. "I hate it when you do this."

"What's that?"

"Play the martyr. You don't have to go alone." He looked up from the knot he tied. "I know you like things to just happen, as if God has laid it out perfectly for you. But it doesn't work that way for me. Some of us have to make things happen and hope God is in it."

Without too much thought, I reached into my vest pocket

and pulled out the U.S. Deputy Marshal badge and studied the simple iron. "I suppose this happened to me." I tilted the star toward him, held it close. "But lately, going after Anna . . ." I looked toward the tower. I had made things happen. Sometimes good came from my deeds. But bad happened as well. Either way, I had made something happen. I acted and wasn't simply acted upon.

I pinned the badge to my vest, reached for my duster tied to the back of Raven's saddle, and tugged the heavy cloth over my shoulders. Time to save Anna. "Let's ride, buddy."

24

Scott and I halted our horses within sight of the enemy's camp. Two guards kept a wary eye for the likes of me, guarding their own mounts. I didn't see Jacob's animal, but one stallion caught my attention. He was beautiful.

I pushed all my weight into my left leg, pressing against the stirrup, and swung my right over the back of the saddle and planted my boot on gravel. I tugged my left foot from the stirrup.

With a gloved hand, I took the tail end of her rein, swung the leather around a thick pine branch at about eye level, and twisted it into a loop. My fingers quickly dropped the rein's end under again to make another loop then swept it through the first loop and tugged. Raven wouldn't pull away, but I could snatch her easily.

I'd brought Alita as well, sure that Anna would be riding away with us.

The two horses stood side-by-side. Raven's jet and Alita's

cream-colored flanks stirred my heart, all that was right in the world.

Get Anna. Take her back to my farm. Watch the horses while we drink coffee.

"Let's go, Scott. Careful, though. Becky's knife is at my throat."

"Makes two of us," he muttered and when I continued to stare at him he said, "Just a joke."

He wasn't convincing.

"If I lost you . . ." It was the best I could do with the swelling emotions.

"Kind of why I'm here." His hands shook, and his face darkened. "If you went down and there was something I could do . . ."

And that was all. We'd said all we could. All we needed. Rare was he speechless.

I pulled the Smith and Wesson. He lifted his Winchester.

We started forward and I paused at a boulder. I peered around and saw no one, so I pressed on. A pine offered cover, and I stopped there.

Scott hid behind a bush that offered no cover.

"Hey."

He glanced over, and I pointed the gun at the bush. "Won't stop a bullet."

"Right." He scurried to my tree like a ground squirrel.

Odd. His presence on my farm, in the restaurant, and at his small home was so different than here. As we moved to the next rock his shoulders were thicker, back straighter, jaw firm as if determination drove him from boy to man. Living for others did that.

Yet his light heart remained. "What's on top of the tower," he asked. "Indian tribe?"

"No idea. Never been up there."

He started for a nearby cleft under the tower. As I

caught up with him he said, "I'll climb it when we're done here."

We kept moving around the tower's base. "Scott, you've any family? Other than your sister, I mean?"

"No, just my sister back East."

"And you moved out here when your parents died?"

"Had a falling out with her after that."

His voice was clipped.

I let it go. If something happened to him, I had enough information to find those who might care what happened.

Movement through scraggly trees caught my eye, and I pressed against a tree. Scott ducked behind a thick pine.

Gunfire exploded. Thunder ripped through the rocks and ricocheted against the tower. Birds squawked and took flight, soaring away as fast as their wings would carry them.

I threw myself flat against the ground and waited for the familiar sound of bullets ricocheting off obstacles.

None came.

Beyond the trees in a small depression, men moved around the rocks like ants. Tiny puffs of smoke contributed to a general haze growing around the fight. Closer to us in a semicircle below, defenders scrambled for cover, their backs exposed to Scott and I.

"Would you look at that," he said, lifting his rifle. "We could even this fight pretty fast."

Tempting.

"Yeah," he muttered after not firing.

"You've every right to defend—" I stopped.

Between the small gaps of gunfire ripping through the air, I was sure I heard a voice.

Not just any voice. "Scott, did you hear that?"

He tilted his head to the side. "Shooting?"

"No." The voice came again. "There."

"I heard it that time."

I faced the tower. "Anna."

"Where is she?"

I looked at the rocks and trees and gravel. "I don't know."

"I thought you knew where the treasure was."

"I do," I said, the frustration high in my voice. "It's just not here anymore."

Scott rolled over. "What do you mean?"

"My father found it." Her distant voice drew me away into a dream, a time when I sat on my porch and watched Anna in the corral with the horses. Their muzzles fit perfectly in her hands as she held out oats.

She had called out to me with laughter in her voice.

Now I heard terror.

"That way."

"Buddy," Scott said. "There's no cover."

"I have to."

Scott looked over the battle. "I'll be your cover." He lifted his rifle. "Go, before they turn around."

I squeezed his arm then started into the shadow of Devil's Tower.

My compass pointed the way, locked on the faint whispers of her voice. The sound cut through the roar of shooting, dragging me forward into the danger of open ground. I didn't care. I kept moving, focused only on Anna.

How many rocks would I walk around this day? At least one more. I would go where her voice took me. Oh, her voice! Despite the terror, her voice to me was a choir of angels hovering overhead. She was alive.

I had been sure I would never hear her voice again, never listen to her soft whispers, never feel her presence.

In front of a cave, flat gravel left plenty of room for Jacob's men to see me. The only cover was a rock that had been rolled to the side.

I holstered my gun, whispered a prayer for protection, and sprinted to the cave's entrance.

I slid to a stop and my boots sprayed tiny rocks. I ducked into darkness, the narrow tube driving straight into a rise and then down.

Now I saw the first difficulty in my lack of planning. Light in a dark place.

Anna's voice came again. Clearer. More real. I made out the word *help*.

My toe bumped against steel, the sound suspiciously like a lamp. Did God work that way?

As I grabbed a match from my pocket I decided if I had to ask, chances were, He didn't.

I lifted the lamp high, the cave's walls a mix of haunting shadows and clear direction.

I followed the path, breathing in the moist air. Thoughts of my father walking through the cave tried to edge in on my mind, but I could only think of Anna. If she were just in my arms again, even for an instant, all would be okay. I could protect her.

Deeper into the bowels of Earth I pushed, my singular focus an uncommon drive of personal bravery. So much dirt overhead, and what was keeping it all from tumbling down?

I stepped over a handful of rocks and stumbled. I let myself fall but stopped just before crashing. I hovered over a precipice so deep I couldn't see the bottom. Gravity pulled me forward, forward, willing me to tumble in. I balanced on the edge for several seconds, and with a yell I pulled myself backward, an inch at a time, slowly shifting my weight away from death.

I regained my balance and peered over the edge. I shivered. Too close. I lifted the lamp a little higher and saw a crate to the right. Dynamite. Were Jacob and his men planning to blow up the cave? I had to hurry.

A log stretched the distance, and it took two steps to cross.

I kept going, the path now covered with sand and small, black rocks.

"Philip Anderson."

I spun, left hand lifting the lamp, right hand on my gun. Across the chasm, Jeb held a rifle on his shoulder, the muzzle pointed at my head. His finger was on the trigger.

I was fast. Not that fast.

Jacob Wilkes stepped into the light and stopped beside Jeb. "Philip Anderson," Jacob said again. Each word was carefully enunciated as he said, "I never thought you to be a treasure hunter."

I couldn't help the growl. "Anna."

"Worry not, my friend," he said, his smile lit in the lantern's gleam. "You'll soon be joining her."

My hand hovered over my Smith and Wesson, ready to pull if Jeb looked away. All I needed was a quarter of a second. But Jeb knew death for either of us was a blink away.

My heart ran cold. Jeb's Winchester.

"Ah, I see you recognize the gun." Jacob looked from the rifle back to me. "Your burning-haired friend was all too eager to give it to us."

I almost pulled my gun. "You killed him?"

"A bullet ended him as we entered the cave behind you. Now I'm about to bury him." Jacob pulled a cigar from his suit pocket, and with a thumb lit a match in his other hand. The tiny light shone bright in the relative darkness. "I've been planning this moment for a while." He put the cigar to his lips and touched the match to the end. Smoke wafted behind him.

"Jacob, you don't have to do this."

"Oh, but I must." He took another puff, and the end glowed. "I must show the world my benevolence. They have to understand that I am a just man."

I knew what he meant to do. "How much time are you giving me?"

My gaze remained on Jeb, but I watched Jacob from the edge of my sight. He dropped to a knee and tugged the log, sliding the beam to his side.

"How much time, Jacob?"

He leaned over, picked up a long string, and took the cigar in his other hand. "Five minutes."

She was the bait. I was the prey. And Scott got in the way. "Where is Scott?"

"A few feet back." Jacob touched the cigar to the string, blew on the end, and the fuse burst into a brilliant ball of light. He dropped it and stood. "Never let it be said Jacob is heartless."

"Jacob, you don't want to know where the treasure is?"

"That's my father's dream. Mine is different. Now go, tell Anna good-bye. My final gift to you." He looked up. "I do wonder if the entire cavern will collapse or just the passage. I guess I'll never know."

I eyed the dynamite.

"Ah. An oversight. I'm glad you reminded me," he said. He took the burning fuse and tugged it toward the other end of the box. "See? I know you're good. Shoot the flame out now, and you'll blow the dynamite early. Now you're wasting your last breaths."

He was right.

I retreated a few steps then turned my back to my worst enemy and tore through the cave toward Anna.

Toward our last moments together.

25

The lamplight splashed against a woman I barely recognized. Her shoulders slumped and her head drooped, reminding me of a willow branch. If it weren't for the ropes holding her to a large rock, she would fall.

I hurried closer, barely noticing a lake reflecting the light.

Her soft cheeks were sunken. Swollen eyes looked at the ground. Water covered her face, from sweat? Tears? Cracked lips opened, and her voice ripped through the cavern. "Help!"

"Anna. Anna, I'm here."

I closed the rest of the distance between us hunched over, fishing for my boot knife.

"Help!"

"Anna." I set the lamp down and grabbed her shoulders. "Anna, it's me."

Her whole body shook as she looked up. "Philip?"

My fingers clasped the knife.

"Philip, is that really you?"

"Anna." All I could do was say her name.

Her face contorted. "Knew you'd come." Her voice was harsh now, almost a whisper. She burst into tears.

With a flick of my wrist, I opened my knife and slit the ropes. The coils slid to the ground, and Anna fell forward. I dropped the knife and wrapped my arms around her while she cried.

I couldn't join her, knowing death was close. I counted to thirty as I massaged her neck and held her close. I pulled away, my chest wet. I ignored the lingering need to keep holding her. "Anna, we've got to find a way out of here. There's a deep canyon and Jacob pulled the log. On the other side is lit dynamite."

"Oh, Philip." She burrowed her face into my chest again. "Don't let me die in here. I'm going to suffocate."

Ideas hit me fast. "Rope." I let Anna go, the hardest act I'd done in quite some time. "He left rope." I reached past her, and as I did, kissed her forehead. "We may get out of this yet."

"You must think me terrible. I smell funny." She glanced down. "And look a fright."

"I've dreamed of nothing but you every night for the past months, Anna. You look more beautiful than I've ever seen you."

She considered my eyes, and in hers I saw the reshaping of a woman who had nearly lost all hope. A flame rekindled. The fires of determination, nearly extinguished by the darkness around her, burned anew. I snatched the knotted hair behind her head and pulled her close and kissed her dry lips.

A world of emotion passed between us, as inexplicable as the sunshine, as powerful as a waterfall, as deep as the chasm that kept us from freedom. Love was more powerful than the danger we faced.

But that didn't stop her from breaking away and snatching the lamp. "Time for that later," she said. "But first I have to tell you something."

"Anna. No time."

She started at an unsteady jog for the tunnel. "Jacob killed his own father. His real father." Her voice was stronger now and matter-of-fact like a school teacher.

The cave walls closed in, and soon we were back in the passage.

Despite our danger, I tried to grasp her meaning. "He killed his... does his evil know no bounds?"

Anna slowed, and the chasm's dark shadow spread before us. She reached out and took the two parts of rope from me and tied them together. Despite the fizzing sound of dynamite and the flame's glow across the way, she was surprisingly calm. "Being raised by a monk, inside cloistered walls, contained his furry until it exploded on the world. Mr. Wilkes just gave the explosion direction." She handed me one half of the tied rope, and my fingers flew over the rope to make a few more knots.

"Two peas in a pod, Mr. Wilkes and Jacob."

"I don't know," she said. "Jacob dismissed him."

I tied a loose overhand knot then sent the tail end back through and tightened a loop. "I've lassoed only a few times. You?"

"No. You're amazing with your hands. Do it."

In the tight cave, I swung the loop close to my body. I reached forward and let go. The rope slid over the crate and fell uselessly to the ground. I tugged it back.

"If I can just turn it, I'll shoot out the fuse."

"Hurry, Philip!"

I swung the rope again, and this time I didn't think. Instead my hands let go when the timing felt right. The lasso arched through the air and hovered impossibly over the crate as if locked in time. I couldn't breathe.

The loop fell over the crate, hugging the dynamite in a tight embrace.

I carefully pulled to the right, hoping the crate would turn. It moved closer.

Anna drew in a breath.

Sweat trickled into my eyes as I jerked the rope again. The crate moved closer and a little to the right, exposing the vanishing fuse. I pulled harder, trying to get a clear view, but every inch I moved it the fuse seemed to burn out of sight.

The bright light marched up the side and disappeared into the crate.

"Philip!" Anna screamed.

Jacob had lied. More like two minutes.

There was nothing I could do. One last chance to save our lives.

I yanked on the rope hard and sent the crate of dynamite sliding over the edge.

Anna and I dove, and I wrapped my arm over her head.

The explosion pummeled my body in a wave of pressure and heat, sucking the air from the cave. Air whooshed back through in a gust. Rocks pelted my skin like hail, and every breath was like breathing dust.

I held an arm over my eyes as a shield. The lamp still shone, but the rocks falling from above were large, some the size of my fist.

The chasm was still there. As if I thought the explosion might fill the bottomless pit.

In the distance I could hear massive boulders breaking away from the roof and plunging into the deep water.

The ground below rumbled, as if a promise the destruction wouldn't stop until the cave was crushed.

A gash crossed Anna's forehead, and blood trickled down her face. But in the pale light, her eyes were vibrant and searching. Searching for a way to survive.

I could try to throw her across the gap. But with the shaking ground, I would probably throw her to her death. I couldn't do it. I just couldn't.

My arms wrapped around her as she pressed close to my

chest. I would be buried with the woman I loved in the shadow of Devil's Tower. A rock would crush us both.

My heart felt no fear, only anguish for all we wouldn't have together.

We sat against the wall. She leaned on me, and I held her up.

A shadow moved on the other side of the chasm.

The light reflected off red hair. Scott!

He reached for the log and tried to push it toward the gap. With his elbows, he pulled himself closer, then lifted the log. I crawled as close as I dared and then held out my arms.

Scott pushed the log over, and I caught the end and held it down.

Anna managed to get to her feet, using the wall for support. She stumbled forward. How would she manage the narrow log?

She hunched as if ready to spring. A hoof-sized rock smashed her shoulder, and she grabbed her arm. I barely heard her yell.

She gathered herself again, took a few breaths, and launched herself to the log's center. She crossed the rest of the distance, tumbling to the ground. My heart cried in relief.

My turn.

Scott still held the log, but I stood at the shaky precipice. I was going to die. Even before I tried to cross the rocking bridge, I sensed the helplessness of falling.

God, help me!

I would rather face one hundred gunmen than this.

One thought destroyed my fears in an instant.

Anna was on the other side.

I stripped off my duster, unbuckled my gun belt in hope of balancing my body. I tied the guns inside with the sleeves and tossed the bundle across.

I dashed onto the log, lamp in hand.

The ground shook on my last step, and the bridge rocked to the side. With the toe of my boot, I managed a foothold and launched myself at the other side.

I crashed into Scott, and we tumbled away from the chasm just as the lamp went out.

"Thanks!" I yelled over the noise.

His reply was soft. "I'll need carried."

I set my duster and guns on Scott's belly. Without hesitating, I wrapped one arm under his legs, the other under his back, feeling sticky wet.

"I can't find the lamp," Anna yelled.

"Leave it. Almost a straight shot. Go! Go!"

I lifted Scott and started running.

As I pressed on the tremors slacked off, but the noise behind us grew.

"You okay, Scott?" He was heavy.

"They shot me. In the back. Took my gun."

"I thought you were dead. And you saved us. You saved us."

"Philip."

"Yeah, buddy?"

"I can't feel my legs."

My blood ran cold. But I pressed on, stumbling over fallen rocks, trying to ignore the screams of my heart. Scott was more than a friend. He was a brother. Without me, he wouldn't have been shot. What had I done to him?

A light ahead beckoned.

The world around me tore apart. Wind swirled from behind, the air screaming in pain. Rocks groaned and vibrated, clinging perilously to the ceiling, finally losing their battle and falling around us in a deafening roar.

Anna disappeared through a veil of dust, and I plunged after her.

The cave collapsed.

I dove into the sunlight, yelling. Scott rolled from my arms as I crashed to the ground.

Scott shouted. Anna shrieked. Dust swirled around us as winds tore at my clothes, ripping off my hat and whipping through my wet hair.

We lay in a heap, trying to catch our breath, feeling the dust clear and the sunlight touch our faces.

Sporadic gunfire brought me to my senses. I crawled to me feet and tried to comprehend what had unfolded around us.

The earth rocked and I tumbled back to the ground. Behind me, the land buckled. The cave collapsed. I glanced up, watching the tower.

The monolith didn't move. Strong roots.

Shouldn't there be more gunfire?

I looked toward the way I'd come—toward the horses—and stopped cold. Jacob stood next to a tree, staring at me.

I stared back.

The distance was about one hundred yards, a futile shot, but we both went for our guns. My fingers slapped against my hip.

The Smith and Wesson was wrapped in my duster.

Jacob held a small pistol pointed at me. His gaze flew past my shoulder, and I chanced a look.

Roosevelt and five men charged toward us.

I turned back and Jacob was sprinting away.

"Philip!" Anna's hand reached for me.

"I've got to go after him." I snatched up my coat and guns.

"Philip, please." Her cry tore at my soul.

"I have to stop this."

Roosevelt pulled up. "They just up an' ran." He noticed I was gearing up, and he saw Jacob's distant form. "Go, Philip. I'll watch them."

I looked down at Anna.

She said, "Go." The resignation in her voice was worse than the pleading. "Then come back to me."

I turned back to Roosevelt as I buckled on the belt. "Meet me at the clearing."

"Why not stay—"

"Other riders might head here. Just go. Fast. I'll meet you there." I wrapped my duster around me. "Scott's injured. Bad. See what you can do for him."

Scott lifted his head, despite his body lying in a tangled heap. "See, I'm fine." He met my gaze. "Buddy. He killed a lot of people. Maybe me. Leroy. Marshal Stone. And Mrs.—" he looked at Anna. "You know."

I started after Jacob. I heard Scott's voice behind me call out. "No mercy, Philip!"

I pulled my Smith and Wesson to make sure she was loaded before racing after Jacob.

Loaded.

The Colt on my left was filled with cartridges as well.

Jacob's leather shoes with thick soles would make him a faster sprinter than I ever hoped to be. For a man who walked with a cane, he ran fast. I wouldn't catch him on foot. Raven, however . . .

I weaved around trees and leapt over small boulders. The gradual slope away from the tower drew me on at speeds I could barely control, but the need to reach Jacob accounted for the recklessness.

He darted like a jackrabbit two hundred yards ahead, and I pulled the Colt and held the iron tool at eye level. Time to motivate him.

I fired a crack shot, with no possible way I would hit him. Hopefully, he would make a mistake. He might trip and break an arm, making this easier.

My toe smacked a fallen log and I stumbled. Several wild

steps later, I caught my balance and kept after him, returning the Colt to its holster.

The ground shook.

A column of thick dust blew through a vent, and my momentum threw me into the rolling clouds. Dust coated my tongue.

I burst out the other side.

My breath came in ragged gasps, and my heart thumped painfully against my ribs. I hated running.

Jacob approached his impromptu corral, coattails flying, blond hair waving in the wind. I was making progress against him.

He mounted the Thoroughbred, yanked the reins, and thundered away.

I passed their corral, the guards long gone, and found Raven with the other horses. With wobbly legs, I mounted.

My tired and battered body might slump in the saddle, but Raven was spoiling for a run. She darted after Jacob with only a touch of the reins.

The late sun lit the world in bright orange, and the air was cooling fast. The green pines were defined in sharp contrast to the darkening blue overhead. Raven galloped past the rocky terrain and gathered speed over the prairie.

Was catching Jacob a matter of mathematics?

Raven's 15-hand height against the Thoroughbred's 17? What of Raven's scooped muzzle, a misshaped look, against the perfectly chiseled nose of the Thoroughbred? Raven's chest was powerful, but the Thoroughbred's shoulders rippled with muscle.

Who had the better horse? Who was the better horseman?

The breeze whipped in my hair, my hat lost somewhere. The fresh wind revived my brain, and I gulped the air like cold water.

I would capture Jacob. He would stand trial. Or he would die.

Except for one problem. Jacob extended his lead.

I glanced behind. The gathering storm clouds beyond the tower threatened the last of the sun's rays. Ahead, the Thoroughbreds' shoes flashed with every lunge. A small trail of dust followed them until they hit a long clearing with a carpet of grass.

The sound of jingling tack, thundering hooves, and heavy breaths filled my ears.

Every footfall, Raven dipped her head and swallowed a breath, her mouth, neck, and lungs a straight line. She lifted her head and exhaled, then scooped for air again. Her curved muzzle and wide nostrils were an advantage now.

I leaned over her neck and whispered encouragement. Her ears were flattened back as she ran. Below her knees, green grass rushed by in a blur.

Jacob skirted the river, the high banks holding him on this side.

He yanked the reins and dove over and out of sight. By the time I approached the bank, his horse was muscling up the other side, water gleaning off its flanks. Still too far for an accurate shot.

Raven's nimble hooves found a path down into the water, her thin ankles making her steps a dance. She drove against the shallow current, then hit a deep section, and swam a few feet before climbing up the bank. We crested the top, and Raven renewed the pursuit, this time about twenty yards closer.

We galloped at incredible speeds as the last vestiges of sun disappeared behind clouds. The meadows were cast in shadows, and the forests turned to night.

I was getting close enough to try a shot. Shooting from a galloping horse was impossible at best, but with a Winchester and this close, I might be able to wing him. I reached for the scabbard and grabbed the stock but paused.

Jacob took a hard right, up a hill bathed in the last of the sunlight.

Several lone pines made a strong go for survival, but the hill's upper half was clear.

Jacob slowed and stopped at the top. He turned his horse toward me, and in the sharp light, I saw every curve of his face. A triumphant look covered his features.

Eight riders crested the hill in a straight line, halting on either side of him.

Many times I'd seen men who plied their trade in death. Hardened by the trail, they had lost the look of regret, of a nagging conscience. But still they harbored the hope of a brighter future, a good-natured dream of an existence that one day they could hang up their guns. Not these men. Their eyes were as cold as the air around them.

The sun gleamed off exquisite guns and supple leather. Every man was clean-shaven, and all rode well-groomed mounts that rivaled Jacob's horse. Their expensive dusters and jackets looked out of place in the wilderness.

In the center, an older man in bowler locked my gaze. He was wiry, with gray hair and a pencil-thin mustache.

Forty yards' distance, and his icy look was clear, the measuring of not just me but who I was. A killer. Like them.

He lifted his pistol.

26

A dream. That's what this was. He couldn't be raising his Colt faster than I could pull mine. Aiming down the hammer. Lining up the sight.

Smoke billowed around him as his revolver jumped in his hand.

The bullet whistled overhead. Common for shooting downhill.

Strength filled my fingers in a quarter second. The image of John Maxwell standing on the Deadwood street facing me filled my mind.

John Maxwell said, 'Like h—' and he drew.

I pulled my gun and fired.

The man's bowler flipped back and dropped behind him.

As the other men pulled their guns, I touched Raven's flanks.

Bullets whipped the air just behind me.

He had been fast. Poor aim, but fast.

Jacob had gotten away, and I had almost died. My mind swirled.

I was but a passenger, sitting atop a cloud. Was it Raven I rode? Or the wind?

She never galloped faster.

I couldn't keep living this way. The family secrets. The fighting. Death and intrigue. No more.

I would find the treasure and go home.

I rode into the jaws of the thunderstorm, a mirror image of the fear and panic in my chest. And more. Exhaustion.

Having been the hunter, I was now chased. And my body felt like a sack of flour in the saddle.

Droplets splattered through the darkening night as a rider galloped ahead. I prepared to pull the Smith and Wesson when I saw Running Deer driving his horse for the clearing. He turned, saw me, but kept riding.

Raven pulled close. She knew Running Deer and his horse's scent, knew them to be friends, and slowed to keep pace with the man who saved me when I was a child.

He surely noticed me hunched in the saddle but said nothing. Instead he rode on.

For miles we rode back toward the tower, the edifice dark. Lightning split the sky, illuminating the rock.

The image burned into my brain.

We burst into the clearing, the darkness complete, the rain falling in torrents. Canvas was stretched over poles, and lanterns sheltered from the wind lit our way.

Running Deer dismounted first and put a hand on Marshal Hill's chest. "Riders." Running Deer wiped water from his face with his other hand. "Nine."

"Bully!" Roosevelt's voice rose over a thunderclap and the sound of rain on wax canvas. "I'll send men to watch."

Scott lay on a cot by the fire.

Anna brushed past Roosevelt, running to me.

I dismounted and dropped to a knee beside Scott, trying to keep swirling terror at bay. He offered a feeble smile, but the exhaustion in his eyes was all I needed to see.

He would have moved his legs for me if he could.

I covered my eyes.

"Philip? What's wrong?" Anna's arms encircled me as she settled by my side. "Did you kill him?"

"He is growing weary," was all Running Deer said.

"Philip?" Her fingers caressed my jaw. "Philip, what happened?"

I had to rein in my emotions. I almost died. He beat me on the draw.

The only feeling I couldn't control was giving me strength. Anger.

I dropped my hands from my face and looked up toward Marshal Hill. "Shovels."

Marshal Hill paused.

I stood and shook water from my duster.

"Philip, it's not in . . . I mean, the treasure isn't buried with your parents."

I stared at him until Roosevelt stepped close and handed me a trowel, the handle as long as my arm.

Rain pelted the canvas above. Thunder split the night.

I looked toward the river. An awful night for this. But my father had come from the river with a shovel. I thought he had disappeared that night for personal reasons. I remembered now he had been gone hours.

He'd found and reburied the treasure.

Fresh sage permeated the night, and I breathed deeply the soothing aroma.

"Scott," I whispered.

"You get him?"

The lump in my throat kept me from telling him, so I shook my head.

He turned away, and the muscles in his smooth cheeks rippled. Finally he said, "Go, buddy. Find it. Then let's go home."

I looked into Anna's eyes. Water had washed away the grime in her hair, her face, cleansing her body and soul. She only nodded.

I stepped out from cover, feeling the rain stream through my hair again, and marched toward the river. I didn't care if the others followed.

Lightning bolts streaked toward the tower and lit the clearing. One second and the concussion rippled through the air and shook the ground.

Someone walked beside me. The next flash showed Anna's determined face pointed toward the river, long streaks of dark hair plastered to her face. Her skin was pale now, the rain done washing away the dirt of the past.

I crossed over a log and walked into a grove, the same copse my father had left so many years ago. The branches overhead helped shield the rain.

Thick grass slowed my progress.

I wiped water from my eyes.

Where could he have buried it?

From behind, a bullseye lantern floated closer. Running Deer, Roosevelt, Marshal Hill, Jackson, Ryan, and Matt appeared beside me, the lamp held high. They looked at me expectantly.

I took the lamp and searched the grass. I knew grass. I had to. I loved my horses.

A patch of green shone just a little brighter than the grass around, as if the blades were fresher, younger. Ten years couldn't hide the past.

I plunged the steel blade into the earth.

Two more trowels started next to mine.

Lightning lit our work.

My hands were small, as if I were young again. I saw Running Deer and the vision was complete, as if I buried my parents again. There had been no rain then. Only my dead parents.

When rain falls on your face it almost feels like you're not crying. I prayed the hole we dug wouldn't be used for Scott.

I barely felt the rain lighten. Wind gusts swept away the sound of digging. The only smell was water.

There was little doubt my father had dug here. The only question was how deep.

The storm slacked its unholy onslaught.

A loud thump gave us all pause.

Anna met my gaze, her wide eyes filled with excitement.

Running Deer, who stood at the light's edge on lookout, turned.

Marshal Hill's keen eyes studied the hole as if examining a problem.

Roosevelt's breath could be heard over the spattering of raindrops and distant thunder.

Jackson and Matt watched with interest but at attention, their soldier's stance returning after the fight.

Ryan stretched his back, his arms crossed at the top of the shovel. He was as impossible to read as ever.

I jumped into the two-foot hole and set my boots on either side of the wooden disc. With shaking fingers, I cleared the dirt from the top of a wooden keg. The barrel was small, and with a few scoops of my hand it opened a space to the side. I reached under and with a heave hoisted it into my arms.

The last time the cask saw open air my father had it. Before him? Hundreds of years?

My anger was giving way to fatigue.

I hefted the keg beside the hole and brushed away mud. The craftsmanship was older, the wood rough and the iron rings aged with rust. The lid had been pried, probably where my father had opened it that fateful night. Iron tabs, however, kept me from opening it with my fingers.

The weariness slammed my body as if the months of chasing, killing, and being near death forced my eyes closed. If I had held all the stars in place, holding them suspended above us, I couldn't have been more tired.

I tried to pull myself from the small hole but fell back in.

Hands gripped my arms and lifted me. My legs barely held but I leaned forward, my hands on my knees.

I would never make it back to camp.

Anna's shoulder tucked under mine and I leaned against her, easing the weight off my feeble knees. All she had been through—the horrors, pain—and she held me up.

"I love you," she whispered.

The warmth of her breath flooded my body.

Marshal Hill wrapped my other arm over his shoulders, and even though both Anna and the marshal were several inches shorter, they nearly carried me back to camp.

Scott's voice rose above the rustling of the grass and distant river. "He hurt? Philip hurt?"

Anna waved a hand and he quieted. She snatched my bedroll and laid it by the fire.

Marshal Hill settled me on the blanket—gun belt, boots, and all—and as he started a fire Anna leaned over me and ran her fingers through my hair. "You hurt? I'm worried."

How could I explain? So helpless. I was a powerful man, and now I couldn't stand, couldn't think, and only wanted to sleep. When was the last time I'd slept?

Days. Weeks. Maybe months.

"So tired."

She settled closer.

Roosevelt set the cask beside my right arm. "This can wait."

Energy surged through my body as if lightning struck, and electricity surged from my head and out my fingertips.

And worse. The vision washed over me like a thunderclap. I was a little boy again. Was it because my bedroll lay exactly where I had sat when I was a child?

The wagon, the fire, the small tree where my parents would be buried. My father read from the Bible as my mother leaned over the pan, stirring.

I put wood in the fire. My hand was a small boy's, and the next blink I was a man again putting wood in the fire as Marshal Hill, Scott, Anna, and the rest watched. "Philip?" Anna's voice. "He's doing it again. Philip, you need to lay down."

Another blink and the wagon was framed in a starry night, Devil's Tower in the distance.

My mother hummed a soft tune in time with the frogs by the river.

Three thugs walked into the meadow.

My fingers tingled.

I blinked again and two worlds collided. My vision of the past and the world as a man were one in the same.

The outlaw that had killed my parents had aged, putting on perhaps fifty pounds, one hundred maybe. The two men beside him were different, their guns covering us, their eyes sharp, their fingers hugging their triggers.

Mr. Wilkes said, "Philip, give me the treasure. The money is mine." Arrogance drifted from him like perfume.

And I knew.

Mr. Wilkes had killed my parents.

How had I not recognized him? His extra weight? His graying hair? His new mustache? Now I saw it. The same chin. The same eyes. The same gun.

I was a little boy again, and my mother looked up from the cooking pot. My father dropped his Bible. He was about to say *we've no money.*

This time I could save my parents.

Oh, how I wanted to stay in the vision, but with the sparking energy I forced myself back into reality. "You killed my parents," I said in a low voice. Some small hope made me think I could stall him. Perhaps I might find a way to keep him from doing this.

More to the truth, keeping me from attempting the revenge I had hoped for as a youth.

His gaze turned from me to the others. He had the drop on us. He'd passed our guards. Conceit born from years of control made him believe he could kill us and take the treasure.

Could I beat him on the draw?

A breath.

Marshal Hill was on my left.

I said once more, "You killed my parents."

I blinked. A boy again.

It was as if two voices spoke as one, "Wrong answer."

I let the past consume me as I defended my parents.

I drew.

In the time it took to pull the Smith and Wesson I knew I would fire two shots. My first struck the man on the right.

As hoped, Marshal Hill cleared leather and gunned toward the man on the left. But Mr. Wilkes was fast. I couldn't stop him from drawing.

I aimed for his heart in a smooth, practiced motion, pulling the hammer back with my left hand and tugging the trigger with my right.

The three men dropped as one.

Not even the sharp smell of sulfur could keep me alert. Energy escaped as quickly as it came. I slumped to the ground.

One thought entered my head as I realized I had two more kills to my name—be careful what you wish for.

Revenge is a fickle master.

I drifted into a fog as the noise and voices surrounded me, but I fought to keep my eyes open. Anna needed me. What if Jacob came now? Then I remembered Roosevelt's men watching. Jacob wouldn't sneak past the guards. He would want to wipe them out first.

I found myself in the bedroll again and all was silent until Scott said, "He hasn't rested, Anna. Not a moment. Since your kidnapping, his sole design was on you and the girls."

"It's true." Marshal Hill's gravelly voice was comforting, and I closed my eyes again. "Horses give until their hearts burst. Philip did the same."

I felt Anna's fingers against my forehead. "He's burning up."

Hadn't even given thought to how I felt. But now with Anna beside me . . .

"Bracing," Roosevelt said. "Heart of courage. But a man needs rest."

I was almost gone when I heard Scott say, "If anyone touches that little barrel, I'll kill him. Or Ryan will."

Anna's voice was soft. "He never lets on how much he thinks about it. How much the secrets burn inside him. Yes, the travesty of someone else opening it would be unthinkable."

The last thing I remember was Ryan grunting his approval.

27

The train jolted, and Anna smacked her head against the window for the hundredth time.

Every time she fell asleep she leaned to the side, and when the car hit a rough track the window smacked into the side of her head. She rubbed the sore spot and glanced through the glass. Pitch black.

She crossed her arms and snuggled deeper into the seat.

Across from her, Philip's chest rose and fell. How long had she watched just to make sure he was breathing?

They'd traveled through Spearfish then directly to Rapid City where they boarded a train. Raven had carried Philip's sick form as carefully as she could. Anna saw it in the horse's eyes. The Arabian knew her master was ill. No, not master. Friend.

Anna looked out the window again at her own image.

She'd always hated her wide cheeks. Well, they were sunken now. Her eyes were dark and hollow.

Anna had the whole seat to herself, just like Philip across the way. They stretched his lean body so he could sleep. His long legs hung over the edge and into the aisle. But she couldn't lie down. Lying meant she wasn't ready for anything Philip needed. She knew the idea didn't make sense. But that's how she felt.

He'd woken several times over the past three days, but he seemed to be reliving his past. His fever broke as they started their train ride and he settled in the seat across from her, and he slept finally, without a dream.

She clutched her hands together as the thought returned. There was a time she had asked him if he really loved her. The question had separated them and caused the entire ordeal with Jacob. No, that wasn't entirely true, especially with the latest revelations of Mr. Wilkes. Since moving to the Dakota Territory, there had always been enmity created for Jacob and Philip.

All the same, Philip had ridden to save her. Against incredible odds, he'd ridden into hell itself and done the unthinkable. He'd led men into battle and saved her.

She didn't deserve him.

Now there's the wrong voice to listen to.

He'd ridden to hell and back. If he wanted her, she was his.

"Hey."

She looked up at the sound of Philip's sleepy voice.

He held out a hand. An invitation. Her heart arrived a moment before she did.

She sat, and he laid his head on her lap. Her fingers slid easily through his hair. "How are you feeling?"

"Rough couple days."

"But better?"

"Much."

His hair was just thicker than corn silk. Piercing gray eyes reflected the lamplight from the train's center aisle. His smile was soft and comforting.

"We made it," he said. A dark look filled his eyes. "I have to tell you about—"

"Scott told me." With her other hand she laced her fingers through his. "He told me everything."

His eyes held the sympathy his lips didn't offer, as if he couldn't say the words that might make all her nightmares come back to life.

Philip sighed and seemed to sink into her lap. She wanted to crowd years of life into this one moment, but she knew to let the feeling go. Just enjoy the aura that surrounded him.

"What was in it?" he asked.

"We haven't opened it." She couldn't hold back a laugh, thinking about Ryan's steadfast devotion to the barrel. "It's under your seat."

They were quiet for a while, trying to wrap their minds around all that had happened.

"How's Scott?"

"He can't feel his legs. We're taking him to the doctor in Mitchell as soon as we arrive."

He closed his eyes, and she felt his anguish. "Anderson's War," he muttered.

So much to say. So much to tell him, but no words came. She let him remain quiet, running her fingers along a wrinkle in his forehead. She sighed. "You're worried."

His eyes pierced her soul with a fervent gaze. "I've . . . I've changed, Anna. I've killed more men than I can count."

She bit her tongue. Such a dangerous man she loved. Her belly warmed at the thought. With no small amount of strength, she kept her hands from seriously roughing his hair.

"What I mean is, I'm not the same man you once knew."

She drew back. "I'm not the same woman. Not mentally anyway."

He shifted and snatched her hand. "I want you to know my intentions."

Her mouth went dry, and her heart pounded. He surely heard every beat.

"Love—our love—is worth fighting for. I intend to help you through any problems that Jacob caused. You and I, together."

Tears slipped over her cheeks and splashed on his face. She drew his head close to her.

In a muffled voice he said, "We'll make it. I know it."

Hope. The feeling gave her strength.

She said, "You'll be there when I face Father?"

"Of course," he said in a quiet voice, sad but honest. "I hope to be there when you face anything."

"When you told me of your past, I know how difficult..." She choked. "I know now." She shuttered, the feeling of terror crawling through her. "I'm sorry."

"That's what I mean when I say I intend to help you." He sat up, groaning as he slowly swung his body into a sitting position. "The body and the brain need to sort themselves out."

"My body's fine," she said quickly. "Buyers want women unspoiled."

He ran his fingers through his hair then over his face. He sighed. "Unthinkable. I've no regrets about what I did in Mexico. I only wish I had gone faster. One day. One day and we could have saved your mother."

She felt small as Philip held her and her tears fell, cleansing her soul. He didn't speak, but he kissed her forehead. After gaining some control she said, "You did all you could. Not your fault."

"Hard, though." He looked at her with a soft smile. "You know, I noticed I use blame to cover up how I really feel."

"Which is?"

"Usually the sadness that comes from losing the one I love."

She leaned into him. "When did you get to be so smart?"

"You're the smart one. Hey look, the sun's rising."

She glanced out to see the first glow of pink line the

horizon. "My mother used to say morning was her favorite. It meant you survived the night, and God had a purpose for you for that day. I suppose now that she's gone . . ."

"How she lived her life lives on in you and Beth." He squeezed tighter. "She's at rest now. I know that's no help, but it's true."

"How do you do it? Living day to day without your parents?"

"One breath at a time. But some days it's just too much."

They watched the reds and pinks brighten into orange.

Philip stretched his shoulders, breaking their touch. "I'm feeling better." He rubbed the back of his head then paused, his hand still on his neck. "I'm finding it impossible to believe we're still alive."

The look he gave her made her stop. She bit her bottom lip. "It was close. Philip, what's in that cask?"

He bent over and slid the barrel from under his seat. The long fingers that wrapped around the side were a pleasure to watch, but the mystery inside took her attention. "Are you going to open it now?"

The sun burst through the window as the train crested a small rise, and Philip shielded his eyes as he looked through the glass. "I want to open this in Mitchell. We're almost there."

"Any guesses what's inside?"

"My father had pulled the necklace from here, I believe." He ran a finger along a knot in the wood. "So maybe jewels."

Anna noted the disappointment in his voice. "That's bad?"

"I'd hoped for clues to my family." His sigh and the way he pushed the cask aside showed her how much disdain he truly had for its contents. "Imagine the small fabric of memories you clung to aren't true. All you believed was a lie. I just hoped for more is all."

"More what? Some redeeming qualities?" she ventured.

He grunted. "Yes, suppose so. You know, I don't care a

whit about my father's family. But my mother's . . ." He held his head. "It hurt to hear me talk of her, after losing your mother?"

"It can't hurt worse," she said and touched her heart.

His gaze took in the other sleeping forms in the car, every person made up of their party. He turned to her and before he spoke again the train jerked and began to slow. They'd paid the engineer to stop on the outskirts of Mitchell to let them off well before the station. Marshal Hill said they could get the town's disposition before anyone really knew they were there. She believed he meant something different. If Jacob had a party at the station for them, they could avoid them entirely. She'd heard Roosevelt say he and his men would sweep the town for any sign that anything was wrong. She was glad Roosevelt felt such a vested interest in Philip.

"Well," Philip said, sitting forward. "We'll stop at your father's house and then I'm going to open it at Caroline's Kitchen."

"Not without me."

"Up to you. Beth. Your father—"

"Can wait a few minutes more after I see them. I love him, love you both. But I'm going to stay with you."

The words, spoken so lightly but so thick with meaning, weren't lost on him.

He offered a somber grin. "Rachel has a vested interest in this as well. Shall we go to Caroline's Kitchen and open this and find out why people gave their lives for what's inside?"

28

I walked through a quiet town, the cask under my left arm. My right arm hung free.

Birds called out to the brightening day. With a wary eye, I glanced for enemies past windows reflecting the sun, around building corners, and down the empty street.

Being in civilization again was good.

My footsteps mingled with the rest—Anna to my right, Marshal Hill to my left. Ryan, Jackson and Matt carried Scott in a litter, following close behind while Running Deer lurked somewhere ahead.

The reunion with Anna's father had been bittersweet. His leg had been amputated, and he greeted her with a crutch under his arm. Beth clung to Anna for five minutes while everyone waited outside. Anna explained to her father what she must do, and with his blessing she had rejoined us.

She promised she would return.

Just off First Street we stopped at Doc Wilson's. I leapt up the steps and pounded on his door.

From below Scott said, "Philip, don't do this."

"The decision isn't yours."

"I want to see what it is."

I ignored him as the door swung open.

Doc Wilson's shirt was untucked, and he whipped his suspenders over his shoulders. He wore no glasses, and his eyes were puffy as if he just woke. "Who's hurt?" His eyes came into focus. "Philip? Is that you?"

"Yes, Doc. Scott's hurt."

The doctor's squint turned to wide-eyed fear. "Dear God. Not Scott. Where is he? What's wrong?"

"Here, Doc," Scott said, sitting up on his elbows. "I'm not a bad as they make out."

"Legs." Marshal Hill rubbed his mustache to cover his already quiet voice. "He can't feel 'em."

Doc stiffened. "Get him inside."

"Wait, wait." Scott held up a hand. "I've got to see something first."

"The back is broken, Scott. I must examine it now, before any more damage is done."

"Doc, I've been slung over a horse for two days and I rode on a bumpy train for another day since the accident." Scott laid back. "A few more minutes won't do any harm."

I glanced at Anna. Shouldn't he be eager to see Becky? He hadn't even asked that she be included. Her furrowed brow told me she might be wondering the same. I turned back to Doc. "Will it hurt, just for a few minutes?"

He considered a moment. "Fine," Doc said, reaching for his bag and stepping into the morning light.

"Wait," I said. "Doc, we'll watch him."

He looked from me to Marshal Hill, who gave a single nod.

"On your head be it," Doc said, returning to the shaded entry and slamming the door.

"Let's go." I jumped down the stairs and marched for Caroline's Kitchen nearby.

"You must be feeling better," Anna said.

"A little weak, but pushing through. I can't wait to see my horses again."

"Ryan, will you get Rachel?" I asked. A small alley cut behind Caroline's Kitchen to the small shack where she lived.

As he hurried around the corner Scott said, "Was he just flitting? Did he just prance?"

"Shut your mouth!" Anna said with a sharp laugh. "He's excited to see her."

We heard a knock. The door opened, a squeal.

"Hey," I said to Scott. "Should we get Becky?"

He shrugged. "In a bit."

Rachel burst around the corner, pulling Ryan behind her like a small horse pulling a huge wagon. I doubted she'd appreciate the comparison to a horse though. "Look at you!" She brought her hands to her mouth, and tears filled her eyes. "I thought I'd never see any of you again." She fell into Anna's arms.

She noticed Scott and she froze.

"Just a scratch." He waved a hand. "I'll be right as rain soon." But I saw lines on the corners of his eyes. He was in pain.

"But—"

"Should we continue?" Scott said, cutting her off.

She turned to me, and I hefted the cask. "Can we use the restaurant?"

It was as if she were waking up. She shook her head, sending long curls bouncing around her shoulders. "Yes. Yes! Of course. Let's go through the back."

"Anna and I will join you in a minute. I'm going to scout the front." I suddenly needed a kiss. Bad. And there was no reason to hold back. None at all.

I took Anna's hand and started for the front, and as soon as the others disappeared down the alley I set down the cask and grabbed her waist in both hands. I wasn't gentle as I pulled her toward me and pressed my lips against hers. With my hand on the back of her head and my fingers in her hair I held her close, hoping the time and pain would be whisked away by the passion between us. Every second locked in her embrace the world slipped away, and the only reality was our two beating hearts against each other.

I broke from her lips and kissed her cheek, then ear, and then held her closer.

"Oh, it's been too long," she whispered.

"I know."

"That was spring water after a long walk in the desert."

I sighed. "You're a poet. But I suppose water does taste better when so thirsty."

She drew back and put her hands on my shoulders. "And you're such a philosopher."

I wanted our relationship to move along quickly. Life without Anna was impossible to imagine, but asking her now wasn't the time. Instead I took her hand and led her toward the front.

"Philip." She tugged, holding me back.

I turned.

She said in a coy voice, "Aren't you forgetting something?"

I smiled and drew her into my arms again, embroiling her in a kiss. Her body shuttered and sagged, and after a moment she pulled away. "That's nice." She brought a hand to her mouth. "Very nice. But I meant that."

She pointed to the cask.

Memories slammed into me like a runaway train. How I wanted to flee from the tracks and escape.

"Philip." She lowered to one knee and hefted it to the top of her thigh. "I know that look. You're closing up on me. Tell me."

I glanced back toward Main Street, the long rows of businesses, a few owners opening shop. With a hand on the butt of my gun and a foot on the edge of the boardwalk I watched. In truth what I wanted most was a place to call home. Mitchell accepted me from the moment I stepped in town. Perhaps Anderson's War hadn't ruined the fact I still had a home, a family here.

Maybe I could hang up my gun.

Maybe I could ask Anna to marry me.

I said, "I like it here."

She stood and laid her head against the top of my arm. "I do too."

"There," I said, pointing across the street. I stepped up onto the boardwalk and took the cask from her. "Remember when the Sioux woman needed help, right there?"

"You were incredible."

"That's the first time I saw you. You were watching me. Remember?"

She leaned against me. "Your eyes."

I couldn't hold back a shudder, and her touch softened as her fingers caressed the top of my hand. The sigh that escaped her lips was like a mother in a store being patient while her children asked for peppermints. "Someday," she said, "you'll see your features through me. A family usually helps you find what's good and bad about you. A bit of refining, I think, in every person's life, is what a family does."

"And I don't have one."

"Do you want one?"

My heart rose to the occasion. She'd asked something of similar importance before. *What do you feel inside?* My answer was *I feel fine inside.* The memory made my gut sick, and in this moment I wanted to answer without an answer. The words almost slipped from my mouth, *whatever you want.*

Anna cared for my feelings. And with any luck, what I wanted would align with her desires.

But why couldn't I say the words? I looked at the cask, hoping for a diversion. Then down the street. All I saw was shimmering windows and blank looks of sleepy store owners.

She deserved to know.

Do I want a family?

"Anna." I licked my lips. "Anna." I couldn't look at her. "Anna." I searched my heart. "Anna, I . . . I'm scared. I want to make a family more than anything." I swallowed. "I don't know how."

She laughed a lighthearted tinkling from her throat but stopped when she saw how it made me feel.

"Oh, Philip." She closed her eyes. "You're nothing like your father. You've already proven yourself a better man." She tapped the cask under my arm. The hollow sound echoed against the Kitchen's wall. "Look. You're standing here, the treasure under your arm."

"Just like my father."

"Exactly my point. You stand here, just like your father, with the treasure. But it isn't open. It isn't your passion."

"Not my dream."

"This," she said, waving a hand from my head to my feet, "may have come from him." She tapped my chest. "But this has been built by a lifetime of loving others, being a good friend to Scott, Leroy, Caroline, Marshal Hill. For loving your parents beyond their graves." Her voice caught. "For loving me." She motioned toward the West. "You've proven to everyone you're not your father. You won't turn into him. Why won't you believe it?"

There was only Anna and the words she dared utter. Didn't she know I could grow angry and never speak to her again? Love does funny things, like take risks.

Her words stripped me bare.

"Oh, Anna. When did you grow so wise?"

She smacked my chest again, only this time with the back of her hand. "And don't you forget it." The corners of her lips curled up so that the dimple on her cheek, now just a vague shadow, reappeared for the first time in forever.

I hefted the cask. "So, you ask me if I want a family. The answer is I do, but there's only one person I trust to help me." As I walked toward the front door I added, "And that's you."

She clung to me as I knocked on the coarse wood planks, and the door to Caroline's Kitchen swung open.

Ryan filled the doorway, and as he stepped aside to let me in I put a hand on his shoulder.

"Thanks," I whispered.

His dull eyes filled with a look that understood my meaning. I'd been wrong about him. Yet he remained my faithful friend.

I stepped past Ryan. Familiar settings would be welcome right now.

The tables had been rearranged.

To my right Rachel pushed in a chair, as if finishing. She looked at Ryan and then back at me. "They helped me move the tables." She shoved another chair home. "I needed a change."

With a thick tongue I said, "Rachel, you've been through much because of me. I'm sorry you—"

"I've felt life to its top because of you." She thrust a hand on her hip. "The bad comes with the good."

Her words washed away the flood of guilt.

I turned to Jackson and Matt. "Thank you for coming to Mexico."

Jackson straightened to attention. "An honor." His pock-marked face was almost handsome in the morning light that filtered through the windows. "Truly."

"What Jackson means," Matt said, "is that he feels it was a cause worth fighting for."

I walked past them, and Marshal Hill's bright eyes and thick mustache were as welcome and familiar as any I'd ever met. "Thank you. Not just for this." I tilted my head toward Anna. "But for showing me what I need to do."

"Just pointed you to the trailhead." He sat on a table's edge. "You led us on the path yourself."

The overwhelming love I felt was impossible to communicate. I put a hand on his shoulder as I walked past him.

Dear God. Scott. Please, God. For a moment I thought I would cry. *God, what can I say to tell him my feelings?* I looked at the rafters overhead, the freshly painted wood telling a story of how much change everyone really needed.

"You have to look at me eventually," Scott said.

I turned my gaze into his calm eyes. How could he see through the long strands of red hair dropping into his eyelashes?

His stretcher was set on the bench near the large center table. He lay on his back, his head turned toward me. A pitiful vision.

I stepped close and he clasped my hand. "This is going to eat at your soul, I know it will," Scott said.

Behind me the girls sniffed.

His strong grip wrapped around my thumb. "All things happen for a reason." He used the grasp to pull himself a few inches to the side. "Could have happened to you as much as me."

Now there were tears and I looked away, embarrassed. "But it *was* you. And I couldn't stop it. This might be the rest of your life, Scott."

"Meant to be." He let go. "If it wasn't a bullet, it would have been a rock from under Devil's Tower. Some fireball from the sky would have hit me. Better helping save the . . ." his voice choked. "The people I love most in this world." He cleared his throat. "Besides, you're the famous one, remember? Can't mar that pretty figure."

I wiped my cheeks on my sleeve. My gaze stayed fixed on my feet. I wasn't normally this emotional. I struggled but could not control myself again.

Scott let go of my hand. "You know, we've happily ridden with you across this country to save our girls then raced to Devil's Tower to rescue Anna. Any of us would give our life for yours." His expression turned hard. "But if you wait one more second before opening the blasted treasure, I'll kill you myself."

Anna's voice was heavy with tears and laughter. "Not if I kill him first. Philip may not want to know what's inside, but I have to know."

I dropped the cask on the bench beside Scott, and everyone crowded around. "I can't open this." I spun the barrel until the bent iron ring was close to me.

Everyone groaned. Rachel bumped me none too gently as she passed then returned from the kitchen with a pick, the handle as long as her torso.

She hefted the tool. "Stand back."

"Wait. Wait." I took the pick from her, tapping the handle's bottom softly on the floor and jarring the pickaxe head loose. I slid it the length of the wood and set the head between two slats.

"So much blood. So many lives. My uncle, my father. Wilkes. Custer. So many."

"You succeeded where the others failed," Anna said.

"Because of you." I didn't look up. "Because life can't be lived alone."

"Okay, fine. You're not alone on your farm anymore," Scott said. "You've changed. Now would you just open it?"

Anna grabbed the pick end and jerked, splitting the wood. "Men talk too much."

Raw cotton peaked through the lid's broken slat.

Without responding, I broke open the barrel's lid. Everyone leaned forward.

I reached in and touched the vague impression in the cotton. "The necklace was here." I snatched a handful of cotton and tossed it on the table. I scooped out more cotton.

My fingers scrapped metal.

Was anyone breathing?

I tugged out the cotton and poked my finger on something hard.

With care I pulled out a crown of delicate gold, laced with rubies and emeralds.

"I knew it!" Anna nearly screamed.

"So beautiful," Scott said with a whistle.

"Ryan, Jackson, Matt, let's keep an eye on those windows." Marshal Hill pulled his gun and started for the front door. He slid the bolt closed. The others took their places but continued watching. Rachel disappeared into the kitchen and I heard a bar slide across the door.

I set the crown on the table and paused before reaching in. A shiver went up my spine.

Cool, smooth pearls slid through my fingers and wrapped around my palm. I pulled out the necklace, eyeing the creamy white gems, each the size of my knuckle. The girls gasped and Scott whistled.

They grew silent as I lifted an emerald ring and held it up to a ray of light. Next to it was a massive diamond, and I held it to the light as well. On the floor the light cast scattered beams.

I set them both on the table.

A silver tiara sparkled with diamonds. I showed Anna a pair of hair combs. Her finger touched a gem, and her voice was a reverent whisper. "Onyx." She tapped the next with her fingernail. "Sapphire."

The next layer was tightly packed in cotton. Gold bracelets, perfect circles lay thin and delicate and pronounced against the dirty white. I set them carefully with the other jewels.

Below, a layer of fabric stretched across the bottom half. I coaxed the material out, feeling the gentle cloth between my fingers. There was more to this fabric than I realized. "Anna, can you help? Just pull. I'll draw it out."

I drove my fingers into the barrel and as she pulled I tickled the cloth out, tugging the attached gems so they wouldn't catch on the cask's iron ring. Soon Anna's arms were high overhead. How did it all fit inside?

The cloth came free, and Anna stepped back with the sound of jangles. Clutched in both hands, her fingers white, she held a dress.

My breath caught.

The bodice front was a white triangle accented by teardrop diamonds. Shimmering gold cloth framed the triangle, but was highlighted with purple and golden gems shaped as flower pedals. The shoulders were crowned with pearls, and diamonds ran down the loose, silk sleeves. A belt, encrusted with diamond flowers, shimmered in the sun.

Anna pulled the dress close and looked down. Looping one arm around the bodice, she ran her fingers over the skirt, touching purple gems. "Have you ever seen anything so beautiful?"

I had to agree.

Marshal Hill's gruff voice broke into the dreamlike moment. "That the last of it? We best find a secure place for that."

"No, there's more."

As Anna laid the dress on the table, I reached back in. Filling the bottom, a golden plate shimmered. I lifted it into the full light.

No, not a plate. A miniature shield.

I ran my fingers over the cold metal, tracing the outlines. Across the top, edged in a golden scroll, was the name *Maxwell*.

Below, one half was painted red with a gold lion. The other half facing the lion was painted gold with a red lion.

Stumbling, I fell back on the bench near Scott's head and stared at the shield.

"Philip?"

I looked at Anna, her concern jarring me from my shock. "F . . . F . . ." I cleared my throat. "Family crest."

Anna brought a hand to her mouth.

She of all people understood the family connection, the bridge through time to pierce my heart.

I held a connection with my mother's family.

How long I sat staring at the crest I don't know, but I felt a touch on my arm and Rachel stood beside me, a cup of steaming something in her hand. I took the handle and sipped, scalding my mouth. I welcomed the burn.

"Thanks."

"Philip?" Anna said from my other side. "Look at this." She reached inside the cask and pulled out a yellowed scroll of paper and handed it to me. A red ribbon wrapped around the paper slipped off and fell to the floor.

I laid the crest on the table and set the scroll beside it. I leaned over, pressing my palms against the rough boards, and stared at the scroll. History—what I knew of my past—was being rewritten. I should be used to this by now. But the feeling was like carving the entire Devil's Tower into something else. Nothing would be the same hereafter. There was no going back.

Every time I learned something new about my past, a little piece of me died. Perhaps that was me changing. The future Philip Anderson wasn't the past Philip Anderson, as if I had to lay the previous man in the grave. He wasn't coming back.

I stood in Caroline's Kitchen, which held so many happy memories. My duster hung over my Smith and Wesson, a weapon I now never dream of being without. My friends were posted at the windows, watching for anyone who looked suspicious. Anna's mother was dead. Jacob, my bitter foe, was still free. I'd met someone out there who might be faster at the draw than me. And here. Here at this table I was laying out riches that would make anyone king.

Might as well take the rest of the bad news. With a finger holding down the top of the page, I slid my other hand along the smooth paper until I pinned it to the table.

A red wax seal adorned the bottom.

Anna laid a hand on my back. "Philip, what does it say?"

I squinted at the faint ink. "Charles, King of this United Kingdom, by the grace of God."

Anna sucked in a breath.

Everyone in the room looked at me.

I continued. "Now know ye that on this day, the year of our Lord Sixteen Hundred Forty and Four, Do hereby bestow for valour in the face of enemies of our High King the God of All upon Philip Maxwell the title of Baron and all the lands that are herein described."

No one spoke. I let the letter roll back up, ignoring the rest.

Questions bombarded me. Baron? Wasn't that a title? Philip Maxwell? A relative perhaps? One I was named after. And King Charles knew him. War hero?

"It's a letters patent."

I looked up at Anna.

"Kings, presidents, anyone in power can write one up and give something to anyone for any reason."

"Ah."

"Philip, you may have a bit of English blood."

"I know. My mother."

"But more than that."

"More than what, Anna?"

"See what I have to deal with?" Scott said. "He's fast with his hands but slow with his head sometimes."

I knew exactly what they meant. But I wasn't going to say it.

Anna, however, could. "He comes from a family with a title."

A knock filled the room.

We pulled our guns and pointed them at the front door.

29

W ho's there?" Marshal Hill asked, his back to the front wall and revolver pointed at the door.

"Marshal? This is Captain Smith. Let me in."

"Are you alone?"

"I've a patrol with me."

Marshal Hill looked at me then called back, "State your business."

"Philip's my business. I must speak with him."

Marshal Hill glanced back at. I nodded once.

"All right, but just you. No one else."

The door opened, and Captain Smith stepped inside. Marshal Hill locked the door behind him.

Captain Smith swept his hat off his head and surveyed the scene. I lowered my gun.

He opened his mouth to speak when his gaze caught the table. His cold eyes, pencil mustache, narrow chin remained unreadable. "Ah." He closed his mouth. "I see."

No one spoke.

"Philip, don't you think it best if you did this in a more secure location?" His tone turned insistent. "Perhaps a fort?"

"He didn't know the contents," Anna said. "And what's more, this is a secure location."

Captain Smith turned and looked past Ryan's double barrel shotgun at the enormous man. "Quite."

I settled on the bench next to Scott, suddenly tired.

"Casualties?" Captain Smith asked, looking at the bench.

"I'm okay," Scott said. "Just resting."

The silence that followed was heavy, as if each person weighed the moment carefully.

"Met Roosevelt at the station," Captain Smith said. "Mentioned you might be here."

Interesting. Roosevelt so trusting of cavalry officers.

I waited.

"Philip," he said looking down at me. "I must take you to the train. We've two days to get to Washington."

The Senate. I'd completely forgotten.

"For all that's holy, man." Marshal Hill walked around to face Captain Smith. "Do you know what this boy has been through the past weeks?"

"I managed to hold off the investigation for this long. As it is, they're not in a good mood waiting on this hearing."

"I know Washington." Marshal Hill holstered his gun but puffed out his chest. "They've short memories and shorter attention spans. This will go away soon."

"Raymond, I'm just looking out for the boy."

Marshal Hill pointed back at me but continued to stare down Captain Smith. "I've ridden through hell with this kid, and let me tell you—"

I let their voices fade away as I looked at Anna, our gazes holding, reading each other's souls. Finding pain so deep it remained unspoken. How long must our passion for life together, for a full conversation that didn't involve Jacob or working out our relationship or saving our lives wait? I would go because standing before the high offices of our land was ordered of me, but I didn't have to like it.

After a sip of coffee I said in a soft voice, "So what other desserts can you make?"

"You mean besides pie?" I could barely hear her over their arguing.

"Right."

She sat on the table and set her boots beside me, resting her elbows on her knees so her lips were close to my ear. "What makes you think it's my duty to make you desserts all day?"

"Touché."

"If you asked nicely though, I'd make you a cake."

I leaned against her leg. "And we'd eat it together?"

"With tea."

I took another sip of coffee.

Marshal Hill and Captain Smith's voices droned on.

"Anna, come with me."

"Next train, I think. I'll bring my father and Beth."

"I can better protect you in Washington."

Anna shuddered. "I thought I could protect myself." She wrapped her arm around mine and rested her cheek against the top of my shoulder. "I was so wrong. God first. Trust Him. I can't put too much of the burden on my knight." She gripped my arm.

"I thought I could save you by myself." I looked at Scott who was listening to the ongoing fight. "I was wrong too."

"In Washington you'll be famous. A gunman. They've all read about you."

I snorted. "The blasted novel."

"It's well-written. I enjoyed it immensely, even if most of it wasn't true." She sighed and kissed my forehead. "The train's going to leave."

"If you have time, check on the horses. They're in the Hutterite camp. A boy named Jake watches them. I like Jake."

She kissed me again.

"Anna, loving me has come with a heavy price. Are you sure—"

"Quiet, boy. Love is worth fighting for."

I closed my eyes, feeling the emotions that swirled around us. How could I leave her again?

I took Anna's hand and kissed the smooth skin. I ran my finger over a soft vein, feeling the comfort between our fingers and enjoying the shiver that ran through her body.

With all my heart, I did not want this. But I let go of Anna and stood. "Stop."

All conversation died. Remnants of words swirled in the air like falling leaves, vintages of a ravage summer coming to an end.

"I'm leaving on this train. Anna will join me in Washington with her father and sister as soon as possible." I turned to Rachel. "I suggest you and Ryan disappear." I pulled out my wallet and shuffled through the bills. "Here's two hundred. It should last for a bit. Maybe leave word with Jon Pole at the saddlery shop where you're going. I trust him."

She took the bills. "I'll pay you back."

"When times are better."

I felt a tap at my arm. "Here's twenty." Scott lay back as I took the coin from him. "Buy me that wicker-wheeled chair across the street. I'm going with you."

"Scott, you're—"

"You need legal representation. You'll get it in Washington, no doubt, but I'm intimate with this story and am nearly a lawyer. I'm going with you."

Before I could interrupt Captain Smith said, "You'll have no legal counsel. You'll probably get off the train that morning and take a hansom straight to the Senate. Scott would be an asset."

"I'd feel better if he went with you," Anna said.

Marshal Hill added, "I know doctors in Washington, a missionary society. He'll get the best care."

"He's broken!" I couldn't hold back the sudden burst of emotion. "Broken because of me! He should be in a hospital right now. This is absurd."

"You know me," Scott said flashing his brilliant smile. "I deal in the absurd daily."

Marshal Hill crossed the room and took the twenty-dollar coin. "I'm coming too. Not much time."

Captain Smith saluted. "Marshal Raymond Hill, I put him back under your care. I don't need to tell you what will happen to both of us if he doesn't stand before the Senate."

Marshal Hill's breath puffed out his mustache an inch.

"Scott, what of Becky?"

"I'll explain on the way out." Scott smacked the bench. "Let's go!"

I slipped the scroll in my pocket and packed the jewels back into the cask. The dress wasn't going to fit. "Keep it," I said to Anna.

"I can't just walk across town with this and put it in my closet."

"I'll escort her." Captain Smith motioned to Jackson and Matt. "These men are back under my command. They will as well."

"Someone will need to find Running Deer."

"Philip." Marshal Hill caught my attention. "Let us handle those things. You need to get on the train."

I looked into Anna's warm eyes. She lowered her head and gave me a sad smile. "I'll see you," she said. "In Washington."

"Then we're coming home for good," I added, but even to me the hopeful tilt in my voice turned sour, hollow. There was a purpose behind us, like a tail wind. And in my gut I felt this entire ordeal was far from over.

30

The garden around us was sparse and ill-kempt. Ahead, the capital building's massive dome reminded me of a lion's head, the two buildings on either side giant paws reaching forward.

To my right along the gravel drive, Marshal Hill pushed Scott's wicker cart, two large wheels on the front, a small turning wheel in the back.

We wore what we could buy at stations along the way, and none of us were the height of fashion. I wore a simple day suit, wool, dark gray, almost black. I kept the top button closed, but the rest of the jacket fell loose by my sides. I couldn't find a hat I liked.

Marshal Hill's black suit set off his keen blue eyes and bushy mustache.

Scott's suit was striped up and down with brown and gray. I'd dressed him. Moving his useless legs through the pants only reminded me of Becky's final ultimatum as we'd left. *If you go to Washington, Scott, don't bother returning. I'll never speak to you again.*

Scott had tried to explain to me that was her way of breaking off the relationship, that she would never be the one to take initiative. He was feeling better daily that she'd cornered him that way. "I'm tired of her making me look bad. Besides, she wants someone to dance with," he had said. "Not cry with."

Directly in front of the building carefully crafted knee-high bushes edged the road. Flowers—golds and velvet reds—added color. Birds bounced along the path in front of us then flew into the bushes. People passed, but all were engrossed in conversation and paid us no mind.

"No one's carrying guns," I said, feeling conspicuous with my own Smith and Wesson.

"Not everyone makes enemies like you do," Marshal Hill said.

Scott chuckled. "Philip doesn't do a thing halfway."

"No he does not."

We paused as the sweet smell of perfume filled the air. Under the capital's dome at the foot of the steps, carriages were parked in disarray. Horses rocked in their harnesses, setting off the jingle of bells. Elegant men in top hats and canes each held a woman on their arm. The dresses were colorful in the morning sun.

My sweaty palms were testament to my churning insides.

I glanced at Marshal Hill. He said, "We'd best keep going. Help me lift Scott up the stairs."

Just before I reached under the chair I heard a cry, "Is that him?"

"It is!"

"Anderson! I've questions!"

"Steady," Marshal Hill said, glancing at my hand that rested on the Smith and Wesson. "They're armed with pencils, not guns. Reporters."

"What should I say?"

"Nothing," Scott replied. "Let's just get inside."

The reporters rushed us.

"What do you think of Dakota becoming a state?"

"Philip Anderson, what do you say to claims you're a vigilante?"

"Anderson, did you execute the members of the Maxwell Gang?"

"What are your ties with Jacob Wilkes?"

I paused.

"Is it true you're cheating on Anna Johnston with Rachel Halliday?"

My hands curled.

Marshal Hill grabbed my elbow and said over the tumult, "This way. Side door."

We followed Marshal Hill. He skirted the bottom of the stairs and closed in on a door guarded by three soldiers. The marshal held up his badge, and they opened the door.

We entered. As soon as the heavy door closed, the waterfall of words abruptly ended.

The three soldiers surrounded us.

"Thank you, gentlemen," I said.

"Our pleasure, sir," the sergeant said, looking into my eyes. "I take it you are Philip Anderson?"

"I am."

"I must insist. Your firearm. It won't be needed. We'll keep it here until the hearing is over and you leave."

"The last time my gun was left—"

Marshal Hill unbuckled his gun. "It's okay, Philip. This isn't a party. And Jacob's not here."

I pulled the leather strap through the loops on the belt and tugged off the belt. My hips felt naked.

"We keep them in this locker," the sergeant said, opening a wooden door. I set my gun next to Marshal Hill's revolver. "You can retrieve them here. Do you need an escort?"

"No." Marshal Hill took his position behind Scott. "I know the way."

Tile floors made rolling Scott easier through the corridors. "You've done this before," I said.

"As a Pinkerton, yes."

We passed murals of animals painted between golden molding. The creatures were so colorful, so vibrant, I wished my nerves were calmer so I could enjoy them. We passed through vaulted passageways so beautiful my pace slowed. A triangle arch opened to a narrow stairway. Hundreds of voices filtered down from above.

I stopped.

"Philip, help me lift Scott."

I just stared.

"Hey, we've got to get going."

My lower jaw trembled. My gut was jelly.

"Philip—"

"Marshal," Scott said. "Give Philip and me a minute."

"We don't have a minute."

"It's not Philip Anderson gunman that's walking up those stairs. It's a farmer more comfortable with horses than people. If you don't let me talk with him, he's not going to make it. Now please."

Marshal Hill lifted his hands and backed away. Scott rolled his chair close.

I looked down at my best friend. I said, "This is why you came."

"We're brothers, you know. Friends. Fighters. We've been through hell and back. I don't know another man like you." He shifted on the cushion. "No one knows you like I do. Anna might. Someday."

"I can't do this, Scott." I eyed the doorway. "Who's walked through this corridor? What great men and women have stood where I'm about to stand? And the power these men hold—" My body shivered violently.

"Breathe, buddy. Breathe."

I wrapped my arms around my middle and tried to take a breath.

"You've always respected power," Scott said. "I don't. Makes me a good lawyer. But you. You care, don't you?"

I looked away.

"Hey, notice that guy right in front of you. The squirrel? He's incredible."

The likeness was striking, the tiny rodent's big eyes looked back at me.

"You know why he's there, buddy?"

I shook my head.

"To remind them of the real world." He said it again, with more power. "Real world. Not the world they live in." He lifted a hand. "Under these ceilings painted to intimidate, they count on the fact you're scared and in awe. Well, put them at the cabin with gunfire. Send them to the village in Mexico, and we'll see who's scared and who's dead."

I grunted half a laugh.

"You're here because they have no idea what it's like past these walls. You're here because they think you might have overstepped your duty. Because how many of them have ever had a real job? How many get their hands dirty by actually making this country great? How many ever had to defend themselves against a gang out to kill them? You've done the work, Philip. They simply set the parameters with which you live by."

"What should I do?" I was surprised how strong my voice was.

"Honest answers." He rolled back a bit. "Keep Jacob out of this." He looked me over. "You're dashing. Young. Hope of a country full of energy. Go show them the Philip Anderson we know."

I rubbed my hands over my face. "Yeah, I'm ready. Thanks for being here."

"Wouldn't miss it. One more thing. You might need this."
He reached under the wicker chair to a basket under his seat
and pulled out a brown canvas. He shook out my duster.
Washed and pressed. "Noticed you're more comfortable with
this as your armor. Now let's go."

I slung the duster over my shoulders, instantly feeling a
newfound strength.

Marshal Hill grasped the other side of Scott's chair, and
we lifted him.

As we ascended Marshal Hill said, "Senate chambers are
up here, but we're off to the Supreme Court chambers. Our
hearing is small, and the court isn't in session today."

"I've dreamed of entering the Supreme Court's hideout."
Scott gripped the sides of his chair as he rocked back and forth
with every step. "Quick rise I've made."

We topped the stairs and set Scott down.

I straightened and gazed at the crowd filling the wide
reception chamber.

I'd never seen more people in my life. No one seemed to
care about the gorgeous lighting, mirrored walls and ceiling,
elegant tapestries and paintings. They were filtering through
several doorways, chatting with each other.

Several men in black wool suits spotted us and ran against
the crowd. Marshal Hill stepped forward.

"Mr. Anderson," one said, his dark hair slicked back by
oil. "We've been expecting you. The hearing will be in the
Senate Chambers today. Bigger than expected crowds."

"I see that." I leaned closer so I could be heard over the
crowd and said the words Scott had made me memorize. "I've
not been made aware of the proceedings. Shall we convene
somewhere so that I can be briefed?"

"No time. The committee is eager to start. Just follow us."

Scott held up a hand. "As Philip's legal counsel, I'd like
the list of questions."

"He won't be needing counsel. He's not on trial here."

"What is your name?" Scott asked.

"Mr. Conroy. Now if you'd like to follow us, I'm sure we can accommodate you near Mr. Anderson."

"I brought my own chair, so I will be directly next to Mr. Anderson." Scott made a motion. "This is highly irregular. I'll be filing a complaint. Lead on."

As they started forward, Marshal Hill leaned over and I just caught him saying, "You're right, Scott. Very irregular."

The men ahead pushed through the crowd, and we followed in their wake.

I turned back. Marshal Hill stood still, a look of concern on his face. He leaned close. "I don't like this. I'm going to mingle. Get the lay of the land."

"Should we leave?"

But he didn't hear. He was already melting into the heavy crowd.

The hosts quieted as we passed. I imagined what they saw, a man purported to be a gunman, straight from a dime novel. His skin was dark, his eyes piercing like a wolf's eyes, a few inches taller than most. Thin but hard, dark hair and a few days' stubble from the train ride. He wore a duster that stretched down to his ankles.

I stared ahead, kept my walk sure, my head erect.

My leg smacked something, and I stumbled to a knee.

A young girl looked directly at me.

Her hand flashed out, and she thrust a note into my palm. "Please, sir. Read this."

Her eyes met mine.

Was I staring into a mirror? Her eyes were as gray as a wolf. "Please sir." Her English accent was soft but firm.

And she was gone, melted away into the crowd.

"You okay?" Scott called from beside me.

"Yeah." I bounced to my feet and grasped his chair again.

Half my brain tried to make sense of what just happened. But things were moving too fast. The crowd was noisy, calling out to me. This wasn't what I expected.

We passed under the sweeping doorway into the massive Senate Chamber. People filled seats, stood along walls, sat in aisles. Long rows of desks stretched on either side, filled with men of huge importance. Scott was right. Their hands were probably soft. Far softer than their backsides, where they'd spent most their time.

As the aisle cleared for us to proceed, I glanced quickly at the paper in my hand. Torn from a larger sheet, the writing was scribbled cursive.

Beware. Do not enter the Senate. Not all is as it seems. Take great care.

A little late.

I stuffed the note in my pocket as we descended the aisle where at the bottom of the Senate floor was a single chair. Above the chair was a high panel with ten empty chairs behind desks in a shallow crescent shape.

I felt like we descended into a Roman amphitheatre. I was the gladiator.

Scott was ushered to the left of the aisle and I was told to leave him.

I was led to a lone seat in front of the empty chairs in front. Hundreds of people at my back and the impossible ten before me.

The night on the river flashed in my mind. My father, reading by the fire.

Devil's Tower was a shadow in the distance.

My senses heightened.

The voices swept away into croaking frogs.

The bushes rustled.

Mr. Wilkes was dead. My parents had been avenged.

I tried to stay in the present, but the night washed over me.

I heard a door open, and ten men shuffled to the seats.
Breathe, Anderson. I closed my eyes. *Breathe.*

I turned to see if there was danger behind me. Scott was arguing with the men who led us in, pointing to my chair.

Three men left the bushes. "Where's the money?"

My father said he had none.

"Wrong answer."

Ahead a gavel smacked wood, and I jumped. Half torn between the gunshot of the past and the Senate Chambers.

The crowd quieted as I tried to control myself.

"We can proceed now that the witness has arrived," the man in the center said. "First, a word from the committee chair. Senator Maxwell, please."

The senator stood, dressed in black robes, a sure look framed by gray hair.

"Philip Anderson."

I stared.

My grandfather.

My grandfather was alive.

My grandfather had a heart attack and died. My mother's grief had been real.

Surely I was mistaken.

A decade of lost time, a whirlwind of hopeless solitude, an isolation of lies that became a hurricane in my heart stood before me.

"You are hereby put under authority of this Senate meeting." His voice. So American. But I could just hear an underlying English accent.

He's alive.

I opened my mouth to speak when his voice boomed through the room.

"Privileges to legal counsel, access to communication outside of this counsel, and public records will be revoked immediately. Please clear these chambers."

The crowd erupted in dismay, and Scott's voice yelled loudest of all.

I kept my eyes on one man.

He was dead.

He is alive.

The one man with more power than I could have ever dreamed just locked the public from this hearing.

And I knew the worst was yet to come.

Historical Note

What's real, and what's fiction?

The Schoolhouse Blizzard of 1888 at the book's beginning was a catastrophe that left children dead, cattle frozen, and settlers stunned at the vicious nature of the Plains.

Theodore Roosevelt. TR's ranch in the Dakota Territory was crushed by the blizzard of 1888, and he decided to retreat to the east and enter politics.

Libbie Custer. As real as I could make her. She was a writer after her husband's death, and participated in several writing conferences.

Maxwell Gang. Created in my imagination, but the gang is a mixture of the most famous bands.

Mitchell, South Dakota. A thriving town with a fascinating history. I've enjoyed the pictures the city's historical society has made available on the Internet. I grew up near Mitchell and ran there during cross country races. Little did I know at the time I'd be writing about the location. I just concentrated on deep breaths and focused on the person in front of me until I crossed the finish line.

Lajitas, Texas. A resort town on the Texas/Mexico Border. I completely made up the history. People of Lajitas, I apologize.

Sex Slave Trade Through Mexico. Very real, and still exists today.

Main Characters—Anna, Scott, Jacob, Marshal Hill, Running Deer, Raven. All fiction. But I love Raven.

Philip Anderson. While a fictional hero, he's based on a cowboy I came across in my research. See the note in the first book of the series, *West for the Black Hills*. Of the many characters I've written, Philip is by far my favorite.

About the Author

Peter Leavell, a 2007 graduate of Boise State University with a degree in history, was the 2011 winner of the Christian Writers Guild's Operation First Novel contest and 2013 Christian Retailing's Best Award for First-Time Authors. Peter and his family live in Boise, Idaho. For entertainment, he reads historical books where he finds ideas for new novels. Whenever he has a chance, he takes his wife and two homeschooled children on crazy but fun research trips. Learn more about Peter's books, research, and family adventures at his website: www.peterleavell.com

Visit the Mountainview Books, LLC website for news on all our books:

www.mountainviewbooks.com

www.ingramcontent.com/pod-product-compliance
Lightning Source LLC
Chambersburg PA
CBHW051334250626
47155CB00007B/2598